BELVEDERE CRESCENT

Misha Herwin is a writer of books for adults and children. Her novels cover a variety of genres from contemporary women's fiction to family saga and time-slip. Fascinated by time, she also writes short stories which have been published in anthologies in the US and the UK.

Misha runs workshops in museums, libraries and schools, and is one of the founders of 6x6, a quarterly event where writers come to strut their stuff to an appreciative audience.

In her free time she reads, attempts to keep her garden in order and bakes. Her speciality is muffins, though her scones are pretty good too.

By Misha M Herwin

House of Shadows
Shadows on the Grass
Picking Up the Pieces

Misha blogs at:
https://mishaherwin.wordpress.com/
and https://authorselectric.blogspot.com/

You can find her at:
www.facebook.com/misha.herwin
and @MishaHerwin

BELVEDERE CRESCENT

Misha M Herwin

Penkhull Press

Published by The Penkhull Press
Staffordshire

ACKNOWLEDGEMENTS

Although a book starts with the germ of an idea, and in the case of *Belvedere Crescent* a particular street, the final version comes to life with the help of many people.

I would like to thank: Jan Edwards for her meticulous and rigorous editing, Hannah Ross and Barry Lillie my trusted beta readers, Tasha Molloy for answering my questions about identical twins, and members of Renegade Writers for their feedback and comments as I brought draft after draft to our regular Wednesday meetings. Also my sister Anuk Naumann for letting me use the painting of hers, that I've always loved, as a basis for the cover.

A special thanks must go to Peter Coleborn for his editing, formatting, and the way in which he has turned a piece of art into a brilliant cover.

Thanks as always to Mike Herwin.

Dedication

Lucy Harrisis

CHAPTER ONE

I never liked going back. Whenever I did, the past wrapped itself around me and the past was a place I did not want to be. But Sadie had called and said it was time.

I fumbled in my bag for the key and was about to slot it into the lock when the door opened and my twin was framed in the dimly lit hall.

"Sorry I'm late," I muttered.

"Hmm." Sadie narrowed her eyes and we looked at each other.

I tried to get here sooner but you know…

Sure.

The words remained unspoken. Identical twins; we could still communicate on a subliminal level though as we grew older the differences between us were becoming more obvious. We had the same pale skin and dark hair but she was thinner, more finely drawn, and had cut her hair short while mine tumbled to my shoulders.

"You haven't missed anything. The nurse says it could happen any time. She's with her now so we don't have to go straight up."

The hand on the grandfather clock lurched to the hour and struck eight.

"Positively Gothic, isn't it?" Sadie said. "The ancestral ghosts gathering for the final moments."

"We're not ghosts," I retorted, more sharply than I'd intended.

"No. But it sounded good. Do you want tea, or vodka? I've got a bottle of wine, if you'd rather. It's going to be a long night."

And one best not spent in a fuzz of alcohol.

"I'll make some tea." I put down the overnight bag that I'd had ready for weeks and led the way down the narrow staircase to the basement kitchen, where a layer of dust softened the collection of crockery on the dresser. Half used notepads were buried among the fliers heaped next to a basket of keys to long-forgotten doors. Brightly coloured milk bottle tops, saved for some inexplicable reason, filled a glass jar, a tangle of rubber bands another.

I lifted the lid on the Rayburn and put the kettle on the hotplate. Sadie took a couple of mugs from their hooks and, ignoring the dried-up dishmop in the chipped Wedgwood jug, rinsed them under the tap.

"I bought milk and teabags," she said.

"How come you're so efficient all of a sudden?"

"Somebody has to be." She shot me an accusing glance.

I flushed. "I've been busy at work."

"Thea the high-flying lawyer," my twin mocked.

"Stop it, Sadie."

"Yeah, well. I haven't won my Oscar yet and there you are clawing your way up the professional ladder. It's got to happen for me sometime soon. We're pushing thirty." Her eyes widened in mock horror that was only partly pretence, for she knew only too well that for an actress age was crucial.

"Thirty-two," I corrected.

"Don't!" Sadie struck a pose, pressing the back of one hand against her forehead, stretching out the other in an attitude of despair, then with that sudden change of mood that was so typical of her she dropped her arms and said, "Come on, sis, where's that tea? The nurse will think we've abandoned the old bag. Perhaps she'll do the decent thing and put a pillow over our great-aunt's head."

"You shouldn't talk like that." I poured hot water into the teapot, swirled it around and tipped it away before adding the teabags and filling it up.

"I don't see why not. It's not as if Aunt Jane ever cared about us."

"She took us in."

"She had her reasons. Great-Aunt Jane never did anything without a reason."

"She scared me."

"You were right to be scared. There was something about her that..." Sadie hesitated; she took the lid off the pot and mashed the teabags with a spoon. Silence stretched between us and I wondered if this was the moment when she was finally going to tell me.

She picked up the bottle, splashed milk into our mugs and topped them up with scalding tea. "I wonder what it will be like—" was all she said "—to watch someone die."

~~~

"Will you be all right?" the nurse asked. "I can stay a bit longer if you want. I've time, yet, before the end of my shift."

"We'll be fine. Won't we, Thea?" Sadie ushered her to the door. "We know who to call if there's a problem."

"I'm sure there won't be. You've managed so well, sitting up with your great-aunt these past few nights."

"I couldn't do anything else." Sadie fluttered her eyelashes.

"And now it's my turn." Battening down a twinge of guilt at not having been there until now, I put my arm around Sadie's waist. I felt her tremble and gave a warning squeeze to stop her overacting.

"We don't have to do this," I said when the front
~~~

door had closed.

"Oh, but we do. We have to be here. You and me, both."

To make sure she's finally gone. The thought floated between us.

In the sickroom, the lights had been switched off except for the lamp that stood on the table beside the bed where our last remaining relative lay. Her skin was jaundiced, an oxygen mask covered her face. Her cheeks were hollow and her hands, seeking an anchor in the airless room, clawed restlessly at the edge of the blanket.

Taking those nicotine-stained fingers in mine would calm and reassure the dying woman. It was what I'd do instinctively if I was with one of my elderly clients but there were too many years of being kept at a distance by Aunt Jane. It would be dishonest to mimic an affection I didn't feel, nor could I summon up any compassion, however hard I tried. There had been no warmth in our childhood. No feeling of ever having been loved. Aunt Jane had done her duty, provided a place for us to live and had paid for our upkeep and education. If we did well at school there had been a glimmer of pride in our achievements, but even that had been tempered by thinly veiled criticism.

I sat on the chair by the bed and Sadie settled herself on the footstool by the fireplace. The shadowed room closed around us and outside the pool of light cast by the lamp she faded from view. We sat in silence. Aunt Jane's chest rose and fell. The hours went by, the gap between breaths grew longer; I kept expecting each one to be the last. It seemed wrong to hope that it would soon be over and yet there was no other resolution. Aunt Jane was not going to recover.

Eternal rest give unto her. The prayer we'd been taught at school came to my lips and was dismissed. Aunt Jane despised the church and would find no comfort there. Her only consolation would be that, after all her years of research and speculation, she'd finally discover what happened after death.

Sadie shifted on her stool and yawned.

"I'll stay if you want a break," I said.

"I'm okay. I'm used to it."

"Shall I bring you a cup of tea? I can get us something to eat. I'm starving." It seemed almost obscene to mention food in front of someone who'd never eat again but my stomach was empty to the point of aching.

"I'm fine. I'm not hungry."

You never are. You'd exist on air and alcohol given half a chance. "Well I am and I'm going to make myself some cheese on toast." The image of melted cheddar slathered with ketchup was so vivid I could almost taste it, but before I got to the door there was a knock.

I'd completely forgotten we were not alone in the house.

"Shit," Sadie hissed. "That'll be The Poet. I didn't want him down here tonight."

The second knock was a little louder. "Let me see her. Sadie? Please. I must see her."

"We'll have to let him in. He has every right to be here. After all, he's known her longer than we have." I opened the door and stood aside as Leo Trevelyan, our aunt's ancient lodger, known to us from childhood as The Poet, came in. Without acknowledging our presence, he bent like a broken marionette over the still figure on the bed and put his hand on hers, holding it there for so long that I was afraid her weakened bones would fracture.

Finally, when I was on the point of edging him away, he looked up and glanced warily around the room, his eyes clouded as if surprised by where he found himself.

"A sharp brain, a cruel tongue, but a kind heart. 'Age cannot wither her, nor custom stale her infinite variety'." He leant over and kissed the top of her head. "Farewell my lovely, my lovely, my lovely." The last words half-sung, half-chanted, propelled him upright.

"It's all right. We're here with her. Why don't you go back upstairs and we can fetch you if there's any change," Sadie said. She took one arm, I took the other and we started to manoeuvre the old man towards the door. Halfway across the room, he gave a violent shrug and broke free of our grip.

"She's gone," he said. "Look to her, kindly ladies."

"No. Not yet," we spoke together. Then Sadie went over to the bed and put the back of her hand against Aunt Jane's lips.

"You're right."

The Poet nodded slowly. His lips, thin and purple with age, trembled and a tear slid from the corner of his eye.

Aunt Jane was dead and all I felt was relief. Our aunt had been ill for months, or more probably years. The cancer feeding first on her lungs, then her brain, until her personality fractured and disintegrated and the woman we'd known all our lives no longer existed.

"That's it then." Sadie drew back the curtains and opened the window. Clean cold air swept through the room.

"To free her soul," The Poet said softly.

If she had one. The thought was shared between us. Then Sadie took her phone out of her pocket and set about the practicalities of death.

I linked my arm with The Poet's and, trying not to breathe in his old man's smell, guided him towards the stairs that led to his rooms at the top of the house. He moved stiffly, as if in pain, and his arm trembled as we started on the first flight. Gripping the banister rail he pulled himself up step by step while I followed behind, ready to catch him if he fell. We were almost at the top when he turned his head very slowly and looked at me.

"I loved her," he said. There was a pause – I waited for him to resume the climb – and he concluded, "And she loved me." Then in a much lighter voice he added, "Or over the years I've managed to convince myself that she did. At the very least my rent paid for the fags that killed her."

"You can't blame yourself." I made the conventional response.

"I don't. Your aunt could never be told. Of course you know that." His glance was keen and knowing. "I've had enough of this. Get me up these bloody stairs so I can pour myself a large whisky and toast her memory."

How will you cope without her? I wondered as we struggled up to the next floor. *She was part of our lives for so long but you were here before we were. You know we always wondered, Sadie and I, if you were lovers. In some ways you seemed so close, yet you were never really together. You led such separate lives, you up in your attic and she shut away in her study.*

"I can manage from here," The Poet said as we reached the final flight.

"No. I'm coming with you. I don't want you slipping and have to rush you to A and E."

"I'm fine. There's no need for you to worry. I

always thought I would be the first to go. When time's winged chariot finally catches up with me it's all provided for. There might even be a little money left over."

"That's not what I meant."

"I know." He reached out and patted my arm.

I could ask him, I thought. *Aunt Jane is dead. His defences are down. He must know more than he's ever said about me and Sadie and what went on in this house.* It was my chance to find out but courage failed me and I opened the door to the attic staircase and watched as he hoisted himself upwards.

When we reached his sitting room, I flicked the switch and the fly-blown bulb sent our shadows cavorting over the sloping ceiling. The Poet wound his way between heaps of books to the chest of drawers, on which he kept his bottles of whisky.

"Will you join me?"

"No thanks. I haven't eaten."

"Neither have I." He measured out an almost full tumbler of Lagavulin. "All the better to dull the pain."

Beyond the grimy window, a line of light edged the roof tops.

"'Tis the nightingale and not the lark, that pierced the fearful hollow of thine ear.' The night has gone and so is she. And so must you." The old man drained his glass, poured himself another, then bottle in hand lowered himself into a chair beside the fireplace.

I knelt down beside the hearth, found the matches in the pewter pot and lit the gas. Blue flames wove erratically through broken toothed burners.

"Leave it," he growled as I straightened the rag rug.

"You'll be warm enough now and I'll be back later to see how you're doing." I was reluctant to leave but his barely concealed impatience was driving me out. "You will let us know if you want one of us to come up and stay with you for a bit. Or anything else you might need." I looked around for the old-fashioned phone, hidden somewhere under drifts of paper and old journals.

"Of course." He nodded graciously and emptied another glass.

I'd just shut the door behind me when he began to weep; a low barely suppressed moan which rose into retching, gasping sobs and culminated in a piercing animal wail. I stood listening on the tiny landing outside his door and pressed my hands against my mouth as if through some sympathetic magic I could will him to stop.

If only he'd let me talk to him, put an arm around his shoulder, anything to stem that overwhelming grief, but if I walked back in he'd be angry that I'd invaded his privacy. For as long as he'd lived there the top storey was The Poet's domain and no one, not even Aunt Jane, entered without an invitation.

A waft of cold air wound around my body. I slid my hands under my sleeves and rubbed my arms. The heating had been on continuously since Aunt Jane had been confined to bed yet the top corridor was icy.

It's because we've been up most of the night, I told myself. *I'm tired and hungry and I need my breakfast. That's why I'm cold.*

In the kitchen the kettle would be on the range, the teapot warming beside it ready to brew builders' tea, and there was always shortbread in the tartan box in the larder. Tea and biscuits was what I needed to chase away the chill that gripped me so deeply that I could hardly move. The stairs seemed an impossible distance away. The air shifted and billowed bringing with it a wisp of laughter.

"Sadie?" Even as I said her name, I knew it couldn't be her. My sister was in the basement three storeys down, The Poet was in his attic, and Aunt Jane was dead. There was no one else in the house and yet the laughter grew louder, beating and echoing through my head. I clapped my hands over my ears but I couldn't shut it out. The sound swirled around me, swooping and mocking. Unable to bear it any longer I was on the verge of sliding to the ground and covering my head with my arms when, quite suddenly, it stopped.

~~~

Thea?" Sadie's voice spiralled upwards, wafting into the darkness that lay in wait at every corner. "Where are you?"

"I..." Short rapid breaths made it impossible to speak.

Stumbling to the top of the stairs I grabbed the banister rail. My hand closed around the polished wood. The landing light came on and my sister was running up the stairs.

"It's okay." Sadie pulled me close, her body warm against mine, and gradually the pounding of my heart slowed until it beat in rhythm with hers. Holding on to each other, our shadows stretching out behind us, we made our way down to the kitchen.

Sadie sat me down at the table, took the brandy bottle from the cupboard and poured two measures into our cups, then added deep brown tea, laced with spoonfuls of sugar.

"Go on, drink it. It's good for shock." She handed me a cup and sat down beside me. "You know, I felt
~~~

it. I felt your fear. My heart went crazy and I couldn't breathe."

I wrapped my hands around the mug to stop them shaking and took a mouthful of hot sweet tea while I gathered my thoughts. "I think it was a panic attack," I said at last. "I was standing there listening to The Poet weeping for Aunt Jane and I was terrified. I honestly thought, if I didn't reach you, I'd die."

"You don't do panic attacks." Sadie's voice sharpened. "You saw something, or heard it, didn't you?"

I wanted to deny it, to rationalise what I'd experienced. I started to shake my head but her glance held mine and I couldn't lie, because she'd know if I did.

"I thought I heard a woman laughing. It was a mean evil laugh, as if she was glorying in Aunt Jane's death. But I can't have done, can I? Because you're the one who—" What I was about to say felt too dangerous to put into words.

"I was." Sadie paused, then said briskly, "You may be right. This could be nothing but a reaction to Aunt Jane dying."

"Or maybe not."

We looked at each other.

"I wouldn't wish that on you," Sadie said.

"Was it that bad?"

"Never anything like you've experienced tonight. There were no horrors, as such." Sadie spoke slowly as if she was choosing her words carefully. "Occasionally I'd see a shadow that was darker than the others. It would give me the shivers but it was only there for a moment and then it was gone."

"That voice – that woman – was laughing. It was as if she'd been waiting for Aunt Jane to die and was making sure she was here when it happened." I drank some more tea. The brandy warmed my body but couldn't erase the chill of that laughter. "Like those black imps in a medieval painting welcoming another damned soul into Hell."

"You don't believe that, do you?"

"No, but that's what it felt like. Anyway, no one knows what happens afterwards."

"Whatever," Sadie said. "Personally, I'd consign our not-so-beloved great-aunt to the heart of the fiery furnace and let the great worm gnaw at her entrails for all eternity. Wherever she is, or isn't, it means that we're finally free." She gripped my hand and our fingers laced together so tightly that I could feel her pulse, and she mine. "Don't think about the bad things. Think about all the things we'll be able to do now."

"We'll sell the house." I loosened my grip. "We'll move on." *There will be no more shadows, no rooms freighted with darkness, crumbling furniture, cracked china, time-stained pictures, and dust-embellished books.* "I can put my share of the money towards the house William and I are going to buy." Sadie pulled a face. "Stop it. You know it's what we both want. Though it won't happen for a while, in any case. There's The Poet to think of. We can't abandon him. This is his home. As it is, he hardly ever leaves his flat."

"He won't be around for much longer. You'll see. He and Aunt Jane were linked, umbilically." Sadie twisted her mouth around the word. "Give him a few months..." She spread out her hands and shrugged.

"Sadie! He's always been kind to us."

"Okay. If you're so worried about him then we'll put him in a home like Mrs K. He'll be fine. So long as he has his books he probably won't even notice."

"You know that's not true. Under all those poetic frills he's razor sharp."

"Well, true or not." Sadie cupped her chin in her hand and continued gloomily. "I'm willing to bet Aunt Jane's left him all her money, which would be a total bugger. The way things are, if finances don't improve, I'll have to move in with Dominic. He might be a good director but he's a lousy lover. Plus, I need some funding for this project I want to do in the Redcliffe Caves. With money from the house all I have to do is to get permission from the council. Which I will, because it's such a brilliant idea. It'll tie in perfectly with Heritage Week. God, Thea—" she straightened up "—with our inheritance we're this close to having everything we ever dreamed of."

But I've got it all already. I'm engaged to the man I love and we're planning our wedding. I love my job. Working with vulnerable people and the Court of Protection makes me feel I'm making a real difference, as well as giving me a really good salary. And then there's Sadie. Infuriating, exasperating, but always there for me, even when she doesn't approve of the choices I make.

"You can buy that car you've been lusting over," Sadie said. "I can have a new one too, though there's probably no point just now, not when I'm going on tour."

"I don't remember you telling me about this. When?"

"Oh, in a couple of weeks. It's that Christmas show."

"You will be here for the funeral? You've got to be. You can't leave me to face it on my own."

"It'll be over and done with by then. If it's not then I won't be here. My career is more important than an old woman who didn't care for us, and we didn't really care for her, either."

"We didn't? We came back to be with her at the end. Why would we do that?"

"I don't know. A weird sense of duty? Being educated by nuns has got a lot to answer for. That and Mrs K always praying over us."

"She was praying *for* us."

Mrs Kowalska, our aunt's Polish housekeeper, with her warm arms and soft hugs, had always done her best for us. In her heavily accented English she scolded us when we misbehaved, comforted us when we cried, and was the one consistent presence throughout our childhood.

"It didn't do me much good. I was irredeemable. Don't pretend I wasn't and don't even try to lay the guilt thing on me. It doesn't matter whether we witness the burning and scattering. If I don't make it you can represent me. 'Sadie Gordon, star of stage and screen, was represented by her twin sister, international human rights lawyer, Thea Gordon.'"

"That's not what I do," I began.

Taking no notice of the interruption Sadie continued. "Wearing a black Armani dress split to the navel and carrying a bunch of deadly nightshade, Thea said, 'This is the most tragic day of my life but I know that, even in this time of sorrow, my twin sister is with me in spirit if not in the flesh'." Sadie threw her arms out in a wide extravagant gesture, then narrowed her eyes and hissed in imitation of a vampire queen, "And blood, my dear one."

"Don't do that." Her fooling reawakened the memory of that cruel laughter. "We shouldn't be talking like this. Not today, not when she's..." I glanced upwards.

"When she's lying dead in the master bedroom?

Nothing could be more fitting. This whole house reeks of pulp horror. Okay, don't give me that look. You're bloody right, it's not respectful." Sadie drawled out the words. "But why should I be? Aunt Jane never knew the meaning of the word. For her, respect was a totally alien concept." She reached for the brandy and poured herself another slug, took a gulp, then leapt up and spat it into the sink. "This stuff is vile. I think I'll stick with tea."

CHAPTER TWO

Rain dripped from the trees onto the funeral procession that wound its way along the avenue of tombs. As the only relatives, Sadie and I walked side by side behind the coffin. We were dressed in the long black coats and boots Sadie had insisted we wear. The Poet walked behind us, shambling along in his usual tweed jacket, corduroy trousers and threadbare tie, though we had persuaded him to put on a clean shirt. The rest of the mourners were fellow academics – brought together by their respect for our aunt's world-renowned work on the traditions of death and the afterlife – and the assorted ragtag that Sadie had dubbed *Aunt Jane's groupies*. Goths, elderly women, pallid young couples, gaggles of students; they'd all come to see how the professor of the occult would be laid to rest.

Hovering around the edges of our group were the tourists. Phones and cameras at the ready, they could hardly believe their luck at witnessing a funeral in the famous Arnos Vale Cemetery. Lining up shots, they whispered and pointed, then straggled away to take pictures of the more famous monuments before scampering back in case they missed anything. If they'd been expecting something flamboyant or outrageous, they were disappointed. Aunt Jane had been adamant that her funeral would be a dignified conventional affair.

The cortege passed the domed mausoleum of Raja Rammohan Roy, then the severely classical columns of a Grecian temple, the ivy-wreathed cross with the hand struggling clear of the earth that held it, before coming to a halt before the statue of an angel, its wings outstretched, its sightless eyes staring into the family grave.

I half-expect her to lift the lid and slide away. Was that Sadie's thought or my own? I risked a glance at my twin but she lowered her head and only the faint twitch at the corner of her mouth revealed that she shared the joke.

As the coffin was lowered, The Poet moved clumsily forward. Positioning himself beside the lichen-stained angel, his grey hair flowing down to his shoulders like an ancient druid, he intoned the eulogy that Jane Gordon had written for herself.

"In life she walked among the dead. In death she will be remembered among the living; counted among those who haunt our thoughts, whose souls linger in this present time. Life may change its form but nothing dies. We come from the stars and return to the heavens."

"Grief." Sadie groaned. "It sounds worse out loud than it did on paper."

I glanced over her shoulder, wondering what those clever men and women were making of the old man's apparent ramblings.

"Oh, don't worry about them. They'll just think he's demented," my sister said.

"It's grief, not dementia. He's not coping very well. Aunt Jane shouldn't have made him do this. We should have stopped it."

"We didn't have a choice. She had it all down in black and white."

The Poet began to sway, his eyes glazed as he declaimed:

"Other women cloy

"The appetites they feed, but she makes hungry

"Where most she satisfies."

"Shit," Sadie hissed. "I've had enough of this."

She dropped the single red rose she had decided we were going to carry, as a symbol of our aunt's vampiric qualities, into the grave saying as she did so, "Earth to earth, ashes to ashes, dust to dust. Fire and fleet and candlelight, and Christ receive thy soul." Then lowering her voice so that only I could hear, she added, "And make sure you stay there."

As she finished, The Poet lurched and stumbled against the stone angel. I moved to stop him falling but Sadie got there before me and taking the old man by the arm she led him away.

The crowd of mourners had begun to thin, drifting away in small groups, when I saw her. Standing a little distance from the grave was a red-haired woman in a long dress. She was watching us. Her face was drawn and her eyes over-bright as she caught and held my gaze. I had no idea who she was, or whether we'd invited her to the funeral, but the intensity of her look scared me. There was such malice in it and it seemed to be directed at me though I was sure I'd never seen her before.

"May I say how sorry I am for your loss." A rotund American with a white beard lumbered towards me. "Professor Gordon was the best in her field. There's nothing that she didn't know about the death rituals of early people. I believe she was about to publish a paper on the Kurumba tribe of Kerala when she died."

"Thank you. That's very kind. If you'll excuse me, I need to…" I was determined to challenge the red-haired woman, to ask her what she thought she was doing at our aunt's funeral, but when I looked at the spot where I'd seen her there was nothing but a tangle of trees and bushes.

"It's a rum place, this Arnos Vale. It's like the best of our Gothic cemeteries in the States. Savannah.

New Orleans. They do death well there," the American continued.

"We used to make much of it here. At least the Victorians did." A tall thin man joined us. "I would, however, argue that since then, Western culture has lost the art of celebrating mortality."

"What about the Mexican Day of the Dead, or All Souls as still practised in Eastern Europe?" Other people joined the discussion, their voices rising and falling as they moved towards the waiting cars.

And now they'll cover her up and she'll be gone. I looked around hoping to see Sadie coming back for me but there was no sign of my twin, only a plump elderly woman leaning heavily on a stick. Her face radiated warmth and concern.

"Mrs K." Still shaken from my encounter with the red-haired woman, I wanted to throw my arms around our former housekeeper and bury my face in the warmth of her body as I had done as a small and frightened child. "It's so good to see you. I didn't think you'd come." I took her hand and she squeezed my fingers. Her grip was less firm than it used to be and I was aware, yet again, of the passage of time. "You shouldn't be standing out here in the cold. Let's get you back to your car. We can talk properly at The Grand."

"No, Thea." She said my name with the beat on the last syllable. "I won't be coming to the tea. I have done my duty and I wouldn't want to intrude. Jurek will take me back to Arlington Court. He's fussing already, bless him. My nephew is such a kind boy." Mrs Kowalska nodded at the middle-aged man standing a few paces behind her.

"Oh, please stay. Just for a little while. Sadie will want to see you too." At the mention of my sister an expression I couldn't read crossed Mrs K's face.

"No, my darling. I don't think so. Jurek, help me please." She handed the stick to her nephew and he held her arm to steady her as she gestured to me to come closer. "Your sister doesn't care enough and you too much." She raised her hand and I bent my head as I had every morning before we went to school.

"May Our Lady and all the saints keep you safe now and forever, Amen." The familiar blessing swept away the last of my unease, Mrs K's scent of vanilla and biscuits taking me back to a time when a prayer and a piece of cake was enough to make everything right. "Now off you go. You have all these important people to look after." Mrs K patted my arm.

No one as important as you, I wanted to say, but Jurek was murmuring to his aunt in Polish and the moment had passed. I said my farewells, kissed them both, and hurried after the others.

~~~

"Get in. Let's get this over with." Sadie stood by the open door of the funeral car.

"What about him?" I nodded at The Poet who was already inside.

"Oh, he'll be all right. We'll stick him in a corner with a glass of whisky while we do our bit."

"I'm not looking forward to this," I said.

"Who is? It's a total farce but one that has to be played to the bitter end."

The driver shut the door and we set off through the centre of the city. The Poet stared in front of him. Sadie folded her hands in her lap preparing to get into the role of bereaved niece. I pressed mine against my empty stomach, trying to suppress its hungry gurgles.

Arriving at The Grand, we took our places in the foyer. The guests filed past, shaking our hands,
~~~

squeezing our fingers, patting our shoulders. Some kissed our cheeks, sighing extravagantly as they did so, others more restrained merely bowed their heads,

"So sorry for your loss."

"A great woman."

"Sorely missed."

Their meaningless phrases washed over me and I struggled to summon up the expected responses. Luckily, Sadie was at my side playing her part almost to the point of parody. Her voice quivered where appropriate, tears pooled in her eyes, and she pressed her lips together at the end of every sentence as if she didn't dare say any more in case she broke down completely.

You deserve that Oscar, I thought as the flow of people dribbled to a halt and the guests drifted off to fill their plates at the buffet. I was hungry but unwilling to join the chattering academics flocking around the table. To distract myself I wandered over to the windows that looked out over the wild tumbles of rock and clumps of trees that clung to the sides of the Clifton Gorge. Above them hung the graceful outline of the Suspension Bridge, below them a greasy thread of river flowed sluggishly between banks of glutinous mud.

The sky was grey with rain filled clouds. Groups of mourners formed dark shapes in the yellow light of the room. As Sadie had predicted, The Poet was slumped in an armchair, his hands clamped around a tumbler of scotch. Sadie herself, her face white, hair shining, moved from group to group, drawing their attention by the force of her presence.

I was tempted to slip away, to pretend I was going to the ladies and not come back. If I left quietly would anyone notice? Even as I planned my escape,

Sadie glanced at me from across the room and shook her head.

I gave an answering shrug and was debating whether to brave the buffet, or help myself to another glass of wine, when a tall woman, with skin so dark it had a blue-black sheen, strode into the room. I watched her cast an all-encompassing glance around the gathering, then dismissing everyone else she homed in on Sadie.

My sister's head went up like a hunted deer's. The connection between her and the newcomer was so powerful it drew the air from my lungs, leaving me weak and breathless. I groped for the nearest seat, sat down and rested my head in my hands.

"Thea, darling." William's hand was on my shoulder, the cool scent of his cologne filling my nostrils. I leaned against him gratefully and closed my eyes.

"Was it as bad as we expected?"

"Worse."

"I wish you'd let me come with you to the cemetery. You could have done with my support."

"Perhaps, but it had to be me and…" I looked up. The woman who had been talking to Sadie had moved away and my sister was sitting at the bar, a glass of prosecco in front of her, chatting to a tall fair-haired professor from Sweden.

"He looks like you," I said. "How odd."

"Are you all right?"

"I am now you're here." I took his hand. "I need something to eat. I'm starving." I cuddled up against him.

"It's hard losing what's left of your family," he murmured.

I've still got Sadie. I resisted looking back at her, angling my head so that I focussed on William's face as he continued. "It can't have been easy growing up with someone like your great-aunt. Clever woman, successful too. But only ever interested in her work."

"We had Mrs K. It wasn't all bad."

"No childhood is. Even so, there are always things buried beneath the level of consciousness. It's too soon to talk but you know I'll be there for you when you're ready."

A prickle of irritation made me draw away. William meant it for the best but I didn't want to be analysed. I wanted to stuff myself full of food, drink a huge glass of wine, and go home.

Freeing myself from his grasp, I could feel him watching me as I went over to the table and started to load my plate.

"The smoked salmon canapes are good." Sadie was beside me. "Go on, have one. William won't mind."

"Why should he?" I said a little too quickly.

"Because he loves you?" There was a slight rise to Sadie's voice which I chose to ignore but my appetite had gone. What was left of the buffet looked stale and tired: the salad garnish limp, bread curling at the edges, tomatoes leaching onto grease-smeared plates, cream solid as cement, or flopping out of soggy pastries.

"The gannets, having fed, are preparing to leave," Sadie said drily as a party of professors clattered their way out of the room. "Shall we hurry the rest of them along? We could strip off and flaunt ourselves along the bar in positions last seen on one of Aunt Jane's funeral vases," she whispered and I bit the inside of my cheek to hold back the giggles. "On the other hand, best play it straight. We don't want anyone dying of shock. Let's do our final bit.

You take that lot and I'll do these."

It took a little time to get through the farewells, condolences and long-winded anecdotes from the departing guests, but the room was almost empty when William came over and took my hand. "Come on Thea, you've done your duty. It's time to go."

I looked across the room at The Poet, still sitting in the same chair, his gaze vacant, his face drained of colour.

"I can't leave him."

"Sadie can take him home." There was an edge of impatience in William's voice.

"I should be there with her," I said, even though Belvedere Crescent was the last place I wanted to be.

"Then let me help you with him."

"He doesn't know you. He's old and sad and it's only for one night."

"So you're not coming back with me?"

I thought of William's sleek white house, its pristine surfaces and large rooms, where each carefully selected object had its appointed place, and shook my head. Tonight I needed to burrow into the warmth and clutter of my small flat.

"It's something I've got to do. I'll see you tomorrow." I stood on tiptoe and lifted my face to be kissed. His lips were warm, the hug he gave me forgiving.

Beyond the curved Art Deco window, the sky roiled with storm clouds.

~~~

"I thought the funeral went well. We even managed to look as if we were sad." Sadie reached for the bottle she'd liberated from the wake and poured us both another large glass of white wine.

"Angels' Tears. How inappropriate," she snorted.
~~~

"Why wasn't there anything called Devil's Rise, or Demon Blood?"

"Too *Buffy the Vampire Slayer*."

"You're telling me we don't need her services?"

I ran my finger along the rim of my glass, raising a high-pitched note that echoed around the kitchen. "At the cemetery..." I hesitated, reluctant to give weight to something that might have been nothing but an illusion conjured up by the surroundings, then decided if there was anyone, I could share this with, it would be Sadie. "I saw someone."

"There were one or two guests." Sadie's voice was laced with sarcasm.

Ignoring her mockery, I continued, "There was a woman with red hair. She was half hidden in the trees but she caught my gaze and the look she gave me was..."

"Yes?" Sadie prompted.

"I don't know how to describe it. It was as if she hated me. No. Not just me. Both of us."

"That's a bit extreme."

"That's what it felt like."

"You mean you were seeing things?"

"I wouldn't say that."

"Okay then. How else do you explain it? I think it was because you'd missed breakfast and you know what you're like when your blood sugar goes crazy."

"You're not taking me seriously. I'm trying to tell you something really important. Why are you being like this?"

"I don't know." Sadie wouldn't meet my gaze. Finally, focussing on a spot somewhere above my left shoulder, she said, "Maybe it's because of all those years when you didn't believe *me*." She gave a wry smile. "It ought to make me more sympathetic but hey, you know me."

"Are you saying I imagined it?"

"No I'm not. It might have been Aunt Jane come to see if we were doing what she wanted for her funeral, or it might not have been."

"I'm sure it wasn't her. This will sound even madder but it frightened me. I had the same feeling as on the night she died."

My sister took my hand. "You're shaking."

"I wish I hadn't said anything." I withdrew my fingers. "What are we doing, sitting here talking about all this stuff? Why did we come back?"

"To put The Poet to bed. There was no one else." Sadie stuck out her lip. "We'll have to make a decision about him soon. Before he starts marching around the Centre in his underpants."

"He won't do that. He'll curl up and die. He's not going senile. He's grieving."

"And we're not?"

"How can we? We don't – *I* don't – feel anything."

"Me neither." Sadie yawned.

"Is it normal to be like this?" I asked.

"I don't know. We've never lost anyone before, at least not when we were old enough to understand. Anyway, I'm tired and far too drunk to go back to Dominic's. He'd only decide that what I need is sex, which I do, but not with him."

"You can come back to mine."

"What about the ever-doting William?"

"I told him to go home. I said I needed to do this with you and he was fine about it."

"It's just us, then." Sadie smiled her satisfied-cat smile.

"Yeah. It'll be good. The heating works, the fridge is full of food, and I'm sure I can find a few more bottles of wine." I got to my feet ready to go – and the room swayed around me. I grabbed hold of the table to stop myself from falling over.

"And how are we going to get there? You're well over the limit," Sadie said.

"I know." I sank back into the chair. "I don't think I could walk let alone drive." Slumping forward, I rested my head on my arms. "We'll get a cab," I mumbled.

"Don't think so. The amount you've had, you're likely to throw up. It looks like one last night in the old house. It'll be all right. It'll have to be." Sadie leaned over and poured us both another glass, carefully measuring out the wine. "I think we've killed it. There's not a single ... drop ... left. The angels have wept the last of their tears. Aunt Jane is dead and buried and I'm going to bed. Do you want our old room, or can I have it?"

"I'm not sure I want to be on my own." I stood up as carefully as I could.

"Don't be then. We can share. The bed's big enough. We can—"

"Pretend we're eleven again." *When we were really close and told each other everything.*

"Yeah, let's." Sadie put an arm around my waist. She waved a hand, as if fluttering a handkerchief. "Goodnight sweet ladies, goodnight." She bobbed her head and smiled as if on stage.

"Don't drown in the bath," I said.

"I'm not going to. It's too cold. Whoever put the heating in this place should be eviscerated. Struck from the plumbing list."

"Stuffed with their own pipework."

"Liquefied in their own gas."

"I don't think that's possible," I said.

Senses blurred by wine, I followed my sister up the kitchen stairs. Like children, we went to the bathroom together. The white tiled walls glimmered under the florescent light giving our reflections a greenish tinge as we brushed our teeth in front of the mirror.

"I've got to get up early tomorrow. I've got an audition for an indie film. Probably won't lead to anything much but who knows." Sadie cleaned off the last of her scarlet lipstick and wiped away the lines she'd drawn around her eyes. Dipping her fingers into a pot of night cream, she held up a dollop. "They swear this stuff holds back wrinkles. Do you think if I use enough of it, I'll stay young forever? Or do you have to be a vampire for that?" She leaned into the glass and curled back her lip. "It's a shame they don't make B movies anymore. I'd be good in shlock horror."

You'd be good in anything. From the moment Sadie had appeared as the fourth angel on the right in the school Nativity play, it was obvious that she had that charismatic stage presence that meant the audience couldn't help but focus their attention on her.

"You go and warm the PJs. I'll be there in a minute." Sadie squinted into the mirror, examining her skin for any possible blemish. In the black dress she had worn for the funeral she resembled one of the silhouettes that hung in the drawing room. Profiles of people long dead; they were our Georgian equivalent of family photos.

Leaving the bathroom door open, I followed the spill of light along the corridor, where a trellis of brown leaves crawled over the dark-green wallpaper and sepia prints in black frames looked down on the frayed runner. When we were little, we'd played that the carpet was a flower-strewn path to a magical land. In the game, monsters and dragons lurked under the floorboards on either side, so Sadie said we had to make sure our feet never touched the bare wood because one wrong step and the creatures would emerge, their eyes burning with hellish fire, jaws dripping blood, to drag us into their lair.

On cross, awkward days, we pushed and shoved each other, jabbing with our elbows and kicking at ankles. The twin knocked off balance grabbed hold of her sister and dug her nails into her arm.

We never let each other fall.

I looked over my shoulder at the lighted doorway at the other end of the corridor. From this angle Sadie's figure was distorted, diminished, like Alice at the bottom of the well. Moving my head sent the walls and floor spinning and I shut my eyes, willing the dizziness to stop. The scent of Sadie's cream wafted past me as she hurried into the bedroom and when I opened my eyes again the lights in the bathroom and in the corridor had been switched off.

In our old nursery nothing had changed. The same shiny eiderdown, patterned with tiny rosebuds that matched the sprigs of roses on the faded wallpaper, covered the white wrought-iron bed we'd shared as children. A collection of kid's books filled the painted bookshelf, our old school desks stood on either side of the cast-iron fireplace, and the tall dolls' house still stood opposite the bed.

Neither of us had cleared out all our clothes when we left. I found a pair of my pyjamas in a drawer, took Sadie's oversized t-shirt out of her bag and put them, side by side, to warm on the radiator.

"It won't do any good. There's no heat coming through." Sadie unzipped her dress. The shift slid to the floor and kicking it aside, she pulled off the rest of her clothes. Grabbing the t-shirt, she had it over her head and was diving under the eiderdown before I'd started to undress.

"Thanks for warming the bed."

"You knew I was going to do that."

"You always have to be first." I got in and stretched a tentative leg along the icy sheet. "It's because I was born ten minutes before you. You're forever trying to catch up."

"No, I'm not," Sadie yawned. "Your feet are freezing. Haven't you got any bed socks?"

"I didn't find any and I'm not getting out of bed again."

Avoiding the dip in the middle of the mattress, I positioned myself on one side of the bed. Sadie lay flat on her back on the other. We were close enough to feel the warmth of our bodies but not near enough to touch.

We're like figures on a tomb, I thought, holding my body rigid to stop myself rolling into her.

"This feels strange but right." Sadie's voice was slurring into sleep. "Switch the light off, sis." I pulled the cord that dangled above the bed and blotted out the room. Only the squares of the sash window etched against the thin curtains remained until they too faded into darkness.

Turning on my side, I sank into the lumpy mattress and with my back against Sadie's, I drifted into sleep.

~~~

"Thea, wake up."

We're eleven years old and Sadie is kicking me, her nails cat's claws nicking my ankle. Snug in a cocoon of eiderdown, sheets and blankets, I struggle out of sleep.

"Did you hear it?" My twin, in her tartan pyjamas, is sitting on the edge of the bed. "She was here. Where you are."

Moonlight splashes on bare boards. Frost
~~~

patterns form on un-curtained glass. Beyond the window lies a cityscape of roofs and chimney pots. Sadie draws her knees up to her chin and stares at the wall. I burrow deeper under the covers but the chill air slides down my back, dispelling the warm fug of our bodies.

"She was crying," Sadie whispers.

"Aunt Jane?" The thought of outspoken, hard-faced Aunt Jane shedding a tear, let alone weeping, is so astonishing that I wriggle up the bed to join my twin. Our shoulders touch but Sadie ignores me and leans forward, her face strained as if she is listening. Whatever it is, I can't hear it.

I tug my ears but it makes no difference. There must be something wrong with my hearing because whatever Sadie can do, I can do it too. It's because we're identical. It's always been like that. Except tonight, when however hard I try all I can hear is the faint tick tock of the grandfather clock in the hall two storeys down. The bed creaks, my tummy gurgles and I wish it was time for breakfast.

~~~

That was the beginning, I thought. That's when it all started.

No. It was long before that. They were always there. I thought if I could hear them you could hear them too. Sadie's voice was in my head.

Before I could reply, the shrill of the alarm and a hand flapping against the pillow jolted me into full consciousness.

"Shit, shit, shit." Sadie sat up. Eyes smudged with mascara, hair sticking up, she looked like a startled porcupine. "I've got to go or I'll be late for the audition. Where the hell did I put my shoes?" She bent from the waist and leaned over the side of the bed. I pressed my head against the pillow and
~~~

willed myself not to throw up.

Sadie stood on the sheepskin rug yelling into her phone. "Pick up, Dominic, can't you. Fuck." She ended the call. "Now I'll have to call a cab." She jabbed at the screen, gave directions then rummaged through her bag for clean underwear. In bra and pants, skin prickled with goose bumps, she checked her messages. Hissed "Bastard." Slid a loose woollen dress over her head, tugged on scarlet tights, and thrust her feet into suede ankle boots.

"I've got time to do my face. I'll grab a coffee on the way," she said and hurried off to the bathroom.

But I haven't asked you. Last night I dreamed... Or was it a dream? It had been so vivid that it was as if I was really there.

Not possible, I told myself. *Too much alcohol, too much emotion and being back in our old room – that's all it was.*

On the other hand, it had spurred me into wanting to ask the questions I'd been avoiding for years. I slid up into a sitting position, ready to get out of bed. It was too late. The front door opened, then slammed. Sadie had gone.

CHAPTER THREE

A fuzz of new leaves softened the branches of the trees. The sky was sharp blue, the light cruel, seeking out cracks in the pavements and lingering on the film of moisture speckling the flanks of cars that had been parked overnight.

I locked the Fiat, slung my bag over my shoulder and ignored the phone vibrating in my pocket. I was already late for our meeting. William had been right when he told me there was no need to call into the office but I'd had to reassure myself that I'd done everything I could on Mrs Blackmore's estate; attention to detail was vital in my work. Now that I'd done that, I was free to enjoy the weekend.

The Lemon Tree bistro stood on the corner of a tree-lined residential street. This early in the year there was still a bite in the air, but tables and chairs had been set out under the bright-yellow awning and a few intrepid customers were sitting outside, drinking coffee and working their way through the Saturday papers.

Pushing open the door, I was enveloped by the smell of coffee, clink of cutlery and murmur of voices. William and Sadie were at a table in the corner. He had an espresso, she a large mug of chocolate; both looking steadily in front of them.

"You made it." Sadie dipped her head over the whirl of cream on the top of her mug and sipped, catlike.

"I've ordered you a latte and a Danish." William moved his chair so that I could sit beside him. Sadie glanced up and, sticking out her tongue, ran it around her lips.

"There's some cream on your nose." I pointed out, reaching for the plate in front of me. The pastry was apricot and almond, my favourite combination.

"Aren't you eating, William?" Sadie bit into a pain-au-chocolat. "Or is it all too fattening?" She chewed extravagantly and gave a little grunt of pleasure. The whole performance was intended to provoke a reaction, though by now she should have known that he wouldn't respond. He never did rise to her bait, priding himself on keeping his cool while Sadie did everything she could to antagonise him, which was why I'd always found it was better not to see them both at the same time.

Behave yourself. I shot a glance at Sadie, who opened her eyes wide as if startled by the idea that she might be doing something she shouldn't. Fighting back the urge to slap her, I took a gulp of my rapidly cooling coffee. It was a little too weak and milky and left a greasy taste in my mouth that had to be countered by the sharpness of the apricot in my pastry.

"Let's get on with it, shall we?" Sadie said. "I've got a dance workshop at two, in Bedminster."

William leaned back in his seat. "I wanted to talk to you both, face to face, because now that probate has been granted we have to decide what you're going to do with Belvedere Crescent."

"We're going to sell it. Thea and I decided ages ago. Neither of us want it. Do we, sis?" Sadie turned to me and I was about to agree when I was silenced by an unexpected reluctance. "You haven't changed your mind, have you? The Poet's gone. I told you he wouldn't last long after Aunt Jane." She snapped her fingers. "It was for the best. He could never have coped in that house on his own. You know that."

"I do." I blinked away the memory of The Poet

padding up and down the stairs in faded tartan slippers, or getting drunk with Aunt Jane in the kitchen. "Belvedere is the only house we've ever known. It's where we were brought up."

"Don't say it." Sadie raised a warning finger. "Don't tell me it's home."

"Where else was there?"

"That was true when we were kids but we got out as soon as we could. You've got your own flat and I've lived all over and when Belvedere is sold, I'll finally have the chance to get my own place. Only I can't do it without my half share."

"To which you are entitled under the provisions of your great-aunt's will. Your aunt was a wealthy woman and a very astute one when it came to caring for her dependents. There was a lot of money in her estate, much more than one would have expected."

"That's okay then. We're sorted. Committee meeting over." Sadie pushed back her chair.

"Wait a moment. Thea—" William put his hand on mine "—you haven't told us what you want."

That's because I don't know. I pressed my lips together, my colour rising as two pairs of eyes, one green, one blue, turned to look at me. Why were they so shocked? It was as if I had failed some sort of test when all I was doing was trying to disentangle the whirl of emotion that had clouded my mind. Could it be that, in spite of everything Sadie and I had agreed and all that had happened in our childhood, Belvedere Crescent represented a security I didn't want to lose? Which made no sense as William and I were getting married and going to live in a house of our own.

"Thea?" William prompted gently and dismissing the sliver of doubt curled in the pit of my stomach, I replied, "I'm fine with it. I don't know what came over me. Forget it."

Cupping her hand in her chin, Sadie let out a dramatic sigh, then glancing up she grinned at me.

"We're all in agreement then. The house is to be sold," William said. We nodded. "There will be a lot of work to do before putting it on the market. If you don't want to tackle it we can get a house clearance firm to do it. After it's been valued, naturally."

"There's some antique furniture and Aunt Jane's books will be worth quite a bit. We'll need a specialist antiquarian bookseller for those," I said.

"I think we should go through it all ourselves first," Sadie said. "There's so much. I don't think Aunt Jane ever threw anything away. We'll do it together. Except for all that paperwork in her study. You know I'm useless at that."

Only when you want to be, I thought, remembering how effectively Sadie could put together a grant application.

"Okay. I'll do the boring stuff but you're not disappearing and leaving me with everything else."

"As if I would." Sadie stretched out her hands. "I can't wait to go through all those trunks in the attic that we were never allowed to open as kids. Think of the clothes. I wouldn't be surprised if some of them were eighteenth century. Genuine period costumes and props. Those I can't use we can sell. I know theatrical costumiers who'll pay loads for anything like that. We can start on it right now. This afternoon."

"I thought you'd got a workshop."

"Oh yeah, but I can come round later. I'll be there about four. See you." She stood up, grabbed her bag and with a quick wave was gone.

"Your sister is remarkably good at getting her own way," William remarked drily as the door of the bistro swung shut behind her.

"That's Sadie." I was not in the mood for discussing my sister. A topic William found endlessly fascinating as he loved to speculate on how the differences between us might be the result of our dysfunctional childhood. Seeking a diversion, I scanned the menu. "It's a bit early but if I'm going to start on the house I might as well have some lunch before I go."

"I won't. Just coffee for me."

"I'm starving." My need to eat was always greater than William's – something he rarely failed to comment on. Right now I was lusting after Mrs K's donuts. Freshly fried, sprinkled with icing sugar, they were bubble light and full of hot sweet jam that, when you bit into them, ran down the chin like blood.

"You're comfort eating, which is not surprising. You'll feel better when the house has been sold. Things will have been resolved and you'll find you're ready to move on. At the moment I feel that you're—" He was interrupted by the waitress wanting to know if we were ready to order.

"A turkey, bacon and avocado panini and a cappuccino," I said, then turned to William. "You don't have to stay and watch me eat."

"I could come to Belvedere with you," he offered. I said nothing and he continued, "You don't think it's a good idea?"

"Not really. You know Sadie..." I spread out my hands, not wanting to say more.

"It's all right. I understand. You two go and spend the afternoon rooting around in your great-aunt's house. I'll catch up with some paperwork, then I'll cook dinner."

"For the three of us?" I teased.

"For you and me," he said.

~~~

I let the front door slam shut behind me, its hollow clang reverberating through the empty house.

Sadie was right. We were the last of the Gordons – and our family had lived in this house since it had been built – so we should be the ones to clear it. Every generation had left their traces. Nothing had ever been thrown out, just added to. The attic storeroom was full of boxes and trunks where goodness only knew what had been stored. Furniture, books, pictures and ornaments from every era jostled for space. Sorting through it would be like an archaeological dig, sifting through layer after layer, to see what could be thrown out, what sold or given away and what, if anything, had to be kept.

Perhaps we'd turn up some document about the family's past, an ancient scandal, or a cache of letters that would tell us about the lives of people we'd never known.

A shaft of sun shone through the yellow square of stained glass on the landing window, bathing the staircase in a warm light. In contrast, the first-floor corridor was dreary and tinged with the smell of a house that had not been aired.

I was about to open a few doors and windows when the smell intensified, the staleness growing sweeter and sweeter until it became a cloying mix of powdery almond, cherry syrup and vanilla that slid down my throat in a parody of the apricot pastry I had eaten at The Lemon Tree.

My stomach heaved and I pressed my hands against my mouth. I had to get to the toilet before I threw up. I spun round, making for the stairs.

The sunlight from the landing window had gone.
~~~

It was blocked by a swirl of dust that broadened and coalesced into a pale figure in a black dress.

"No," I cried. "You're not real."

The woman from the cemetery smiled and took a step forward.

I held up my hands. "Go away. Leave me alone."

She glided towards me and I backed away, banging into the wall as she cut off my escape.

CHAPTER FOUR

"Thea. Thea? For God's sake, let me in." Sadie was yelling and banging at the door. At the same time my phone was ringing. And the figure in front of me was fading.

My legs shook as I crept down the stairs. Getting to the door was like wading against the tide with the sand sliding beneath my feet. I turned the key; the door burst open and Sadie rushed in.

Seizing my hand she cried, "I've been out here for ages. I rang the doorbell, then I knocked and when you still didn't answer I rang your mobile. What were you doing? What's going on?"

"She was here." I gripped Sadie's hand, clinging on to her for reassurance. "At the top of the stairs. I couldn't get past her."

"It's all right. I've got you." Sadie put her arm around me and pushing open the door to the drawing room she helped me inside. I sank down onto a sofa.

"I don't know what I would have done if you hadn't come."

"I had to. I got this feeling." Sadie's hand closed over mine. "I knew there was something wrong and as I came in something cold brushed through me." She shuddered and I hugged her. "It was like an electric shock. Only of the icy variety. One minute I was sweating like stink from running all the way here, then I was swamped by this wave of freezing air. If the bloody car hadn't decided to die on me I'd have got here sooner."

"I'm glad you're here." My voice shook.

"So am I."

Fighting to stave off the fear that lapped around the edges of the room, we curled into each other. Sadie's head rested on mine, our breath mingled, our heartbeats synchronising as they'd done in the womb. Our limbs relaxed and gradually my grip loosened, allowing Sadie to move out of my embrace. My hand was still on her hip but the cocoon-like intensity had gone.

The room was filled with a dingy half-light out of which, like boats beached on a long-forgotten shore, loomed the familiar shapes of worn chairs, sofas covered with throws, and side tables cluttered with books and ashtrays. On either end of the mantelpiece was one of a pair of brass candlesticks, dull with lack of polish, the space between them crowded with a random selection of objects: a Chinese horse; a terracotta warrior; a marble bust of a Greek god; a bronze Kali with her necklace of skulls; a tiny bottle, its glass opaque with age; a seashell; a pile of opened envelopes.

Sadie's nostrils widened. Her eyes narrowed and she put her head to one side as if listening. After a while she said, "I think she's gone."

"Are you sure?" Sweat prickled on my shoulders.

"Not completely. But I don't feel I'm under attack anymore." Sadie stood up. "We should get the place exorcised. Or do you think it would be a good selling point? 'Georgian mid-terrace house, in exclusive neighbourhood, resident ghost included in the asking price'."

"Sadie, be serious."

"Why? It's over."

For now. The words lingered unspoken between us.

"We don't have to stay long. We can go right now if you want. But it would be a shame not to take a look at that stuff in the attics." Sadie gave me that sideways glance that I found so hard to resist. The one that said, *I'm braver than you,* while at the same time asking me to be the big sister and help her to get what she wanted.

I took a breath of dead air. "Sorry. I can't face it right now. We can do it another day." I heaved myself to my feet.

"There's no changing your mind?"

"No." Now that I was leaving, the heaviness that had sapped my energy was gone. "Do you want a lift to where you left your car?"

"No. It's outside the flat. I went back to have a shower after the workshop and when I tried to start it the bloody thing wouldn't go. I'll get Tom from the garage to fix it. Shit, Thea, I can't. He's away on holiday and I've got this audition in Bath on Monday." She paused. "It's really important."

"You want me to take you?"

"Could you?"

"I will if I can but I do have work to do. Anyway it's not far. You can get the train."

"It costs too much." Sadie pouted. "And there's always engineering works on that line and if they put on replacement buses, I can't be sure of getting there on time." She moved her shoulders in a barely perceptible shrug. A tiny movement that somehow managed to convey both disappointment and disbelief that anyone could deny her something so vital.

You're manipulating me, I thought as I went into the hall to fetch my bag. *But, hey, you're the only sister I've got.*

I took out my phone and scrolled through the calendar to see if there was any time during the day when I could slip out of the office, but there was no leeway in the list of appointments, interspersed with meetings, that I couldn't miss. If I were still in my own flat I would ring in sick, but I lived with William, who was a partner in the firm, so this was not an option.

"Sorry. Monday's full of client meetings. If you're broke, I can lend you the money for the train – or a taxi if there's any disruption. Better still, I'll give it to you."

"No thanks. I'll be fine. I'll manage, somehow." The slight emphasis on the last word conveyed a world of hurt. "Being that your job is more important than my whole career." She slid from the role of patient sufferer into that of petulant child.

"That's not what I said."

"It's what you meant."

"I did not." We were descending into childhood scrapping and I couldn't do anything to stop it. The pattern was set, the next line inevitable.

"It's all right. I'll get there without you." Sadie flounced out of the room.

I waited, determined not to call out or be sucked into feeling that it was my fault that she couldn't have what she wanted. Then the front door banged and I had to fight down a rush of guilt. It didn't matter that whatever I said or did, Sadie would get to her audition. I still felt bad.

My twin could be totally selfish, infuriating and manipulative or, when it suited her, entrancing, loveable and loyal. She might take advantage of me but it was always the pair of us against the rest of the world, and when she'd thought I was in danger she'd come running, so how could I let her storm off in anger?

I fumbled with the catch and flung open the front door. Shielding my eyes from the sharpness of the light, I peered down the street but I couldn't see her. When Sadie was angry she moved fast and was probably halfway down the hill. The only chance I had of catching up with her was to get into the car and follow the route back to her flat. Even then I might miss her and from experience it was better to let Sadie stamp and swear until she'd calmed down. It never took long – her moods were fleeting – but if the process was interrupted she'd sulk for days.

Tomorrow, I'd send her a text wishing her luck. By Monday evening, we'd be back in balance, this afternoon's spat forgotten in the triumph of Sadie's totally deserved success; or her despair at being rejected for a role that was not only made for her but would have been the first step in her stellar success, if only the terminally stupid director had recognised her talent.

That's how it'll be. That is how it always is. Nothing changes. I comforted myself with the thought as I locked the door on whatever was inside.

~~~

My phone lay on the desk in front of me and I was doing my best to ignore it. It was mid-afternoon and apart from a quick kiss, texted the night before, there had been no word from Sadie.

Mrs Norman was staring at me blankly. Her face was grey with exhaustion, her hair lank. Her husband's behaviour was becoming increasingly erratic and I suspected that it was too late to start the process of granting his wife power of attorney.

"We must be able to prove to the court that your husband is capable of making a decision," I said. Mrs Norman stifled a nervous cry. Before I could explain further my phone buzzed. Startled, she jerked back in her seat.

"I'm sorry about that." I stretched out my hand to
~~~

switch it off.

"Got the part!" Sadie's message flashed across the screen and the feeling of inertia that had weighed me down lifted like mist in sunlight.

"That was my sister," I explained but my client barely responded. I gave her a reassuring smile. "Let's see what we can do for your situation." My head was clear, the throbbing behind my eyes had gone. I talked Mrs Norman through her options, leaving her resigned, if not hopeful, and completed the paperwork.

Afternoon slid into early evening. The office lights buzzed and flickered, the staff began to leave, hurrying to collect children from school or nursery, or to avoid rush hour in the city centre. I turned over the final page of the document I'd been working on, closed the file and stood up. Pain sliced through my head, stealing my breath as the room whirled. I grabbed at the desk but couldn't stop myself from falling. Vague shapes surrounded me. I heard words I didn't understand, then darkness swept over me.

"It's all right, darling, the paramedics are on their way." I was lying on the floor, William kneeling beside me his hand on mine, his long fingers pressing lightly, holding me down, keeping me from floating into endless sleep. The part of me that had become untethered looked down on my body, its eyes shut, arms and legs limp; the office girls ranged around it like a Greek chorus; William's white-blonde hair falling over his forehead, his blue eyes willing me to stay. I didn't want to leave, nor did I want to slide back into the heaviness of flesh and blood, the clumsy weight of arms and legs. Without them, it was so peaceful, drifting, feeling nothing.

Then came a sharp tug, followed by a dragging sensation, as if my insides were being slowly pulled from my chest, and a painful gasping and gulping down of air thick as water. My ribs ached, my head pounded. My heart leapt, fingers and toes prickling as the blood flowed back through my veins.

The rim of a glass was pressed against my lips. Water slid down my throat and I swallowed awkwardly. Liquid dribbled down my chin. William took out his handkerchief and dabbed at my skin. A duo of footsteps clumped up the stairs. The members of the chorus fell back, yellow jackets crackled and creaked.

"Thea, how are you doing, my lover?" A female paramedic knelt down beside me. "Do you have any pain?"

"Thea?" William's voice was sharp with anxiety. I had to say something but my tongue was too big to form the words I needed to describe the never-ending emptiness that stretched out before me.

"We'll have to take you in, my lover."

They carried me out of the office into the waiting ambulance. A plastic mask was put over my face and from time to time the paramedic checked to see if I was still breathing. The insistent calling of my name buzzed in my ears, something bleeped, the vehicle swerved and bounced. Everything fell away and for a single moment there was nothing but darkness, then lights dazzled, voices cajoled, murmured, questioned and I was being wheeled into a cubicle and the curtains were closed around my bed.

~~~

"They've done all the tests." William looked pale and drawn. "They've found nothing wrong but they want to keep you in overnight just to be sure." He squeezed my hand. "I'll fetch your things as soon as we know which ward you're in."
~~~

"Is it all right to come in?" The curtains around the bed billowed and, without waiting for a reply, a nurse entered. She looked at William, then at me. "Thea, there's someone who has to see you."

A feeling of such intense loss swept over me that I closed my eyes and prayed that I could stay in this moment, however painful, for what lay before me was far, far worse.

"Thea Gordon?"

In contrast to the pale greyness of the hospital, the police were squat black shapes, wired to their radios. The woman was the one that spoke. "I'm afraid I have some bad news."

CHAPTER FIVE

The June sun blazed through curved windows. Black glazing bars bisected the view, holding me trapped in a wide white bed. I wished that I could slip back into the dreamless dark that had saved me in those first weeks after Sadie's death. Now my nights were broken and I lay awake for hours, unable to sleep. By morning I would be drifting off into a shallow doze which left me, as it had done today, with dry eyes, cracked lips, and skin stretched tight over my bones.

I looked at the carafe of water that stood on the mirrored bedside cabinet and was wondering whether I had the energy to pour myself a glass when William came in.

"You're awake." He kissed me lightly on the forehead and I smelled his clean scent. The reek of my unwashed skin wafted up from beneath the covers and I slid lower into the bed. "Do you feel strong enough to get up? Or shall I bring your coffee up to you?"

There was a splash of sunlight on the deco dressing table. I watched it shimmer and spread, washing over the white pot that held my makeup brushes. Like everything else in this house it had been carefully chosen. Had William had me in mind when he bought it? Or was it there before he'd even met me, waiting for the woman he'd chosen to share his life?

"Thea?"

I had to make a decision. I ought to get up, have a shower, go downstairs, sit beside him at the pristine breakfast bar in the pristine kitchen, drinking freshly ground coffee and feasting on pain-au-chocolat, meltingly hot from the oven.

The thought of the sweet stickiness of the pastry and bitter taste of coffee, which once would have been so appealing, brought the acid to my throat. My hands moved to my stomach, which lay flat between my hipbones, its soft roundness gone. If only I could lie here until the rest of me dissolved and I could slip between those bars and escape into a place where there was no more feeling.

"I'll make you a latte. That's what you need. I'll bring it up."

Or I will. The flash of grim humour surprised me. The image of vomit, a violent splurge of colour in all this whiteness, amused and appalled me. The thought of milk, heavy and hot, made my stomach churn.

"I don't want anything, just a glass of water."

"Thea, you can't keep doing this." William sat down on the bed. "You have to eat. Darling, you're fading away. I can't bear to see you like this." He reached under the duvet and took my hand.

Would William, with his aversion to germs, kiss those unwashed sweaty fingers? Did he care for me that much? Did I care if he didn't love me anymore? My hand, as he raised it to his lips, was limp and unresponsive.

"I know you've had a terrible shock. We all have. But I promise, things will get better. Given time."

Of course they would. And it was time I began my recovery was the subtext. There were, according to the experts, seven stages of grief, all of which had to be negotiated before I became whole again.

William never said it but I knew from his attitude that he considered a couple of months was long enough for stage one, so by now I should be moving on to the next. Was that one anger? An uncontrollable rage at God, or the universe, or whoever I could find to blame for what had happened? If it was denial I was living through, then I was doing it wrong. I knew that Sadie was dead; that a blood vessel in her brain had burst as she was crossing the road.

Afterwards, when I'd been discharged from the hospital, I'd gone to the mortuary to say, "Yes that's my twin. That's Sadie."

She'd looked as if she was asleep, as if at any moment she'd open her eyes, give me that wicked green look of hers, and say the whole thing was a brilliant joke and it was time to get off this trolley thing and get a drink.

To celebrate getting that part in the audition.

The audition I was too busy to drive her to.

"Oh." I breathed out as the sharpness of my guilt briefly pierced the grey fog in which I spent my days.

"What is it?" William tightened his grip.

"Nothing." The response was automatic. What else was there to say? There were no words that could describe the numbness that enveloped me.

"It would help to talk to someone." William got to his feet. "How about if you had a shower, got dressed and came down for breakfast? In the meantime, I'll research who'd be the best person for you to see."

I didn't reply. William would do what he thought was best for me and perhaps he was right. I should be talking out my grief, letting it spill like water from a broken bottle, draining away into the earth where it would moisten the soil, making it damp and warm, ready for new growth.

Bollocks to that!

Was that Sadie's voice or mine? It was the sort of thing she would say, cutting through the crap, telling it how it was.

A surge of energy sent me to my feet. I walked into the shower and let a stream of hot water beat down on my head and shoulders. It washed away the grime and sweat, taking with them some of my exhaustion. I made up my mind that from now on I'd ignore all the advice people kept giving me and do only what I felt was right for me.

My sister had always done what she wanted. Now it was my turn.

"Great timing," William said as I came into the kitchen. "I've warmed a croissant and your coffee is ready."

Why hadn't he listened when I told him I wasn't hungry? I didn't need anything to eat, my stomach wasn't aching and being free of the desire to stuff my face was liberating.

"When it happened. When Sadie died and you brought me—" The word *home* hovered but couldn't be expressed. "Here," I compromised.

"Yes?"

I stared out of the window at the expanse of lawn, bordered by dark conifers that shut off the view. Beyond them was the sudden drop into the Avon Gorge, a jaggedness of rocks, where Alpine plants clung to sheer stone above the unforgiving surface of the road.

"I don't know what I would have done without you but—" my eyes strayed to the row of white kitchen units, their surfaces rounded and glossy reflecting the sharp morning sunlight and I had to force my gaze back "—I have to start doing things for myself."

"That's good. You're making progress."

I took a sip of coffee, crumbled the pastry on my plate, lifted a flake to my mouth, and put it down again. The taste of butter and sugar revolted me. I longed for the cool juiciness of a peach, the slightly tart sweetness of black grapes, the subtleness of watermelon with its red flesh and large flat seeds. When we were little, Sadie and I had collected those pips and dried them and Mrs K had shown us how to thread them up into necklaces.

Outside the window, the contrast between conifers and sky was stark.

"I'm going to start by clearing the house." I pushed away my plate and got to my feet.

"What? We sold your flat, remember? When you were ill?"

I wasn't ill. I was in shock. I was grieving. "I haven't forgotten. I meant Belvedere Crescent."

"You mustn't do too much. Not to begin with. Okay?"

"I won't. Doing something practical will help clear my head. And this is something I have to do." I paused, surprised at strength of my conviction. It was the first time I'd stepped outside my grief since Sadie had died. William was shaking his head but I went on: "It was what we were doing before the accident."

"If you and Sadie were doing that together, then going back there will be a big step. You're not strong enough physically or emotionally to deal with that."

"I'll be fine." I thought of that last afternoon, but the figure I'd seen on the stairs didn't raise a shudder. She was a premonition and the worst had happened. Sadie was gone. Nothing could be worse than that.

"You might be right." Seeing I was not going to change my mind, William changed his approach. "The house does have to be cleared before we put it on the market. But only if you feel up to it. There's no hurry to sell. We can finance the new one easily enough without your aunt's money." He pulled me close and kissed the top of my head. I let him hold me, for a moment, then stepped away.

"You're not going now," he protested.

"I thought I would." I kept my voice light.

"Without eating breakfast? That's not the Thea I know."

"I'll get something later. At the deli," I improvised hastily as the urge to leave became increasingly more urgent. "Don't worry." I reached up and kissed him.

"I can drop you off on my way to the office."

"No. I'll take the car," I said, even though the thought of driving after so many weeks made my hands clammy and my insides churn. "It's not far."

It won't take long. You can do it. You've been driving for years. There's nothing to be afraid of. I turned the words over and over in my brain, chanting them silently, creating the mantra that would give me the strength I needed to get in the car and drive away.

"'Bye, darling. See you tonight. I love you." William's voice floated up after me as I climbed the curved staircase to our bedroom.

CHAPTER SIX

I'd done it. I'd escaped William's care and made it safely back to Belvedere Crescent. The first few minutes had been scary but after that my confidence had returned. The Fiat was parked in its usual spot and I could begin clearing away my past.

The light, streaming through the stained glass of the landing window, threw splashes of colour onto the black and white tiles: pools of sickly yellow; flecks of scarlet, bright as arterial blood. The fanlight over the door was clotted with grime and junk mail lay in drifts where it had been pushed against the skirting board.

I dropped my keys into the brass bowl. Metal against metal echoed emptily. Once it would have been full of keys: Sadie's, if she'd not lost them; Aunt Jane's held together by a tab covered in hieroglyphics; The Poet's secured with a piece of frayed string. Mrs Kowalska's would be the only ones missing. She kept hers safely ensconced in her capacious handbag.

I leaned against the dark-green wallpaper and breathed in the familiar smell of the house. A residual trace of damp underpinned the lingering tang of cigarette smoke and the faintest suggestion of bleach, which grew stronger as I opened the door that led down to the basement kitchen. The steps were steep and I moved cautiously, my head light, my legs heavy with sudden exhaustion.

There was no milk in the fridge and what coffee was left in the jar had compacted into a solid brown lump. Jabbing at it with a spoon, I levered out enough to make a dishwater weak cup of coffee, took a couple of sips then threw the bitter liquid down the sink. I should have stopped at a supermarket but driving away from the safety of William's house had taken all my energy. My stomach rumbled and I realised that not only was I thirsty but for the first time in weeks, perhaps months, I wanted to eat. I took my phone out of the back pocket of my jeans and texted Domino's Pizzas.

While I waited for the delivery I searched through the pile of papers on the dresser. Writing lists helped me organise my thoughts and, when I found an old notepad, it felt right that I should start with an old fashioned biro and paper rather than my phone or laptop. That instinct was confirmed when I opened the notebook and saw the faint indentation of lists written all those years ago.

Logically, the best place to start was the study. It was where Aunt Jane had spent most of her time, and it was overflowing with box files, folders and piles of papers, while the filing cabinets were stuffed so full that not all the drawers would shut.

Once Aunt Jane had learned her cancer was terminal she'd told me who had charge of her will and where I'd find everything relevant to the house. She'd begun to catalogue her papers but had grown weak very quickly and not got far. There was so much left to sort through, all of it valuable resources for academics and researchers, as well as Aunt Jane's publisher.

Get in touch with the university, was the first item on my agenda. But who in her old department would be the best person to deal with Aunt Jane's estate?

The Poet will know, was my next thought before I remembered that he too was dead. Three funerals in six months. Was it any wonder I was exhausted? A strand of hair had come loose from my pony tail and

I twisted the end of the biro through it and stared at the page in front of me.

If Sadie was here we'd laugh and joke about what we had to do. Our humour might be black but it would make everything easier. Mud brown tea would help and maybe a bottle or two of wine. But Sadie was gone and the only way to tackle the job was to break it down into small manageable tasks. If the office was too much I'd start with the attic and work my way down. In The Poet's rooms there would be works in progress as well as finished material, all of which had been saved for a possible biography. Perhaps the best thing to do was to get rid of all the everyday items, like clothes and bottles of whisky, then ship what was left to the press that published his poems. Or maybe—

A sharp rap on the door announced the pizza delivery. Once the box was in my hand, I could scarcely wait for the driver to leave. He was still climbing the steps up to the street when I began stuffing a greasy mix of melting cheese and tomato into my mouth, gulping it down with water from the tap. After a couple of slices I was full and pushed the box to one side. The food had made me feel steadier, more able to think, and I decided that I'd go up to the attic and assess the extent of the problem.

The house was hot and still, the final staircase narrow and airless. The Poet's sitting room, high under the eaves, looked as if he had slipped out for a moment to share an idea, a conundrum, or a piece of word play with Aunt Jane. The air was thick with the woody scent of his tobacco and the acrid tang of old and unwashed flesh. The wastepaper basket overflowed with bunched up balls of paper. Long out-of-date literary journals and newspapers lay in heaps on the floor. A thick layer of dust furred the rickety bookshelves that lined the walls. One was full of The Poet's work, slim volumes of highly acclaimed verse; on another were rows of black notebooks, each identical in size and shape. There had been a crisis when the local stationer had stopped selling them and we'd had to source them on the internet.

I wound my way through the detritus and opened the window. The smell of a city summer hung in the afternoon. There was no breeze and my t-shirt, sticky with sweat, clung to my back. Plump white clouds sailed past in a blue sky but I couldn't catch the breeze.

Go on. There's no one to stop you.

"Sadie?" I drew back into the room. Had I heard my sister's voice? Or was I caught in a tangle of memories.

I dare you. Go out on the roof like we used to. The words were as clear as if Sadie was at my side, urging me on, taunting me for my lack of courage.

"I will if you will," I countered, then waited, tense with expectation and hope, but all I could hear was the distant hum of traffic as it laboured up Park Street.

It's my imagination, I told myself. *Part of this magical healing process they keep telling me about.* A spurt of anger at all those well-meaning people who assumed they knew what I was feeling and what I should be doing spurred me on. There might be no rational explanation, it might all be in my mind, but I no longer cared. So long as there was the faintest chance of reconnecting in some way with Sadie, I'd take it.

I sat on the windowsill, swung my legs over and climbed out onto the roof. Sliding my feet along the narrow gully between the roof and the parapet, I edged towards the slope of the tiles, where I leaned back and stretched out my arms.

Come on, Sadie. Be here. Talk to me.

A pigeon plumped down on a chimney pot. Beyond it, Bristol spread out below me, the terraces of Georgian houses like the tiers of a wedding cake, the red brick of Cabot Tower, the lawns of College Green lying between the golden stone of the cathedral and the curve of City Hall, where the two unicorns on the roof glinted, harsh and metallic. If I turned my head to the right, the river crawled between thick banks of grey mud. Above it hung the Suspension Bridge. Spanning the wildness of the Gorge, it was a place of suicide and despair.

What would it feel like to climb up the metal struts, stand balanced on the top, hold out your arms, and let yourself fall? What if you couldn't climb? Could you squeeze through those elegant bars, snaking sideways, one hand gripping hard until the fingers loosened and you launched yourself into the air?

It would be easier for me. All I had to do was lean forward, tilt from the hips and let the momentum propel me over the parapet. There'd be a moment of excruciating, agonising pain, then nothingness. What the past months had taught me was that, whatever William tried to do, life without Sadie was grey and meaningless. Unless time could be peeled back and our story arc wrenched into a different shape, nothing would change.

I shut my eyes. Orange and yellow light danced behind my lids and my weight shifted onto my toes. One small thrust and it would be over.

Don't be so bloody stupid. Life's for living. Don't throw it away.

Sadie?

My eyes jerked open. I bent my knees and stretched out my hands, searching for the parapet. Below me lay the flag-stoned pavement and the iron railings that hedged in the basement yard. With each violent beat my heart seemed to swell, constricting my lungs, leaving me gasping as slowly, very slowly, I let myself fall back against the tiles.

Spread-eagled, every muscle pressed against the safety of the roof, I slowed my breath. I didn't dare look down. My toes curled inside my trainers, gripping against a fall. A movement of air brought the barbequed scent of charred meat from some distant garden, then a cloud, its edges fraying into wisps, sailed into view. Keeping my eyes fixed on it, I inched towards the gable and the open attic window.

Climbing onto the roof had been easy, getting back inside demanded all my concentration. My whole body resisted as I pulled away from the slates, half-turned and, clutching hold of the window frame, hurled myself into the room.

"Out on the tiles again, twin?" The Poet was sitting in his chair; his outline hazed by dust-filled sunlight.

"I didn't think you knew," I answered, for it seemed perfectly normal on this strange afternoon that he should be here, where he'd always been. I was filled with the crazy hope that if he were here then Sadie would be close by.

"Oh, I knew more than you and t'other one could imagine. You'd wait until I went to the pub then you'd be out there, playing your games like a pair of cats at midnight."

"It was never midnight. We were always in bed by then." The phone in my pocket vibrated and I muted it. Whatever was happening, whether it was a ghost or a hallucination, was more important than whoever was trying to get in touch with me.

"Infernal machines," The Poet grunted.

"You always refused to have one."

"I had no need of it." The Poet tamped down his pipe and took a long pull, filling the room with the sweetish scent of his tobacco. "You can call me a Luddite but those things are instruments of instant miscommunication. You might assume that you are conveying information to the other party but truncated language breeds nothing but mis-understanding."

"That's what you might think."

"I might indeed, twin, but compare a Shakespeare sonnet with one of those images of a heart and you'll agree with me. Go on, girl, check your message."

"Later," I said but my eyes strayed to the screen.

I love you, William had texted. *A whole day without you is too long. I'll come round after work and we can go home together.*

No. You'll ruin everything. I've got to be here on my own.

If he came, he'd intrude into a place where the dead were not gone, where my sister was still with me. He'd insist on finding a rational explanation for what I'd seen and heard and I knew there wasn't one.

I pressed delete and looked at The Poet but his chair was empty, the worn plush pitted with burn marks where the ash had fallen from his pipe. The table beside it was stacked with books and there was an empty tumbler, the crystal stained with the residue of dried-up whisky.

"That's not like you to leave a drink unfinished," I said.

There was no reply and, sitting down in the battered wing chair, I curled my knees up to my chin, hoping that if I waited long enough Sadie would return. It was like playing hide and seek, except when we were children it was hard to hide because we always knew where the other one was. This time the rules were different and I had to work out what they were.

Cradled in the chair, I tried to bring back the sense of her I'd had on the roof. It was no use. The room was empty. My legs and arms were stiff, my back ached and my throat was dry. What I needed was a drink of water, clean and cold from the mains, not the tepid liquid from an upstairs tap.

Halfway down the first flight of stairs, my phone rang and I let it go to voice mail.

"Thea where are you?" William said. "You haven't replied to my messages. Are you all right?"

I'm fine, I texted. *Busy sorting stuff.*

Don't do too much. See you later, x.

I twisted my ring and as I turned it the diamond bit into my palm. The phone rang again and this time I answered.

"You are coming home tonight, aren't you?" There was a hint of uncertainty, even fear in William's voice.

I hadn't planned to stay, but I didn't want to go back to that sterile house where William would spend the whole time fussing over me.

"I thought I might sleep here. I've got such a lot to do."

"Is that a good idea?" He was making an effort to keep his voice steady, his tone rational. "You're not well. If you couldn't take the pressure of going back to work then should you be staying over all on your own?"

Stop it, I thought. *Stop going on about me being ill. It's not helping. Anyway being here and being at work are two different things.* I sat down on the bottom step and rested my head on my hand, my forehead against the wall. Seen close to, the foliage on the dado panel burgeoned with obscene growths, bloated and grotesque.

"Thea?" Somewhere close to my ear William was still talking and I couldn't shut him out any longer.

"I see it as part of my recovery. You've said often enough that I've got to face my past. Well that's what I'm doing."

"The next step then will be to go and see someone. I've found a Dr Radik who comes very highly recommended. I'll book you an appointment. It'll be good for you to talk to a professional."

And he'll believe me? He'll believe I'm hearing my sister's voice and talking to my aunt's dead lover?

"Okay." I fought to keep the flippancy from my voice. *It'll be no use but I'll go.*

And it'll get William off your back.

"Yes," I said out loud and somewhere Sadie smiled.

CHAPTER SEVEN

A stream of water splashed into the Belfast sink. I filled a glass and drank. Through the iron railings that topped the basement yard, I watched a procession of legs, half-listened to the drifting voices. A small black cat twisted through the bars, padded down the steps and leapt onto the patch of sunlight on the window ledge. It raised one rear leg and began to wash.

What was it doing here? As far as I knew none of the neighbours had a cat, so where had it come from and why did it look as if it belonged? Cats did sometimes move from house to house looking for the perfect home. But if that's what it was doing it had chosen the wrong place.

"There's no one living here," I told it. "At least I don't think there is."

Sadie, The Poet, the people I was seeing couldn't be real. So what were they? A physical manifestation of my grief? I knew that could happen. People who'd lost someone they loved often thought that they could see them after they had gone. In most cases those sightings didn't last, gradually fading away over the course of time until there was nothing left but memories.

Even that second loss would be better than slipping back into those terrible days when a blanket of greyness blotted out everything except my need for Sadie. Maybe I should have listened to William when he said I wasn't strong enough, and coming back to Belvedere Crescent had sent me sliding down into some desperate mental state.

I could be suffering from hallucinations. Or I

could be seeing things like Sadie used to. When she'd talked about hearing a child crying, or seeing a little girl from the past, no one had ever said she was ill. Aunt Jane had been delighted, treating her as if she had a gift. Now that she was dead, had Sadie passed that gift on to me? If she had it wasn't something I wanted.

Trying to block out the memory of that mocking malicious laughter, the hatred that had come from the figure barring my way at the top of the stairs, my hand tightened around the glass. The cat raised its head and glared at me through the window. Its eyes were yellow, its pupils slits of darkness. It held my glance, flicked its whiskers with its paw – and went back to washing its bottom. It looked so comical that I almost laughed.

Thanks cat. I nodded in its direction. My grandstand view of its furry genitals had brought me back from horror to the warmth of sunlight and the smell of the kitchen.

William was right. I needed to talk, not to a doctor or a psychiatrist, but to the one person still alive who knew both Sadie and me, who was here when we were growing up and might have some insight into why anyone would wish us ill.

~~~

The lanes are full of danger. Sunlight dazzles; tractors block your view; reckless drivers accelerate past slow-moving farm traffic; and there's nothing you can do in a headlong collision. The voices whirled in my head as if something was holding me back, telling me not to leave the safety of the house.

Forget it. I'm going. Determined not to give in, I walked across the road, patted the warm body of my car and slid into the driver's seat. Driving out of the crescent the feeling that I was being reckless
~~~

persisted but by the time I reached The Downs the sense unease had gone and I felt as if I'd been released into the bright afternoon. The summer lanes frothed with cow parsley; the hedgerows were green with bramble, blackthorn and hazel. I swung around the bends eager to arrive at Arlington Hall but as I came closer my foot eased off the accelerator.

Did I really want to know? Would having the answers make any difference? If what I suspected was true and I could see people from the past, then why did I think Mrs K could help me? Could anyone, or had I been left to face things on my own?

Damn you Sadie, not being here when I need you. My hands tightened on the steering wheel, my palms damp with sweat. I took some calming breaths, blew through my lips, and my shoulders relaxed. As I drove on, however, my reluctance to arrive grew stronger.

Treat it as an interview with a difficult client, I told myself. *Besides, it'll be good to see Mrs K again. Won't it?*

Stone mastiffs, teeth bared, shields in their claws, topped the gateposts at the entrance to the hall. Looming over me, they distorted my sense of space so I crawled past expecting at any moment to hear the screech of metal against stone. Having successfully negotiated the gates, I parked some distance from the other cars. I got my bag from the back seat, locked the Fiat, checked the doors, then came back to check again. The walk from the carpark to the house with its heavy portico and rows of symmetrical window felt interminable.

"Thea Gordon to see Mrs Kowalska." I pressed the intercom and the door slid open.

The entrance hall, with its graceful pillars of white

marble, soft apricot walls and ornate fireplace, resembled the lobby of an exclusive country house hotel rather than a care home.

The last staging post before the narrowness of the grave. They must have another way out for the coffins. I stared at the red and orange lilies standing stiffly in their burnished holder, a display so extravagant that it almost obscured the girl at the desk.

"Miss Gordon, how nice to see you. It's been too long." The receptionist smiled. "Mrs Kowalska is expecting you."

Then all shall be well. All manner of things shall be well. With the words of Julian of Norwich on my lips I was seized by a ridiculous urge to make the sign of the cross as I used to when entering the school chapel.

"You know your way, don't you?" the receptionist prompted.

"Of course. Thank you." How sane and normal I sounded. No one would guess the effort it had taken to get out of the house.

Sadie's not the only actress in the family, I thought as I went into the residents' annexe. The corridor was lined with honey-coloured panelling, the walls above it painted white and on each door was a brass holder with the name of the occupant. The tag was neatly typed and easily replaceable. Halfway down I stopped and knocked.

"Come in." Mrs Kowalska's voice was warm with welcome.

Sunlight lingered on the rich red rug, the side tables laden with wooden boxes, carved figures, photographs and ornately framed icons. More dark-skinned saints with stern expressions stared down from the walls, but my gaze focussed on the plump little woman with smooth white skin, her grey hair pulled into a bun on the top of her head.

When she saw me her face lit up in delight, which quickly morphed into a tender sadness as she struggled to her feet and holding out her arms, cried, "My poor, poor darling."

Stepping into her embrace I breathed in her scent and my eyes pricked with the tears I found so difficult to shed. For a moment I thought I was going to weep. I'd not cried properly since Sadie had died and would have welcomed the relief of letting go, but with a single blink my tears were gone.

"Come, sit down." Mrs K led me to a small sofa by the window. She sat down and patted the seat beside her. "Losing Sadie was a terrible thing. Terrible." She stroked my hand. "Your heart is broken, my darling. I know."

Then make it better. Tell me that it'll mend. That I won't be like this for ever, I begged silently, pointlessly.

"It will always be with you. Your loss is part of you. How else can it be?" Mrs Kowalska's eyes turned to the photograph of two little dark-haired girls on the table at her side. She leaned forward, her chins wobbling, her stomach spreading over her lap. "You are so sad now but there are still good things in your life." She lifted my hand and the light caught the huge diamond in my engagement ring. "You have someone who cares for you. You deserve it, my Thea. You were always such a good girl. Sadie now—" Mrs K shook her head sadly "—that one was troubled."

Sadie couldn't help it. That's how she was. It wasn't easy. It wasn't easy for either of us but I tried. I really tried.

I waited, hoping for some revelation, and when it

didn't come searched desperately for anything that would prompt Mrs K into saying more.

"As for your Great-Aunt Jane…" Once again, the meaningful headshaking, followed by a censorious tutting.

"It must have been hard for her. Bringing up two little girls on her own," I said. A shadow clouded the old woman's eyes and I added quickly, "She couldn't have done it without your help."

"That house was not a good place. I did my best to shield you from that woman's heathen ways."

"You did. You were our security, when we were growing up."

"Thea." Mrs Kowalska sighed and squeezed my fingers. The gesture gave me the courage to continue.

"In what way was the house not good?"

"My darling, I am so glad you came to see me. If you hadn't I would have phoned to tell you to visit." Mrs K increased the pressure on my hand. "There is so much sorrow and I can do nothing, though you know I would give my life to help you. But don't despair, my Thea. You are the strong one; you always were. Now, listen to me, we will have tea. As the English say, tea will make it better. Personally, I would prefer a shot of vodka but you are driving and will refuse and I do not want to drink alone. So I will ring the bell, the girl will bring the tray, and it will be like when you were little and came home from school."

If only I could go back to being eleven again. The pair of us clattering down the area steps, Sadie in front, I behind with my school bag heavy on my shoulders. Out of the dank fog of a November evening we'd come into the light and warmth of the basement kitchen, where soup bubbled on the range, washing hung from the wooden airer, and the room was filled with the smell of baking.

"Take off your coats and wash your hands," Mrs K would say and we'd run to the white tiled lavatory with the square sink and wooden draining board, elbowing each other out of the way to grab at the translucent bar of Pears soap. A perfunctory lather, then a quick dry on the rough towel and a race to get to the table where mugs of steaming chocolate waited beside plates of biscuits, warm and crumbly from the oven.

It was safe down there in Mrs K's domain. We were protected by the Black Madonna of Czestochowa, whose face was disfigured by a spear thrust by a Tartar invader. As a guardian against evil she was even more potent than the Sacred Heart of Jesus, who, the nuns at St Cecilia's said, had sacrificed himself for all mankind and still suffered for those that sinned.

Sadie said it was all balls. Though not in front of Mrs K, who would have washed her mouth out with the block of yellow soap that lived next to the sink. I wasn't so sure. Everyone I knew, except for Aunt Jane and possibly The Poet, believed in God, so how did my sister know that he didn't exist? What if her lack of faith was the Devil tempting her to despair? Best be on the safe side, do what the nuns said and pray that Sadie would return to the fold.

Another copy of that lurid painting with the exposed heart surrounded by thorns hung above Mrs Kowalska's door. Together with the icons it formed a protective ring around us. I sank back against the cushions and half-closed my eyes.

"Rest, Thea, it will do you good." Mrs K's voice soothed and comforted and I'd almost slipped into a doze before the girl returned with the tea things.

"Hot sweet tea with plenty of milk, that is what you need." Mrs K poured me a cup then sweetened it with spoons heaped full of sugar.

"Eat, eat. You are too thin. Never would I have thought that my lovely plump little Thea could have lost so much weight. You are a skeleton, my darling. It is not good." She nudged the biscuits in my direction. Disks of thick dark chocolate, like mud over sand, lay on white china. My throat closed against every bite. I took gulps of cloying tea to wash down the jagged pieces and wondered if this excess of sweetness was a deliberate ploy on Mrs K's part to make sure I wouldn't be asking any more questions.

Was the old woman protecting me, or was she unwilling to face the truth about the house and the evil I'd sensed there? If she was not prepared to tell me what she knew then my visit was a waste of time.

"I'm sorry. I have to go." I rose to my feet, bracing myself for the customary torrent of reasons why I shouldn't leave, but instead of her usual cajoling Mrs K nodded briskly.

"Of course you must. Before you do, there is something I have to give you." She pointed to a wooden box decorated with a pattern of hearts picked out in wirework. I handed it to her and waited as her arthritic fingers struggled with the close-fitting lid. Once, those fingers had embroidered flowers on a little girl's party dress, sewn lace on to petticoats, mended ripped hems and teddy bears' ears. Mrs K had prided herself on her pretty hands, the nails pink as the inside of a shell. She might have spent her time cleaning, washing and cooking, but her hands were the hands of a lady, as she was in the habit of reminding us.

"There!" The lid finally gave, revealing a nest of

white velvet on which lay a gold cross and chain. "Take it. Put it around your neck and wear it always. You must do as I say, Thea, you understand me? It is very important that you never take it off. You will do that, won't you? To please me. Yes?" She held my glance and I nodded. It was easier to give in than to fight, as I had learned from Sadie's confrontations with Mrs K.

The cross lay lightly against my skin, the chain so fine, the crucifix so small, that it scarcely registered. And yet it had such power. As my fingers curled around it I was filled with the certainty that I was loved.

Mrs K's expression softened. Shaking her head, she said, "Thea, darling, this slimming is no good for you. You must take those biscuits Jurek brought on his last visit. They are, unfortunately, not homemade but..." she sighed and held out her hands. "I cannot cook any longer and Mr Marks and Mr Spencer, their biscuits are made with real butter. You must eat them with your coffee at eleven o'clock."

Once again I did not argue although the thought of the sweet richness made me queasy. For Mrs K, food was life and love and to refuse was a denial of both.

"Remember, coffee with milk and a good breakfast. If you do as I say, the colour will soon be back in your cheeks. Now, my darling, if you really must leave me..."

I was being dismissed. Mrs K wasn't going to tell me anything and she wanted me gone as quickly as possible in case I asked any more awkward questions.

"Don't forget to come and see me again. Next time you will bring photos and you will tell me all about the dress.”

The dress? I almost spoke out loud before I remembered. The wedding date had been set, the venue booked, and yet, although we had a year to go, I hadn't chosen a dress. It was another thing to put on the list and I was grateful for a practical task that anchored me to a world where people didn't fade in and out of shadows, or speak when they were no longer there.

“Of course I will,” I promised.

“I will pray for you.” Mrs Kowalska's hands were already searching for the rosary that lay on the cushions beside her and before I had reached the door she was telling her beads.

CHAPTER EIGHT

Whether it was Mrs K's blessing, the cross fastened around my neck, or that I'd set myself a task and completed it, I drove back to Belvedere Crescent feeling much more in control than when I'd left.

Dropping my keys into the brass bowl, I turned towards the stairs and found the black cat sitting on the second step.

"How did you get in? Was it through the basement window? I'm sure I shut it." The cat looked at me with unblinking eyes. "It's a bit much. You know, you don't live here. We've never had animals. We weren't allowed to have pets." The cat made no sign of having heard. "I don't know what to do with cats. I've got nothing for you. Why don't you go back to where you came from? Go on. Go." I flung open the door and, waving my hand, tried to usher the animal towards it. The cat opened its mouth, displaying small sharp teeth and a rough tongue. Then it rose and padded up the stairs.

I hurried after it. The cat, tail erect, sauntered down the corridor to the bedroom I had shared with Sadie, slipped through the door that I was sure I had shut and leapt onto the bed. Curling round once, then twice, it settled down and began to purr itself into sleep.

Not knowing what to do I stared at it. The cat opened its eyes and stared back, daring me to chase it away.

"Okay," I said. "Have it your way."

My phone bleeped. It was William wanting to know how I'd got on at Arlington Court. If I didn't answer straight away he'd keep on until I rang him.

Glad of a diversion from the confrontation with the cat and promising myself I'd deal with the creature later, I read his text.

Darling Thea, as luck would have it, Dr Radik has a cancellation for tomorrow. I've booked you in and will come over and fetch you. All my love, William.

"No you won't," I muttered. He might think I'd agreed to see this psychologist of his but when, or if, I did, it was my decision. I swiped the screen but before I accessed William's number I was startled by a low growl. The cat, having gained my attention, lifted a paw and began to clean its face.

"You're right. I'm being childish," I told it. Since Mrs K had made it plain that she wouldn't answer my questions, perhaps it might be useful to speak to a professional. "Annoying though it is, Puss, William did reach that conclusion long before me. And that's because he loves me. Sometimes I underestimate him. There's no one left in my life who cares for me the way he does. I have to remember that William only wants what's best for me."

Or what he thinks is best for you. Sadie's voice slipped into my mind.

He wants to spend the rest of his life with me, I replied.

So he can mould you into the sort of woman he wants.

He doesn't do that. I'm my own person.

Oh yeah!

Stung by Sadie's response I messaged, *Thanks for sorting it out but I'd rather go on my own. Thea x.*

The cat, having finished washing, flicked its tail over its face and fell asleep.

~~~

Dr Radik's consulting rooms were in Rodney Place,
~~~

an easy walk from Belvedere Crescent. The hall and staircase were so similar to those at number fifteen that walking up to the second floor felt both familiar and strange. The white walls and uncarpeted floors were what our house would be like if it was stripped to the bone. Clean and stark, free from the burden of the past.

The psychologist was younger than I'd expected, only a few years older than me, with a round pleasant face, gold-rimmed glasses and a welcoming smile.

"Thea." He held out his hand. His grip was firm and confident. This was a man who could untangle the knots in my brain, put an end to the hallucinations and banish the dark figure and her evil laughter. But if he did, would I lose my ability to see Sadie?

"Please, sit down."

I hesitated. What had seemed so clear when I first came in was clouded with uncertainty.

"Your fiancé has told me something of your history. He says that you need help to come to terms with your loss." I nodded. Dr Radik took the chair opposite mine. "I have to take your details first. Basic stuff. Then you can tell me what you want from these sessions and we can go from there." He picked up the pen and clipboard from the coffee table and as I answered his routine questions my shoulders loosened and I began to relax.

"The relationship between twins can be deep and complex," Dr Radik said. "No one but a twin can really understand what it must be like to share the same DNA." He stopped and waited.

While I was working out what he wanted me to say, I looked over his shoulder out of the window. The shadows of the trees in the leafy street stretched across the pavement. An insect buzzing against the glass was the only sound in the room as I searched for words. They were the tools of my profession that I used every day to draft legal documents, tease out people's wishes and calm my clients' fears, and they were slipping from my grasp.

"I've never known anything different. Sadie's always been there and now she isn't," I said at last.

Doctor Radik nodded. I watched a fly fall onto the windowsill, legs scrabbling in its death throes.

"And how does that make you feel?"

As if part of me is missing. As if all of me is unravelling and I don't know what's still here and what's gone.

"Sometimes, when someone has died those left behind feel guilt."

"There was nothing I could have done." My hands knotted. My palms were damp, the engagement ring tight on my heat-swollen finger.

"I understand. That is the rational position but how do you *feel* about it?"

"I don't know. There are things... We didn't always agree... People think twins do but some-times..."

"Is that something you'd like to work on?"

For God's sake you're the expert. You tell me.

"If you would like to explore that side of your relationship and delve deeper to see if there are any issues, we could try hypnosis." I must have looked startled because he continued: "Don't worry, I won't make you do anything you don't want to. That would be unethical and not very helpful. Used thera-peutically, hypnosis can be a useful tool to unlock deep-seated memories. It could help us understand why you've reacted the way you've done. It could give you closure."

I don't want closure. I don't want to move on. Not if that means being without Sadie.

"I just want to be able to sleep."

"Sleep will come. It'll be part of the healing process."

No more lying in bed, limbs tensed, braced against some unknown disaster, heart racing, unable to switch off the thoughts that beat through my brain.

"Would you like to give it a go? There's nothing to be scared of, I promise. It'll be like watching the movie of your life, or those parts of it you choose to focus on."

"That doesn't sound too bad."

"It isn't. Now, if you're ready sit back in your chair. Close your eyes and count backwards from a hundred... Right. Relax and tell me what you can see."

I am in our bedroom. Sadie is insisting that I can hear the crying but I can't.

"That was the first time she did something and I couldn't do it too, and then—" The words snagged on my lips and I couldn't form the sounds. I was too far back in my past.

~~~

In the morning Mrs K clucks over our pale faces.

"I've made your breakfast and you must both eat or you will get sick." She puts two plates of porridge on the table. A golden dollop of butter is slowly melting into the warm oats. Sadie wrinkles up her nose and doesn't move. I eat eagerly, relishing the salty buttery taste.

"That's better. There's a good girl." Mrs K pats my cheek. "Now you are ready for school. Your sister—" She looks sternly at Sadie, who lifts her spoon to her mouth. Holding the housekeeper's glance, her hand wobbles. The spoon drops to the floor and is followed
~~~

by the crash of the plate.

"Ai, ai, ai! What a waste," Mrs K cries as porridge spatters everywhere. "Now you must clear up the mess you have made."

"We're going to be late." Sadie runs to get her coat. I pick up the pieces of blue and white china.

"She knows I can't eat that stuff. It makes me sick." Sadie is waiting for me at the top of the basement steps.

I shrug. There's no point in getting into an argument. Sadie's behaved badly and I've tried to make things better, but there are more pressing things on my mind. My eyes are heavy with lack of sleep and there's a pain in my belly. It's the last Friday of the month, the day we're given our report books to take home for Aunt Jane to sign. I think I've done well. I've been in the top three in our class for two months running and my marks this time have been high. Sadie, on the other hand, has slipped lower and lower down the rankings and will be in for a scolding.

~~~

"We could lose the reports. Drop them down the drain, or something." Sadie walks out of the school gates, gathering speed as she hurries up the hill.

"We can't do that," I protest as I struggle to keep up.

"Why not?" Sadie whirls around to face me.

"Cos..." I flounder, convinced that nothing can be hidden from our form tutor Sister Anne.

"You're scared," Sadie taunts. "Scared of getting into trouble."

I lower my head. She's right. The fear of doing something wrong never leaves me. It twists my insides and sends me running to the toilet on test days. Added to this is the guilt and fear that comes
~~~

from the nuns. It's at its worst in chapel when all the Catholic girls go up to Communion and Sadie and I are left in the back row, because we haven't been baptised so we can't take the sacrament and when we die we'll be going to hell. Religion is full of mystery and terror and there is no escape from it. At school we start every lesson with a prayer and at home there is Mrs K and her icon of Our Lady of Czestochowa in the corner of the kitchen.

At least Our Lady is kind and, in contrast to what we are taught at St Cecelia's, it doesn't seem to matter that we don't belong to the one true church. All the same, to make absolutely certain that we won't be damned Mrs K blesses us every night before she goes home. Sadie stands with her fingers crossed behind her back, but I love the feel of Mrs K's hand tracing the sign of the cross on my forehead.

When we reach the main road, instead of going left, which is our usual route home, Sadie turns right. It's the long way round but there is no stopping her and I trot after, past the Georgian mansion that is now a private hospital and through the gateposts that stand at the entrance to the cemetery.

Overhanging branches drip dismally onto a path slippery with moss and lichen. Headstones lean crookedly into the ground. A marble angel, wings outspread, lifts a warning arm, the hand long gone. Sadie stops in front of a tomb. The slab on the top lies at an angle and a deep crack runs down the side. She rummages in her bag and with a flourish pulls out her report book.

"I'm going to post it in here for the ghosts to read." She edges the book towards the gap. Her name is on the blue cover and I want to snatch it out of her hand, but I'm scared that if I make a sudden move she'll do what she threatened and once the book is gone there'll no way of getting it back. I bite my lip and stare at the dark line in the stone wishing there was some way of stopping her.

"You believed me! You really did." Sadie laughs, tosses her head and, with the book still in her hand, runs towards the gate and the comforting glow of the streetlamp.

We walk the rest of the way in silence. Sadie is waiting for me to speak but I'm too angry with her for teasing me and with myself for being taken in. It's hard to hold back the tumble of words fighting to get out and, by the time we reach Belvedere Crescent, my jaw is aching.

Sadie runs down the steps but waits for me at the bottom and holds out her hand. I take it because I hate being cross with her and she's going to need me when she has to face Aunt Jane. Nothing is said as our fingers lace and we walk in to face our interrogation.

The kitchen is hazy with smoke. Sitting at the table Aunt Jane stubs her cigarette into the overflowing ashtray and leans back in her chair. Her face is strong and hard, lines deeply grooved on either side of her mouth. Thick grey hair hangs to her shoulders. Her voice is rough as gravel.

"How have you done this week, twins?" She stretches out her hand for the report books. Her fingers are stained with nicotine, nails varnished lipstick red, breath ashy and stale.

"The children are hungry. Let them have their milk and biscuits first." Mrs K clicks her tongue in disapproval. My mouth waters in anticipation of sweetened milk and butter-rich pastry. Sadie is white, her bones stand out against her skin. Seeing her like that, my appetite is gone and my stomach gripes.

"We haven't got all day." Aunt Jane drums her fingers on the table. Sadie's nostrils flare. She's going to say something. She's going to cause a fuss because she's not done well in her tests. My legs tremble. I can't let Sadie take the full force of our aunt's anger. I have to deflect her attention.

"We came home through the cemetery. One of the graves is broken and—" I falter. Aunt Jane looks bored, Mrs K anxious. "Sadie said last night that—" My sister draws in her breath. It is a warning but the words spew from my mouth, unstoppable as vomit. "She hears things. She hears people talking."

"Thea!" Sadie gasps.

"*Jesus kochany*," Mrs K crosses herself.

Aunt Jane smiles. She turns slowly and looks at Sadie. "Is this true?" Sadie's glance is fixed on the wall. "Well?" Our great-aunt's voice takes on a dangerous tone. On the range the kettle comes to the boil as steam bursts from its spout.

Sadie shifts her weight from one foot to another. I cross my legs.

Don't let me wet my knickers, I pray, but fear makes the need more urgent. It's going to happen, I have to go, but as long as Aunt Jane fixes us with her Medusa stare I can't move.

"Yes," Sadie says. "I can hear them. Can't you?"

The expression on Aunt Jane's face changes. The anger is gone. It's followed by surprise, then excitement and a fleeting glimpse of triumph.

"Come with me." Grabbing Sadie by the arm she marches her out of the room. Released, I race to the downstairs lavatory. Make it just in time. Sit, bottom on cold porcelain as the pee pours out of me, hot and steaming in the icy room.

"Have you washed your hands?" Mrs K places biscuits on a Willow Pattern plate. I watch as the figures disappear beneath a corral of pastry. When I take one what will I see first? The two birds in the sky? Or the lovers running away across the bridge?

"We will save some for your sister." Mrs K pours a mug of milk. "Careful now, don't burn your mouth." I purse my lips and blow. A ripple moves across the surface like the edge of a wave breaking on the shore. I bow my head and drink. Mrs K puts her hand on my shoulder and I want to turn and bury myself in her ample softness but already the touch has been withdrawn and Mrs K is at the stove, tutting and muttering in Polish as she stirs thick potato soup.

Lifting the spoon to her mouth she tastes, shakes her head and adds more salt. Her back is turned and she doesn't see me dunk a biscuit into my mug then suck the soggy mess into my mouth. The melted crumbs dissolve on my tongue.

The clock on the wall ticks loudly. By now Aunt Jane should have looked at our report books and we should be going upstairs to start our homework, but Sadie isn't here. Did I get it wrong and what I said made Aunt Jane angry? Is Sadie being punished? Or is my twin getting all the praise that would have been mine?

If I hadn't told her about Sadie and the voices Aunt Jane would have been pleased with me. I wriggle on my seat and kick the legs of the chair.

"Thea." Mrs K's voice is full of reproach. Wiping the back of my hand across my face I stand up, relishing the annoying screech of wooden legs on the tiled floor and fetch my school bag. The strap bites into my shoulder as I climb the stairs.

The door to the basement closes, shutting off the

last of the heat from the range. The chequered floor is chill, the stained glass in the landing window dull. Wraiths of cigarette smoke hang in the air. On my left, the door to the study is shut. Neither of us has ever been inside. Great-Aunt Jane's study is strictly forbidden, even to Mrs K or the girl who comes to clean.

But Sadie is in there. I sit on the bottom step with my bag beside me and link my hands around my knees. Shutting my eyes, I rock backwards and forwards. Sometimes, when I do this, I can feel Sadie so close to me that I'm not sure where I end and she begins. When we were little this happened all the time. Now we're older all sorts of things get in the way, like school and Sister Anne and report books and...

The door opens. Sadie comes out through a veil of smoke. I jump up, catch a glimpse of a book-laden desk, and in the red glow of an electric fire Aunt Jane is smiling. My eyes water, a cough sticks in my throat and I can only whisper, "What did she say?"

"Nothing." Sadie shrugs. She smells of cigarettes and stale ash. It is the first time my sister has refused to share a secret with me. I purse my lips to hold back a sob.

"All right then, don't tell me." I'm not going to show her how much it hurts and picking up my bag I run upstairs to our bedroom. Slamming the door, I lean against it. She'll have to knock if she wants to come in and I'm going to make her wait. That'll show her. Hot with triumph, my heart beats fast.

Any minute now she'll be coming along the corridor and begging to be let in. I set my feet firmly on the floor and thrust the whole of my weight into my shoulders.

A thin line of light slants in under the door.

Opposite me, the window is eight black squares divided by bars of flaking paint. The rest of the room swirls with shadows. The cast iron bed stands ghostly on the rag rug. It'll be dark soon and I wish I'd put on the light. I stretch my arm as far as it'll go. My fingers don't quite reach the switch. There's a sharp pain in my middle and a burning feeling in my back. If Sadie tried to push her way in I'd overbalance and fall over.

I straighten up. I'm going to have to wait in the dark. It can't be much longer. I squint at the alarm clock perched on the chest of drawers beside the bed, twisting my neck to get a glimpse of the luminous figures. My skin cools, goose-bumps break out on my arms. Downstairs in the hall the grandfather clock tolls five.

Slowly, very, very slowly I slide to the floor. My eyes prick and I rub them with my fists. Part of me wants to fling myself on the bed and let the tears flow but there's no point. No one will hear. No one will come. Sadie is downstairs in the warm kitchen where Mrs K is cooking supper.

I hug myself. A draft swirls around my knees and nips at my ankles. It's not fair. I kick out a leg and drum my heel on the floor. Sadie has won again. Why does my twin, younger than me by ten whole minutes, always get the better of me?

Slippers shuffle past the door followed by the scent of tobacco.

"Twin? Is everything all right? Are you locked in?" The door handle jiggles. I get up and smooth down my skirt, push the curls from my eyes and tuck my hair behind my ears.

CHAPTER NINE

"Thea." Dr Radik's voice tore through the image. The Poet, with his tweed jacket flecked with holes where the ash had dropped from his pipe, his face, deeply lined, kind eyes beneath his bushy eyebrows, was gone.

I opened my eyes.

"Sadie was the special one, the favoured twin?" Dr Radik steepled his hands and looked at me over the top of his glasses.

While I was the good girl. I passed my exams and did what I was told, but it was never enough for Aunt Jane because I didn't have whatever it was that Sadie did.

"I suppose, it did feel like that sometimes."

"That's something we can work on. I can book you in for a session in two weeks' time. Unless you want an earlier appointment." He scrolled down his screen. "Of course, you don't have to agree but I feel that we're getting somewhere."

"I'll ring you." There was so much that had not been, and possibly never could be, said.

"I think this session went well." Dr Radik was standing up, his hand outstretched. Politeness demanded an answer but I merely nodded before hurrying down the stairs.

Out in the street the sunlight was harsh, the heat sapping. My bag was heavy, my legs as weak as if I'd been lying in bed for months. The air was oily with exhaust fumes, cars clogged the streets, and a knot of tourists, chattering loudly, strolled in front of me, blocking my way and forcing me into the road in my rush to get past. My phone vibrated, quivering with impatience as I fumbled through my bag to switch it off. William would have to wait. I had to get home and gather my strength before submitting to his analysis and dissection of every phrase and sentence in his attempt to come at what he thought was the truth.

Which won't be what I feel, or what I think.

A spurt of irritation drove me on. The streets merged into a backcloth of light and shade; sound muffled by the beat of blood in my ears. I shouldn't have given in to William's pressure, however well meant. My instinct had been right; going to see Dr Radik was dangerous. Whatever fears and horrors lurked in my past were best left unexamined.

Down the hill, around the corner, and I was in the crescent. Half tripping over my feet I broke into a run. Past the sweep of houses, their shadows stretching out towards me, I went before stumbling up the steps of number fifteen. The door fell open and the house welcomed me inside.

Propping myself against the wall I almost wept with relief. The cat, tail curved into a question mark, sauntered down the stairs. It twined around my legs, purring and nudging at my ankles, demanding I bend down and stroke it. The feel of warm fur, the solidness of the small body, calmed me. This hysterical reaction to Dr Radik and his questions was not like me. I'd always been the sensible rational one who reviewed all the options and made logical choices. Sadie's death had knocked me off balance but if I took things slowly and at my own pace then I'd be back to normal.

The cat lifted its head and I tickled it under the chin. I sat down on the floor and it jumped on my lap. Sunlight, filtering through the dusty fanlight, spiralled into a waft of cigarette smoke. The cat gave a sharp urgent meow and leapt up. Tail spiked, it made for the door to the kitchen.

"It's okay," I said, more to reassure myself than the cat, whose fur bristled and whiskers quivered.

Halfway down the basement stairs my stomach cramped so violently that I had to put my hand out to steady myself. The cat slinked past and I crossed my fingers and kept them crossed until I was standing at the sink waiting for the water to run cold. The cat jumped onto the draining board, a silhouette against the dazzle of light that streamed through the railings. I screwed up my eyes and I was eleven years old again.

~~~

"You're my best sister," I whisper as I climb into bed beside Sadie. My twin lies on her back. Her eyes are closed, her chest rises and falls, but I know she's not asleep. "Tell me what it was like."

Sadie lets out a small snore. I kick her leg.

"Aunt Jane's study," I persist.

Sadie stretches her arms above her head.

"I can't," she says.

"Why not?"

"I promised."

"But we tell each other everything!" My voice rises in disbelief.

Sadie turns on her side and burrows under the quilt. "Aunt Jane said it was our secret and no one else must know. 'Specially you."

I draw my knees up to my chest.

"I'm sorry." Sadie's voice is muffled by the covers. She stretches out her hand, her index finger extended in the gesture that means we are one, together against the rest of the world, but I don't respond and lie wallowing in misery. Sadie snuggles closer. "It's cos you can't hear them." She's trying to
~~~

make me feel better but I'm not ready to be friends. Biting my lip I screw up my eyes and pretend to be asleep.

The bed is warm, Sadie's breathing regular, soporific. On any other day, lulled by that rhythm, we'd slip together into sleep, but tonight my stomach hurts and my legs twitch as if insects are running about under my skin. If I got up I'd get my torch and sit on the window seat and read until I feel better. I put my arm over the edge of the eiderdown and quickly draw it back again. It's too cold and I am too tired. I yawn loudly so that Sadie will hear me but she doesn't stir and the pain in my belly becomes a dull throb that travels up under my ribs.

If Mrs K knew how I was feeling she'd make me a hot water bottle, wrap it in a towel and tuck me into bed. But Mrs K goes home at the end of the day. If I want a hot water bottle I'll have to do it myself. There will be plenty of water in the kettle that stands permanently on the range. I slide out of bed and search for the slippers hiding in the mess on the floor. Our dressing gowns are on the bedrail and I put mine on and set off to the bathroom, where the hot water bottles hang on hooks screwed into the back of the door. Mine is the blue one, its ribbed surface is cold and rubbery.

A single lamp dangling over the stairwell lights the hall. Shadows, eager for ambush, crouch in corners. They rear up over the ceiling, as step by step I creep downstairs. Outside Aunt Jane's study I stop and listen. I can't hear anything, but just in case I tiptoe past the door and race down the final staircase before reaching the safety of the kitchen steps.

The staircase walls cocoon me, the smell of last

night's supper of meatballs mingles with the bleach Mrs K uses to wipe the kitchen surfaces. I am halfway down when I hear the slow lumbering voice of The Poet with its rich cadences, interspersed with the rasping tone of my aunt, eager and sharp.

"Lap of the gods." My aunt slurps her drink. "I swear it couldn't have worked out any better. Identical twins. One who can, the other who can't. Leo, I have a subject and a control. Heaven sent, I tell you."

"You can't use her."

"Why not? I won't be doing her any harm."

"How can you know? As you said, this is all uncharted territory."

"I'd—" There is the click of a cigarette lighter followed by an indrawing of breath. "Of course I'd make sure she's okay. That both of them are. For God's sake, stop worrying. I tell you, no harm will come of it. All I want to do is carry out a few simple tests."

Tests? I tense. What does that mean? What are they going to test us for? Was it like exams at school where you had to revise, or are we going to be experimented on like research monkeys? No. It couldn't be that. No one is allowed to do that on humans. Are they?

"Is that all?" The Poet is not shocked or angry so it must be all right. Whatever it is I'll do it. I'm good at tests and I'll pass. But what will happen if I fail or worse still, if Sadie does?

"That's what I said and I meant it. I am aware that I have a duty of care for the brats."

"Really?" The Poet drawls. "I know you, Jane. Once you get an idea you become obsessed. Your research comes before everything."

"I've waited a long time for a chance like this, Leo,

and I'm not going to let it slip away because of your spurious ethical concerns. Did you know I heard something once—" She stops as if she's working out what to say next and I almost burst with waiting. "It was a long time ago and nothing came of it. Oh, what the hell, give us a refill."

"You drink too much." The tap runs, a tumbler is being washed out, a clink of glass on crystal as more whisky is poured. I back up a step. There will be no comforting hot water bottle tonight.

"Sometimes, it all feels so nebulous that I want to jack the whole bloody thing in. Start a new life. Get rid of the house. Move."

My legs wobble.

"Where would I go if you did that?" The Poet puts my fear into words.

"Where *would* you?" Aunt Jane's voice is light and playful. This is the only home we've ever known. If Aunt Jane goes what will happen to me and Sadie?

Perhaps we could live with Mrs K, I think as I trudge back up the stairs. But Mrs K's flat is tiny. There's only one room plus a very small bedroom crammed with furniture, rugs and icons. Remembering the sad-faced Madonna with the wooden Christ Child on her knee, I hang my hot water bottle back on its peg and make the sign of the cross as the nuns have taught me.

Please, I pray as I get back into bed, *let it be all right.* Sadie rolls over. Our faces are almost touching. We breathe in each other's breath and I know that, whatever Aunt Jane decides to do, so long as we're together everything will be alright. The pain in my insides washes away, my limbs are heavy, my eyes impossible to keep open.

~~~

We hold hands as we go down to breakfast, only
~~~

letting go when we come to the narrow staircase leading to the kitchen. It's my turn to go first but I let Sadie lead, the words from last night, *Move, get rid of the house,* beating through my head.

It's Sunday morning and Mrs K has gone to Mass. I wish we could go with her like we did when we were little. In those days Sadie and I, dressed in our best clothes with Mrs K holding us firmly by the hand, walked to the cathedral where we sat either side of her in the white tent-like space. Sadie wriggled and fidgeted on the hard chair but I loved the singing and the smell of incense. Then there was the mysterious bit when the wafer the priest held up became the body and blood of Christ, and Mrs K went up to take Communion while we had to stay in our seats and promise not to move a muscle.

"When you are seven you can go to classes and then make your First Communion," Mrs K told us.

"Can we?" I asked Aunt Jane.

"Never, not on my watch. In fact, that's it: no more Mass for you. You're intelligent children and you can make your own choices when you're old enough. End of discussion."

So who is going to save us now? At the thought of being locked out of Heaven my lip began to tremble.

Aunt Jane held up her hand. "Don't even think about crying, Thea."

"When will we be old enough to decide?" Sadie stepped in to save me.

"You'll know when you are," Aunt Jane replied.

I'm eleven and I'm old enough now. I know there's a God but Sadie says she isn't sure and when I ask her what'll happen to her soul when she dies, she shrugs.

"Anyway," she says, "all that praying was boring. The only good bit was when we went back to Mrs

K's."

"And had hot lemonade and pierniczki." I love the heart-shaped honey cakes covered in dark chocolate. The Polish shop around the corner from Mrs K's flat is the only place you can buy them. Sometimes she brings them to Belvedere Crescent for a special treat.

There won't be any today. Aunt Jane is making toast. She stands by the range, lifts the lid of the hot plate, peers at the two anaemic pieces of bread suspended on the wire rack, sighs impatiently, slams down the lid and reaches for the coffee pot bubbling on the other plate.

"There's milk in the fridge." She waves a vague hand, pours a mug of thick black sludge, sits down at the table and opens *The Observer*. Sadie brings the milk bottle. Reaching for our mugs on the dresser, I wrinkle my nose. I am sure I can smell burning but with the Rayburn it's impossible to tell.

"Shall I see if the toast is ready?" I ask.

Aunt Jane grunts and reaches for her packet of cigarettes.

"Unemployment looks as if it's going down," she mutters. "Put some on for me, will you?" she says as I juggle the two blackened slices onto our plates.

"The infamous burnt toast. Incinerated, its blackened carapace blooms with darkness." The Poet wanders in, dishevelled and unshaven, and pulls a notebook out of the pocket of his tartan dressing gown and a pencil from behind his ear.

"I wasn't expecting you this morning," Aunt Jane says.

The Poet yawns. "I came down to remind you about that film you wanted to see at The Watershed." He strikes out what he's written.

"Are you going to come with me?" Aunt Jane's

laugh is harsh.

The Poet considers. "Probably not," he says at last. "I'll be off to The Albion."

"I might join you for a drink, after." Aunt Jane gets up and stretches. "Girls, you can look after yourselves." She drops her arms to her sides. "That's what I brought you up to do. The whole purpose of being a parent of any kind is to make the offspring independent." She glances sideways at The Poet and blows derisively down her nose.

~~~

Rain pours down the windows. A grey relentless curtain shutting us off from the rest of the world. Sadie lies on our bed. Propped up on her elbows she is immersed in *Mizz* magazine. She's wrapped herself in the patchwork blanket that we knitted with Mrs K's help. My hands and feet are cold and my nose feels as if I've been eating ice lollies. I try to slip in beside her but Sadie jerks the blanket away.

"If you could go out with anyone, sis, who would you go with? Liam Gallagher or Damon Albarn?"

"No one." Left out in the cold I'm not going to play.

"When I'm a famous actress, when I go up for my Oscar, I'm going to say, 'I couldn't have done it without my twin. She's—" Sadie makes her voice low and husky "—everything to me'." She pauses. "Then you'll cry and—"

"I'm hungry." I get off the bed. "I'm going to get a biscuit."

I hurry down the stairs. My footsteps echo on the thin carpet. My shadow follows and I take great care not to look behind me. The emptiness of the staircases at Belvedere Crescent scare me. There are too many unexplained corners and pockets of darkness, where anything could hide. I don't want to see what's lurking there – but I'd look if I thought
~~~

it would make me a special twin and I could go into the forbidden room, like Sadie.

Passing Aunt Jane's study my palms prickle. Taking this as sign I go back. There's no one in the house except for me and Sadie and this is my chance to find out what happens behind that door. If I sneak in, touch nothing, and am quick as can be, no one need ever know.

The brass doorknob is warm, the mahogany door smooth under my fingers, as I turn, push and push again.

"You won't get in." The Poet's voice is warm with amusement. "Come on, twin, you must know by now no one ever gets into the inner sanctum without her say-so. Not even me."

I flush, a bright embarrassing red. I want to run but am determined not to give ground.

"Why not?"

"There are things in there that children shouldn't see."

But Sadie can. Resentment bubbles. *Why are there secrets everywhere in this house? Why does everyone know what they are, except me?*

CHAPTER TEN

The tap dripped into the stoneware sink and the cat pressed against my leg as the kitchen came into focus.

Afraid that if I moved my head everything would spin out of control, I kept looking straight in front of me. I filled a glass with water, took a mouthful – and spat it out. It was cloudy and tasted flat. I emptied the glass and ran the tap until it came clear. My throat was blisteringly dry and I took great gulps, not pausing to swallow fully so that water trickled down my chin and left wet patches on the front of my t-shirt. When I'd finished the pressure in my chest was so painful that there was only one way it could be relieved.

Opening my mouth, I let loose a loud belch, something I'd never have dared to do when Mrs K was in charge, but there were no ghosts here, of the living or the dead. That strange sensation of being back in the past must have been caused by not having anything to eat or drink, then walking home in the blazing heat. Talking about my childhood with Dr Radik had triggered a hallucinatory response. If I'd drunk some water as soon as I'd got in it wouldn't have happened.

Unhelpful though the session had been, it had made me realise that there might be some deep-seated issues that had to be resolved. Losing Sadie was like losing part of myself, a part that was both integral yet separate, which was why we fought so hard as we struggled either to get free of, or to dominate, the other.

At the same time we were so close that it was

impossible to imagine being alone. Until that day when Aunt Jane had taken Sadie into her study we'd shared everything, whether we wanted to or not. Our guardian had created a divide between us for a while, but that closeness had returned as adults, so that whenever anything important happened I turned first to Sadie and Sadie to me.

Until I met William. If only she could have accepted him as I would have accepted any partner of hers, but my love for him had become a barrier between us.

You don't need him, sis. Sadie's voice slid into my mind.

I love him and he loves me.

So long as you do what he wants.

Go away. That's not helpful. My relationship with William is not relevant. What I'm trying to do right now is work out what's going on in this house.

What if it's all linked?

Then I'll find the answer. It starts and finishes here. Beginning with Aunt Jane.

We were never told where we had come from nor why we had been adopted into this family, and even Sadie had eventually learned not to ask. Absorbed in her academic life Aunt Jane was volatile and irrational. At times she was full of anger and everything we did appeared to irritate her beyond bearing. Then, in a sudden swing of mood, she'd be full of pride at my achievements at school, or Sadie's zaniness, only to swing back into an impatient dismissiveness of everything we did as if she couldn't bear to have us around.

As a child I had been afraid to ask about our birth mother in case Aunt Jane called Social Services and had us taken away. Sadie maintained that not knowing who our parents were didn't matter, that it was not relevant to who we were, but she was lying. She was either as scared as I was about what we might find out, or she already knew, because that was what she and Aunt Jane talked about in those long sessions in her study, from which Sadie emerged drained and distant with dark shadows under her eyes.

I don't know what she did to you. You refused to tell me and after a while I gave up asking. Why was that?

She made me promise, was Sadie's reply.

As if that ever stopped you from doing anything. We were only eleven, for God's sake. Too young to know what we were doing.

I wasn't. Anyway, she said you were part of it too. Remember the questions. When she'd ask you—

If I'd seen or heard anything? I was the control, wasn't I? The other twin in the experiment. God, Sadie, why didn't I see it? How could I have been so stupid?

You weren't. You didn't say anything because you didn't want to upset anyone. Anyway, it doesn't matter anymore.

Yes it does. From now on I'm—

You're going to what?

Not care so much about what everyone feels.

As if.

You'll see.

I shoved open the kitchen door and in that brief moment sensed, rather than saw, Sadie beside me. The feeling was so strong that I was convinced that if I turned my head she'd be there, standing at my side, egging me on to be brave and stop worrying about what might happen. Powered by this feeling, I ran up the kitchen stairs and flung open the door of our aunt's study. Even as an adult there was that odd flicker of fear associated with that room. When Aunt Jane was too ill to get out of bed I'd stayed only long enough to gather up the papers she'd laid out for me on her desk. Knowing she was dying she'd put all her affairs in order. The only thing she'd left undone was what she should have told her adopted daughters.

Like why we were left in a basket on the front doorstep. Sadie's presence filled the room dispelling the musty aura of unwashed ashtrays, dust covered papers and the residue of inhaled and exhaled breath.

"Don't do this to me," I said out loud. "Either be here or don't, but this..." I shook my head and screwed up my eyes, hoping that when I opened them I'd see Sadie, and at the same time knowing that I wouldn't. "Maybe I am going mad," I speculated.

It depends how you define madness, Sadie replied airily.

An inability to deal with reality, constructing your own alternative world. A world in which we are still together.

If I were you— my sister began.

"Oh, shut up." I was losing my grip. If this went on I'd end up locked away, a hopeless case, drugged to the eyeballs.

The curtains were drawn, the blinds down. Moving into the semidarkness was like wading into a slime-filled pond and my feet dragged, held back by an undefinable dread. The skulls Aunt Jane had collected in the course of her studies leered down at me from the shelves. The piles of journals on the floor blocked my progress.

A hand slipped into mine, her fingers exerting a gentle pressure before being withdrawn.

Sadie! It had to be her. My sister giving me the courage to go on. *You're doing it again. You're messing me about.* I strode to the window and pulled back the curtains, stifling a scream as a brown shape fluttered out of the worn velvet. Berating myself for my pathetic reaction, I brushed away the moth and raised the blind. Sunlight poured into the room. I felt for the catch and pushing up the window let in the reassuring murmur of the city.

If Sadie was not going to stay with me then I'd do it on my own. The first place to look was in the filing cabinets. Wherever there was space, and even where there wasn't, another set of drawers had been added. There were two in each of the alcoves on either side of the marble fireplace; a row of them masked the bookshelves along one side of the room, with another four facing them on the opposite wall. The final pair stood by the door. On one of them was a stained tumbler, an empty bottle of Macallan, and an old copy of *The London Review of Books*.

The paper, lying lopsided, half-hid the label F-G. To my surprise the drawer opened easily. It had not been locked, which saved searching for the keys, but implied that there was nothing important hidden inside.

Flicking through the folders I had a sudden feeling that I was being watched. I turned. The room was empty but my unease grew, my fingers becoming increasingly clumsy as I discarded file after file. If there was any information about us it wasn't here. So what had Aunt Jane done with it? Where were our adoption papers?

Throughout my childhood I'd longed to fit in and be like everyone else. While Sadie thrived on the attention, I'd hated being singled out at school for not being a Catholic and for being that weird thing, an identical twin. When we were small other children would come up to us and stare; adults felt free to comment as if our looking the same made us too stupid to understand what they were saying.

At least Aunt Jane's complete disinterest in anything to do with clothes meant that we were never dressed alike. Mrs K also had her opinion on how we should look.

"You are Thea and she is Sadie and the world should know who is who," she'd say if we ever chose the same jumper or t-shirt.

"Or who is which and which is who," Sadie would reply, to be reprimanded by a sharp clicking of the tongue.

I raked my fingers through my hair. In the past we'd wondered if there was a family connection, which would explain why our great-aunt had taken responsibility for two baby girls. If there was I wasn't going to find the answer neatly filed away. Was it because her adopted daughters mattered so little to her, or was there something in those papers that had to remain secret? In which case it was possible that she'd destroyed them and searching through her mountains of paperwork would be a complete waste of time.

Frustrated, I slammed the drawer shut. It closed halfway then stuck. I shoved it with my foot and it slid open revealing the corner of a folder that had become lodged in the track. As I yanked it free my arm knocked the pile of books and papers on the top of the cabinet. They cascaded onto the floor and only a deeply ingrained respect for written material stopped me from kicking the whole lot to the four corners of the room. My anger surprised me, even more the tears that flooded my eyes. After months of feeling nothing my emotions had become violent and unpredictable.

I took deep breaths until the anger subsided and the tears ebbed, then bent down and began to pick up what I'd scattered. The papers I bundled together. The books I stacked one on top of the other, a Jenga tower of different shapes and sizes which I made no attempt to straighten. One volume was smaller than the rest. It was brown with a mottled cover so that the word *Journal* had almost merged into the background. Had this belonged to our great-aunt? I opened it. Inside, written in a child's hand, was a name, *Amelia Edwards*.

The study was drowsy with late-afternoon warmth. The air, drifting in through the raised window, brought faint smells of cooking spices, the distant cry of a seagull, the muffled clunk of a car door.

Go on read it. The voice nudged at the edge of my consciousness. *It'll tell you what you need to know.*

It's a diary. It's secret.

Written by a dead girl! 'The grave's a fine and private place, but none, I think, do there embrace.' Nor do they bother about someone looking at their diaries. After all, it's a kind of immortality. Why not? I would.

"Sadie!" I could almost see her. Perched on the edge of the desk, one leg swinging carelessly, a black pump dangling, about to fall to the floor.

The image dissolved. Even as I moved towards her Sadie disappeared. My insides curdled with a mixture of rage and disappointment.

"Be like that then," I said, as I used to when we were children to distance myself after we'd had a fight. Then, quelling all my doubts about intruding into someone's most private thoughts, I pushed my hair behind my ears and began to read.

January 10th, 1905

My name is Amelia Victoria Edwards. I am eleven years old and I am starting this journal to record the strange things that have been happening, because I am certain that if I tell Father or Mother they will never believe me. Particularly Mother. She will say that I am always seeking to be noticed and that good girls should be seen and not heard. Father does encourage me to give my opinion but not until I am asked, and speaking out of turn is precisely why I have been sent to my room.

Mother had one of her headaches and Father suggested she might call Dr Donaldson, which made Mother very cross. She does not like Dr Donaldson because she says he does not understand her delicate constitution. Father teased her and said that in that case she perhaps she should consult one of these new lady doctors.

He winked at me and I said, "That's what I want to be when I grow up, a lady doctor."

Mother was so shocked! She believes that young ladies must do nothing but get married, and that I am a lady because her family comes from a noble line. Her great-great-great-(I think) grandmother was a French noblewoman who lost everything in the French Revolution. Father's family are only merchant traders. Father says this is nothing to be ashamed of because we are in the twentieth century now and must move with the times.

I went to my room with a heavy heart especially since I had not meant to upset my parents. I accepted that I had to take my punishment, which was not as harsh as it might have been because in some families children are beaten and sent to bed without their supper and all I had to do was stay in my room until I had apologised. Then I would be forgiven.

To make the time pass more quickly I sat on the bed, pulled the quilt around me, and tried to read, but not even the adventures of the *Treasure Seekers* could distract me. However hard I tried to concentrate on how Oswald and the others were going to restore the fortunes of the House of Bastable, the thought that Father was angry with me made me miserable. I kept looking at the door hoping he would come and ask if I was truly sorry for what I had done. I would say I was even though it is not completely true. I was sorry that I had upset him and Mother but I do not see why, just because I am a girl, I cannot do more with my life than get married. If I cannot be a traveller and venture into the heart of the Dark Continent then I want to be a doctor and cure people of terrible diseases, or a fossil hunter and find an enormous dinosaur, or write stories like Mrs Nesbit.

The grandfather clock in the hall struck ten and I heard Father helping Mother up the stairs. The door to their bedroom opened and shut. I waited and waited but still Father did not come. I tried to be brave and not cry, but I was too miserable and I sobbed and sobbed until I fell asleep. I dreamed that Father and Mother had died and I was an orphan and there was no one to love or care for me. The nightmare frightened me so much that I woke up and when I opened my eyes I could see a faint outline of a figure sitting on the end of the bed.

"You were crying," the person said. It grew more solid as it spoke and I saw that it was a girl wearing plaid trousers and a loose shirt of a kind I had never seen before. "I heard you."

"You can't have because this is my dream. I'm still

dreaming and in a minute you will fade away."

"Then I'm dreaming too. I'm dreaming that you are in my bed, in my room. I live here with my twin sister Thea, and you—" she pointed at me and laughed "are the ghost. Not me."

"I am Amelia Victoria Edwards and you are a figment of my imagination. I shall shut my eyes and when I open them again you'll be gone."

"I don't think so." She reached out and seized me by the wrist. "I'm as real as you are."

~~~

I stared at the page in front of me. Was Amelia Edwards the girl Sadie had heard that night? She'd once lived in this house and was as real as we were. Or had been. The journal entry was dated 1905 so Amelia was long dead. Yet Sadie insisted she'd seen Amelia and, more significantly, now I had proof that Amelia had seen Sadie.

Putting the journal face down on the desk I tried to make sense of what I'd learned. Two eleven-year-old girls living at opposite ends of the twentieth century had been in the same room at the same time. That was not possible, unless time had fractured or doubled back on itself. I'd read somewhere that linear time, when one event followed the other, didn't exist. It was a construct humans had built to keep themselves sane. If that were true, and everything was happening at the same time, then if I stayed where I was long enough Sadie and I would be together again.

I took out my phone and sent William a text.

So much to do. Will stay a few more days, love Thea x.
~~~

CHAPTER ELEVEN

The cat was waiting in the kitchen. Sitting by the larder door, it meowed loudly as I searched for something for it to eat.

"Go home if you're hungry," I told it. In response it twined around my legs, its cries becoming increasingly plaintive until I found a tin of tuna in the back of the cupboard. It was well past its sell by date but by now the cat was becoming frantic and I decided to risk it.

"If it kills you, you can join the other ghosts," I told it, scooping the contents onto a chipped Spode plate. The cat gave me a scathing look and began to eat.

For myself I opened a more recent tin of baked beans, tipped them into a saucepan, put it on the Rayburn, then took it off again.

Thea if you don't eat you will fade away to nothing, Mrs Kowalska's voice echoed in my head.

That would be good. To float away into nothingness, not to feel anything ever again. I threw the beans into the bin.

The doorbell rang, its solemn clanging note like the tolling of a funeral bell. I splashed water into the pan and waited for the bell to stop. It rang again and was followed by the shriller note of my phone.

The gate at the top of the area steps opened and William descended into the Stygian world of the basement. He moved quickly and purposefully, his summer clothes and white blonde hair marking him as out of place in this world of chaos and uncertainty.

He knocked once then pushed against the

kitchen door. It was locked and he didn't wait for me to open it but came to the window and tapped on the glass, making it obvious that he wasn't going to leave without seeing me.

I was going to have to let him in.

Why? He doesn't belong here. Was it Sadie's voice, or my own suppressed thought rising like scum to the surface? If it was my sister interfering in my life again then she was wrong. William's calm logic and unwavering support was what I needed to confront this swirling morass of shifting images and voices that came and went, sweeping me one way then the next until I was beginning to lose all sense of who I was.

William, in contrast, was always in control of himself, of work, of whatever went on around him.

Of you too. Sadie's whisper spurred me into action. Opening the door I stepped back to let him into the house.

"I had to come. I was worried." He didn't touch me but kept his distance, waiting for me to make the first move. The difference in our height made me feel even smaller than usual and I was acutely conscious of the greasiness of my hair, the faint smell of sweat from my unwashed clothes.

"I'm okay." I took a small step back. The cat pressed itself against my calves and was gone, a whisk of fur disappearing into the shadows.

"Of course you are. But you haven't eaten, have you?" Our eyes moved simultaneously to the half-washed pan in the sink. "Let me take you out for supper. Then you can come back to your—" he paused for a beat, searching for the most innocuous phrase "—house clearing."

I wanted to say no. The thought of leaving the house was oddly disturbing but I didn't want an argument. If only he would leave and let me get on with what I needed to do, but once William had decided on a course of action there was no deflecting him. In the early days I'd found this trait attractive. Later, I'd begun to stand up to him and demand to be heard but after Sadie died nothing mattered anymore and it was easier to give in.

"We'll go to Marielle's. I'll call a cab. You've got thirty minutes to shower and change."

"We can walk." A cab could whisk me away, take me further out of the city than I wanted. If we walked I could easily slip away and run home.

"Are you up to it?"

"I'm not ill. I was never ill."

"You had a breakdown."

"It didn't take away the use of my legs."

A faint frown crossed his face, then he smiled wryly. "Get up the stairs then."

"I won't be long." I hurried up to the second floor and he followed me into our old bedroom where I left him flicking through our books, then opening the doll's house and inspecting the muddle of miniature furniture like a prospective buyer before an auction.

"I brought you some clean clothes." William was standing at the bathroom door when I finished my shower.

"There are times when you're simply amazing." I reached up to kiss him. "How many other men would have known that I was in desperate need of clean knickers?"

"You didn't take much with you."

"I wasn't planning to stay." I put my arms around his waist, my head against his chest hearing and feeling the beat of his heart.

"You're still wet. You're dripping all over my shirt," he said. I let go, shaking my hair to pay him back for breaking the moment, when I'd felt safe and normal again.

We walked hand in hand along the crescent. William had brought my blue-green dress. The gauzy fabric twisted around my legs throwing me a little off balance. I tugged the skirt free, lengthened my stride to match his, and the slight feeling of dizziness and unreality that had made me drag my feet disappeared.

Princess Victoria Street was full of people enjoying the summer evening. Cafés and restaurants had set tables out on the pavement but William chose to eat inside. "Away from the dirt and the fumes," he said, as with his hand on my back he steered me towards our table.

William's steak swam with blood. My salad was a mountainous arrangement of lettuce leaves slimy with dressing, pale flakes of chicken, and shiny olives black as rabbit droppings. I poked warily at it with my fork hoping to find something I could eat but the sheer volume defeated me and I took refuge in the wine.

"You're not eating."

"I'm not very hungry. I think it's the heat."

"Or you're doing too much."

He's going to tell me to come home so he can look after me. I gripped the stem of my glass preparing to defend my decision but William surprised me.

"How far have you got with your house clearing?"

I put my elbows on the table and rested my chin in my hands.

"Not very. I'd planned to start at the top and work my way down." William nodded approval. "It hasn't worked out like that, though. I got caught up with Aunt Jane's papers."

"I thought all that had been sorted."

"Yes. It has been. I was browsing." For some reason I didn't want to tell him about Amelia's journal. "I should have kept to my schedule."

"You have a schedule?" He smiled indulgently. "How much time have you given yourself?"

Before you come home. The words hung unspoken between us.

"Summer's the time to sell that house." William put down his knife and fork. "It won't look so good in the winter. Not even when you have cleared away all the clutter. Those terraces are always dark and gloomy. Let's aim to get rid of it by the autumn."

Then someone else will live there. Will it be empty or will the others still be there? Will they be waiting for me or will I lose them completely?

"You're not changing your mind, are you?"

"No." The word came on a sigh and the moment I said it I wished I hadn't. "It's been in our family since it was built."

"I know. But we were never going to live there, were we? We talked it all through when we got engaged. The plan is to sell my house and buy somewhere that's ours. A house with a big garden with plenty of room for kids. It's what we both want."

I couldn't deny it. It's what I'd agreed to: a home and family of my own. So why did I feel so miserable?

"I thought you might manage something sweet. Your favourite, tiramisu? Or would you prefer coffee?" William asked.

"Coffee keeps me awake and—"

"You want to get back." William gestured to the girl to bring our bill. The waitress took her time, sharing a joke with the boy at the coffee machine, smiling at the other diners as she wove her way through the tables, then chatting to William as he slipped his card into the machine and added a generous tip.

"See you again."

"You will. This is one of our favourite places, isn't it, Thea?"

I nodded and edged towards the door. I'd been away from number fifteen for too long and, irrational though it was, I had to get back as soon as I could.

"Hey, calm down." Out in the street William slipped his arm around my shoulders. Walking like that would slow us down so I moved out of his embrace, took his hand and swung it as I might have done with a child, to reassure him that there was nothing wrong, that I was fine, that we were a couple. My palm was hot against his, my heart flickering in my chest, but I made myself adjust to his pace and we strolled like lovers through the velvet evening.

"As soon as we have a buyer we can start looking for somewhere in the country. Not too far from the city. I was thinking of Long Ashton or Easton-in-Gordano," William mused. "With what we make on my house we should be able to afford whatever we want." His words swept over me in a meaningless stream. As the road dipped down the hill I was desperate to shut out the babble in my ears and run from the clammy heat back to the coolness of the house.

"Yes," I said and, "Yes." Anything to hurry him along.

Conscious as always of any change in mood he pulled me gently to a standstill. "Are you all right?"

"My headache's back. I shouldn't have had the wine," I lied. This time I didn't resist his arm around my waist. Submitting to his protection would get me back sooner.

The curve of the crescent was already in view, its leafy shade promising relief. I could see number fifteen, blinds down, curtains drawn, front door deep in shadow. When we reached the house William put his arms around me again. I stood very still willing him to let me go.

"Will I see you tomorrow?" He kissed the top of my head and I was flooded with remorse.

"Of course." I kissed him hard on the lips. Startled, it took him a moment to react and when he did I swayed towards him, the strangeness of the evening, the pull of the house forgotten.

"I love you," I whispered. *And I'm going to marry you and we will be happy for the rest of our lives.*

Snogging on the doorstep like a pair of teenagers, the voice in my ear was full of derision. William's arms tightened, constricting my lungs. His head lowered towards mine was heavy, his lips greedy, choking my breath. I pushed hard against his chest and he let me go.

"Thea, what's wrong?"

"I don't feel well," I gasped.

"Then let me..." His hand was on my elbow ready to steer me inside.

"I'll be all right." My fingers closed around the key. My breathing slowed and I found I could smile. "Honestly." I put as much conviction into my voice as I could. "I'm tired, that's all."

"Are you sure?"

I'm not sure of anything. Only that I have to get inside and be on my own.

I nodded and kissed him. "See you tomorrow." Then the key was in the lock, the door was opening and I was safely back in the house.

The air, which had been disturbed by my entrance, settled around me. The sense of unease and incipient panic that had been with me all evening drained away now that I was back where I should be. The cat padded along the landing and sat down, watching as I hauled myself up the stairs. I was so exhausted I could scarcely move and, when I reached the bedroom, all I could do was pull off my clothes and fall into bed.

~~~

I woke late the next morning, heavy with sleep. The cat nudged at my arm and then, when there was no response, thrust its face into mine and it occurred to me that the creature might be hungry or needed to be let out. While I could lie corpse-like beneath the sheet all day the cat had needs that couldn't be ignored.

I sat up slowly, swung my legs over the side of the bed and got to my feet. I slipped the blue-green dress over my head, went down to the kitchen and opened the basement door. The cat padded up the steps and was gone.

I brewed a cup of black tea and sat down at the table.

It'll be back. I think it likes you. Sadie's voice was bubbling with laughter.

I don't do pets. I studied the tea-stained ring on the inside of the cup. If I turned around there would be no one there. If I waited then, maybe, Sadie would return.

The black hands on the white face of the kitchen clock measured out the minutes. One by one they ticked inexorably onwards. It grew hotter, the air denser, the old kitchen smells of cooked cabbage and stale cigarettes stronger.

Why was it that however many times the place was aired and scrubbed these were the smells that lingered? Or was it all in my mind? A sharp meow
~~~

and the cat was butting its head against my leg. I reached down to stroke its head and it nipped lightly at my ankle.

"You're hungry again, aren't you? All I've got is the other tin of tuna. Well, the first one didn't kill you so this should be okay." The cat sniffed delicately, decided I wasn't going to poison it, and began to eat.

I sat and watched it. Every room in the four storeys above was full of things that, like the cat, could not be ignored. Each item, however small, carried its history, its importance, or lack of it, demanding that I either keep or discard it and, even after I had made that decision, I had to work out what was to be done with the things that couldn't be thrown away.

If Sadie had been there to help me, clearing Aunt Jane's house would have been completed in a matter of weeks. Alone it would take me months,

Or even years, a small triumphant voice murmured.

"Years," I sighed. Folding my arms on the table I let my head drop forward and, half-lying, half-sitting as we had been made to do at primary school, I drifted into semi-sleep.

Hours swum by and I was sucked deeper into lethargy. The cat jumped onto the windowsill and purring contentedly stretched out in a patch of sunlight.

Tomorrow, I thought. *I'll start tomorrow.* I'd told William I wasn't feeling well and it was true, I had no energy. A day's rest, taking things easy, and I'd be fine. William, however, wouldn't be happy if I didn't come back soon. Raising my head I tried to work out how long I could reasonably stay away.

You do know you're free to do whatever you want.

Of course, I shot back.

But you're still driven by the need for approval.

Oh sod off. A flash of pain shot through my neck. I rolled my head and heard the bones click. Muscles loosened. I got up and the musky smell of my sleep-laden body rose from the crumpled blue-green dress.

Upstairs in the shower I turned the water to cold. Icy drops pricked my overheated skin, stimulating and energising me and when I finally stepped out into the bathroom I was ready to get down to work. The house was drowsy and still. If I worked on Aunt Jane's papers, or starting sorting through The Poet's detritus, it would lull me back into sleep, or that grey half-state which was neither sleeping nor waking. To stay alert I needed fresh air and exercise, even if it was only a walk around the garden in the middle of the crescent. I put on the blue-green dress, tied my damp hair onto the top of my head, slipped on a pair of sandals, and went out.

The air was a little cooler and the light had softened from the bright promise of morning into a mellower golden tone. The street was empty, there were no cars parked along the kerb, and the persistent hum of traffic was missing.

The gate into the garden stood slightly ajar. Trees shaded a lawn edged by neatly clipped shrubs and bisected by gravelled paths. One led to the centre of the garden, another, the most secret of them all, the one Sadie and I had used in our games, meandered towards the rockery. It wound past patches of hostas and ferns, their primitive foliage uncurling from rusty clumps of growth. The ground was damp as were the boulders that ran with water spewing from the stone head of the satyr set in the wall above the rocks.

In all the time we had lived in the crescent I'd never seen the fountain working. The residents' association must have paid for its renovation, which was strange because neither we, nor Aunt Jane, had been asked to contribute. The whole garden looked neater and the wild tangle of rhododendrons, where we used to make dens, had been cut back.

Looking around to see what other changes had been made, I saw three children, two girls and a boy, walking down the path.

~~~

One of the girls has long red hair, the other's hair is dark. They wear white pinafores over their dresses, and tightly laced black boots. The boy is in a sailor suit and his blonde curls hang down to his shoulders.

"This is your special place, is it?" The older girl's voice is full of contempt. "You should see the gardens at Coombe Magna."

"I didn't say it was my special place. I said it was somewhere I can come to play," the dark-haired girl replies.

The other girl sighs extravagantly. "I can't bear these town gardens, can you, Louis?" The boy looks from one girl to another but says nothing. "Come on—" the red-haired girl continues "—let's go back to the house. There is nothing to do or see here."

"Hortense, Mother said we were to get some fresh air."

"Mother!" Hortense shrugs her shoulders. "I don't know why she brought us here to *play* with Cousin Amelia." She shoots a venomous glance at the dark-haired girl and walks away.

"Wait for us." The boy starts after her but Hortense doesn't stop, the heels of her boots throwing up spits of gravel as she strides towards
~~~

the gate.

Amelia stands watching them. They are halfway along the path when Louis looks over his shoulder. He hesitates then runs back, curls flying like some Edwardian cherub.

"You mustn't mind Hortense. She can be—" he puts his head on one side "—what Mother calls 'difficult' at times. Poor Mother, she's had so much trouble and worry since Father died."

"It must be a terrible thing to lose your father. If anything happened to mine I don't know what I would do." Amelia holds out her hand; Louis takes it and they walk down the path to where Hortense stands scowling at them. As soon as he reaches his sister Louis drops his cousin's hand. He says something to Hortense that I don't catch, then they were gone and the roar of traffic was pounding in my ears.

~~~

I rubbed my eyes, expecting to find that I was sitting half-asleep at the kitchen table, but the garden was still there, the grass scrubby and parched, the dark-leaved shrubs twisting their ancient roots through the thin soil.

I didn't see that, I told myself. *I imagined it. It must have come from looking through those papers yesterday. I'm not hallucinating. I'm hungry. I should go to a café or something.*

Oh yeah. Sadie's voice again. *You're trying to pretend it's not happening.*

"It's not," I said defiantly and walking through the gate I locked it behind me, then checked to see if the road was clear to cross.

~~~

The light shimmers and I'm a teenager sauntering along the pavement, my schoolbag full of books, my blouse sticky in the July heat. As I near the house I see Sadie sitting on the steps, her face turned to the sun drinking in the heat.

"What took you so long?" She smiles her pleased cat-like smile. "I've been waiting for ages."

"I stayed behind to see how I'd got on with my politics assignment."

"I don't know why you bother. You get straight A's all the time."

"You could too."

"If I could be bothered." Sadie gets up. "There's no point. Not if I'm going to be an actress. Don't look at me like that. You know it's what I'm going to do."

"I wish you weren't. I wish—"

"That I was more like you. That's never going to happen. Anyway, you'd better let us in. I've lost my key again. I rang the doorbell but they're all out. So I've been waiting ages for you."

~~~

I reached for my bag, looked up and found myself stumbling through the front door. In the hall I could see the faint outline of Sadie's figure as she went down the stairs to the kitchen.

Oh God, you are still here. I started after my twin. The door had shut behind her. I wrenched it open and raced down the stairs but even before I reached it I knew the room would be empty.

"Okay," I said, softly, "I'll wait. I'm not going anywhere. I'm staying for as long as it takes."
~~~

CHAPTER TWELVE

I opened a drawer in the dresser, found an old exercise book, took a biro out of the cracked Wedgwood mug, and sat down at the table.

The cat, sunning itself on the windowsill, watched as I drew a line down the middle of the page. In one column I put what I'd seen and heard: The Poet in his attic, the three children in the garden, Sadie on the front doorstep. In the second I listed possible explanations: dehydration, lack of sleep, hunger, heatstroke, hallucinations, memories so vivid that they became waking dreams, past life regression, grief, insanity.

Or was I being haunted? I put down the pen, the familiar room suddenly alien and threatening. My hand went to the cross Mrs K had given me. The old housekeeper had known there was something evil in this house. To keep it at bay she had put up her icons and made us say our prayers every night and taken us to church until Aunt Jane had put her foot down and decreed that her girls were not to be indoctrinated.

My fingers tightened around the crucifix, burying it in my palm. The cat had slunk away and I was alone.

Determined not to be intimidated, I stood up and shook out the folds of my dress. The list that was meant to help me apply logic to the situation had done the exact opposite and I was in danger of scaring myself silly. The simplest, most obvious explanation, and the one I was refusing to face, was that I was still suffering from the breakdown I'd had when Sadie died. What I should do now was make another appointment with Dr Radik, then go back to William's, get my laptop and do some research on the psychological effects of losing a twin.

And argue it all out of existence? Sadie mocked. She was sitting at the other side of the table, her eyes very green in the shadowy room. *It's happening, sis. Go with it. You have to.* Sadie's voice grew more urgent.

And if I don't? I gripped the top of the chair. *What happens then?* But Sadie was gone.

"Shit!" I kicked the table leg. The energy that I'd lacked for months flooded back. I stretched my arms. After my shower my skin and hair were clean but the dress smelled of sweat.

The washing machine was musty from lack of use so I rinsed out my underwear in the bathroom and set it, battened down with a piece of coral and an old tooth mug, on the windowsill. The dress I draped over the top of the ancient shower where it dripped its blue-green dye into the copper-stained bathtub.

It would be a while before it dried and in the meantime I had to find something to wear. There was nothing light or cool enough among the clothes Sadie and I'd left behind. The alternative was to search the trunks in the attic or, the idea was almost heretical, I could look in Great-Aunt Jane's wardrobe.

Standing with my hand on the doorknob, a flutter of unease pricked at my bladder and I crossed my legs as I would have done as a small girl summoned by Aunt Jane for some misdemeanour. Torn between the need to run to the toilet and the knowledge that if I went it would be harder to summon up the courage to return, I was about to open the door when I sensed a hand on my shoulder.

You're doing the right thing. The voice wasn't

Sadie's. Screwing up my eyes, I prayed that whatever it was would go away, and when I finally dared open them again the corridor was empty.

Aunt Jane's bedroom was exactly as Sadie and I had left it after the funeral. The medical equipment had been returned, the drugs disposed of, the bedding washed and put away. Nothing else had been touched and, apart from the stripped-down bed, it looked as it had when Aunt Jane had slept there. Unused for months, it was in need of airing and I opened the windows, pushing them as high as they would go, not caring that my towel slipped to the floor and any passers-by could look up and see my naked breasts.

The late-afternoon sun was warm on my skin and I lingered longer than I should before I turned my attention to the tallboy. Pulling open a drawer, I was surprised by a waft of perfume. I'd never known Aunt Jane smell of anything but tobacco and now I was breathing in complex layers of lavender, citrus, patchouli and amber with an undercurrent of musk, that emanated from what looked like a small nineteenth century medicine bottle nestling among piles of skimpy knickers, silk slips, suspender belts and lacy bras.

I took a pair of black lace knickers, the silk soft and sensuous against my skin, and I wondered why Great-Aunt Jane, who dressed carelessly in loose woollen dresses or baggy tops and men's jeans, had drawers full of erotic underwear. It was unlikely they'd been chosen to entice The Poet, a man who scarcely noticed what he ate let alone what anyone wore. Was this evidence of a past lover? A time when Jane Gordon had been a young woman who wore *Jicky* and sexy underwear? If so there would be clothes to match.

There were two wardrobes in the bedroom, both large Victorian pieces with mirrored doors. The first one I opened was full of what I recognised as Aunt Jane's clothes. A row of shapeless grey garments interspersed with one or two of a richer aubergine or maroon. The second wardrobe billowed with colour, texture and shape. Full-skirted dresses from the fifties hung next to sharply tailored suits and flirty flapper dresses sparkling with sequins. It was a treasure trove of vintage and Sadie would have loved it.

If she were here we would have spent the day trying them on, inventing characters for each outfit, posing and prowling like models on a catwalk. Or rather Sadie would; I'd be her audience. We'd have taken pictures on our phones and posted them on social media.

I swallowed down a sob. I was here to find something to wear. The rest could wait although the contents of the cupboard, given the current rage for vintage, were probably worth a bit of money and sorting them out would have to go on my to-do list.

The clothes from the forties and fifties were the most desirable, but not everything I'd seen looked as if it had belonged to Aunt Jane. Flowery, candy striped, chequered, pink, blue, and yellow dresses hung limply from padded hangers faintly scented with lavender. Behind them were silks, satins and brocades from a different era, and at the very back of the wardrobe, what had to be an Edwardian wedding dress – a slim white column of silk and lace, with a high waist and a train that had been carefully looped over the hanger to prevent it trailing on the floor. It was so beautiful that I couldn't resist taking it out. I held it up against me. It looked like a perfect fit and I didn't think I do any harm by trying it on.

The silk slid easily over my head and shoulders. I had to twist my arms and neck to fasten the buttons that ran down the back, but I managed enough of them, and straightening the train I turned to look in the mirror.

The black line of my knickers showed through the delicate material and when I moved there was a trace of mothballs, or was it camphor? But the dress looked good and, if there had been someone to help me with the buttons, it would have been perfect.

It is a perfect fit on the girl who looks back at me in the mirror. The girl who is not Thea, whose eyes shine with happiness, whose dark hair is pinned up in an elaborate style under a wreath of flowers. A rope of pearls hangs from her neck and there are more pearls in her ears. "Today is the best day of my life," she murmurs and as the image fades I was suffused with a feeling of joy and expectation.

I caught hold of the train and, holding my head high, twirled around. The dress, I was convinced, had been waiting for me. William with his love of vintage would adore it. For our wedding I'd carry a bouquet of lilies, or would roses and stephanotis be more true to the period? I'd have to google it. I had to make plans.

The dress slipped from my shoulders and fell in a pool of white onto the flowered carpet. I picked it up and laid it on the bed. Taking a yellow shift from the cupboard I slid it over my head, then carried the wedding dress to my room.

It ought to be wrapped in tissue paper and kept away from the light, but having only just found it I couldn't bear to hide it away. Hanging it on the wardrobe door I stroked the sensuous line of the skirt, fingered the fine lace, visualised myself with fresh flowers in my hair, and the cross Mrs K had given me around my neck.

A faint disturbance in the air lifted a lock of hair from the back of my head.

Don't do it, sis. That dress is not for you.

"Get lost, Sadie. I know what I'm doing."

Oh yeah?

I know you don't want me to get married. You never did. But tough – you're gone. I'm going to look wonderful on my wedding day and you're not going to be there.

Slamming the door behind me I stormed down the stairs, deliberately channelling my anger into the clatter of my footsteps. Sadie could think what she wanted, I was going to William's to begin serious preparation for our wedding and my sister was not going to stop me. I was almost at the front door when my phone rang.

"Thea?" William sounded surprised that I'd picked up. "You sound ... better?" The question in his voice fuelled my anger. He'd been so adamant that staying in the house on my own was a bad idea that he couldn't admit I'd made the right decision.

"I'm okay." I was careful to keep my tone neutral. First Sadie, and now William was questioning my judgement, ruining the elation I'd experienced when I'd seen myself in the wedding dress.

"That's good. That's great." There was a pause. "You haven't forgotten tonight, have you?"

"No," I lied, hurriedly shifting through the jumble of days and dates in my brain.

"Our party," William prompted.

"Oh yes," I said quickly. Too quickly judging by his reaction.

"We're having friends and colleagues around for our engagement party." William spoke more slowly than necessary as if to make sure I understood. I twisted a lock of hair around my finger.

"No problem. I'll be there."

"I never thought you wouldn't be." Another pause, fraught with disapproval. Or was I looking at his reactions through Sadie's jaundiced eye? "The caterers are coming at four to set up."

I was about to say that I was on my way and would be there in about twenty minutes when a band of pain tightened around my head.

"Thea?"

"Sorry. I've got that headache again. I'm going to take some paracetamol and I'll be with you as soon as I can." I waited for his response and when it didn't come added, "I am looking forward to tonight."

"I miss you," he said and a twist of warmth impelled me to reply, "Miss you too."

Slipping the phone back in my pocket, my fingers felt for the ring on the fourth finger of my left hand.

"Oh shit." The exhalation of breath was accompanied by the faintest touch on my shoulder and a glimpse of a bone-white face that triggered a surge of panic as I realised that the ring had gone.

Think, I told myself as I swallowed the painkillers. *Stay calm. Work backwards. You had it when you came in so it must be somewhere in the house. It's not lost. It's misplaced. You wouldn't have worn it in bed so did you put it on when you got up? If you didn't it will be where you left it last night.*

The ring was not on the chest of drawers. It was not beside the bed, in it, or under it. It was not on the bathroom windowsill or among the debris on Aunt Jane's dressing table. A few miles away a party was being prepared. The invitations had been sent, received and accepted, the caterers would arrive shortly, William would be waiting, and I'd lost my engagement ring.

"It has to be here somewhere." My voice sounded thin, uncertain. I screwed up my eyes in an effort to recall the last time I'd seen it on my finger.

The sun had moved to the back of the building. The downstairs hall was gloomy and dark. My headache was fading, and thinking that more light would help in the search I felt for the switch beside the study door. My fingers ran over blank wallpaper.

~~~

I smell the coal fire before I see it through the half-open door. It must have failed to draw because there's a hint of smoke in the air that melds with the sulphurous tang of the gas lamps. The room is lined with glass-fronted bookshelves. There is a large desk, a leather chair, and two further chairs on either side of the hearth. Above the mantelpiece hangs a portrait of a woman in a blue gown. She has dark hair and a pretty face and bears a close enough resemblance to the little girl who sits on her father's knee to be the child's mother.

"Daddy, you promised to read more from *Alice in Wonderland*."

"So I shall, Amelia. Can you remember where we got up to last time?"

"I think—" the child puts her head coquettishly to one side "—we had reached the chapter with the caterpillar."

"Then Mother called you away for your supper. I do believe I have marked the very place. If you bring me the book we can begin where we left off." The child slides from his knee, goes over to the desk and picks up *Alice in Wonderland*.

It's the same one that Sadie and I had when we were little.

Amelia settles herself in her former place.

"If you are quite comfortable, we can begin."
~~~

"Will you do the voices, Daddy?"

"Of course. It is part of the pleasure of reading to you, my darling." He clears his throat. "The Caterpillar and Alice looked at each other for some time in silence: at last the Caterpillar took the hookah out of its mouth, and addressed her in a languid, sleepy voice.

'Who are *you*?' said the Caterpillar.

This was not an encouraging opening for a conversation. Alice replied, rather shyly, 'I... I hardly know, sir, just at present ... at least I know who I *was* when I got up this morning, but I think I must have been changed several times since then.'

'What do you mean by that?' said the Caterpillar sternly. 'Explain yourself!'

'I can't explain *myself*, I'm afraid, sir' said Alice, 'because I'm not myself, you see.'"

~~~

This described my situation exactly. I didn't know who or what, where or even when I was. The thought was so ridiculous I began to laugh. It was so long since I'd found anything funny that I couldn't stop. Laughter poured from me, bouncing off the walls and floating down the corridor and when, muscles aching, I finally rocked to a halt, I was alone in Great-Aunt Jane's study.

I went to the desk and flicked through Amelia's diary in case the ring had slipped from my finger and got caught in its pages.

What happens if you don't find it? Sadie murmured.

Then it's insured. It was the logical response.

Do you think he'll forgive you?

Of course he will. You don't understand about love, do you?

I whirled around to confront her and my foot
~~~

caught one of the towers of paper that jutted like stalagmites from the carpet. The unsteady pile swayed crazily then, one by one, files and single sheets slid slowly and inexorably to the floor.

"Shit! Now look what you made me do. I haven't got time for this." I shuffled the litter of handwritten notes, typed papers and stapled files to one side until all that remained was a scatter of photographs. Their colour had faded into that strange greenish tinge that characterised pictures taken in the seventies, and it was this that caught my attention.

The first one I picked up showed a girl of about sixteen wearing a loose flowered dress. A woven band held back her hair, which was reddish blonde and curled around her face, half-hiding her hooped earrings. The same girl appeared in the next photograph, this time with a pair of twins. She was holding the tiny babies awkwardly, her head turned to one side as if caught talking to someone off camera. There was a large basket at her feet.

That's us, was my first thought. *And that girl, could she be our mum?*

"Don't be ridiculous," I said out loud, as if hearing the words would reinforce their meaning. I'd never seen this picture before. If the girl was our mother then surely Aunt Jane would have shown it to us. But who else could it be? It was too much of a coincidence to find that photograph of a girl with a pair of twins in our great-aunt's possession.

I took it over to the window and studied it carefully. There was enough of resemblance between the girl and our aunt to make me wonder if they were in some way related. They couldn't be mother and daughter for not even at the end of her life had Aunt Jane mentioned a child, nor had Mrs K or The Poet. Another possible explanation was that the girl was

Aunt Jane's niece, but it was much more likely that she was one of Jane Gordon's students and, in my heightened state, I was making connections where none existed.

This did not, however, explain the mystery that surrounded our adoption. Whenever we had asked about it our questions had been ignored or deflected, which in this house was highly unusual. Aunt Jane thrived on debate. She schooled us to take nothing for granted and praised us when we questioned accepted beliefs. She'd relished and encouraged Sadie's rebelliousness – until she refused to go to university at which point I, who was taking the path our fiercely academic aunt had laid out for both of us, had become the favoured twin.

Turning the photograph over I searched for a name or a date. I found nothing. Nor were there any clues in the rest of the pictures. If I wanted to know more then I'd have to search on the web, but for that I had to have my laptop, which meant leaving the house.

Would it let me go? The idea of being held captive by a building was crazy, yet my fingers were clumsy as I scrabbled in the brass bowl to retrieve my keys. Scooping them up something snagged against my hand and I saw I was holding my ring. It must have slipped off my finger when I'd come back with William. How I'd missed it, I had no idea.

Or maybe it wasn't there.

"Stop it." Clamping my hands over my ears, I ran out into the daylight, slamming the door behind me.

CHAPTER THIRTEEN

The car was parked opposite the house, its bodywork dusty in the queasy afternoon light as if it had been left to rust in the shade of the overhanging trees. Standing on the edge of the pavement, I turned my head from right to left to check if it was safe to cross. The road was clear, stretching beyond the curve of the terrace into the noise and rush of the city. There was nothing to stop me but like the rumble of an incipient storm the pressure tightened behind my eyes and my toes curled inside my sandals holding me in place.

It would only take a few steps and I'd be back in the safety of the house, and once inside I'd text William to tell him I was feeling too ill to be at our party. The laptop I'd collect another day.

If only Sadie was here. Knowing she didn't want me to go would give me the push I needed. Or an excuse for staying at home.

You've got to make up your own mind, sis. I can't do it for you.

Will you be here when I get back?

What do you think?

I stepped into the road, clicked open the door and slid into the overheated Fiat. I started the engine, jabbed on the aircon and drove reluctantly out of the crescent. Joining the flow of traffic around the Victoria Rooms was like plunging into white-water rapids. Then it was up the hill, across the open spaces of The Downs and into a suburb of expensive houses, hidden behind flowering hedges and long-established trees.

William's house, our house I reminded myself,

was at the end of an avenue. Once through the security gates a circular drive led up to a building as starkly elegant as its owner. Built in the thirties, its white walls were topped by a flat roof of green tiles. The windows were wide and curved except for the portholes on either side of the heavy oak door.

I drew up beside William's car and glanced at the clock on my dashboard. It was too late to go and get my laptop. My investigation into the history of the Gordon family would have to wait. If I'd not taken so long to leave I would have had at least an hour to start my research, but getting out had been so hard. It was as if the house was refusing to let me go, denying me the chance to discover more about my past.

I didn't feed the cat, I thought. For a crazy moment I debated whether to drive back before telling myself firmly that the cat would survive and what I had to do was to go and get ready my engagement party. I pushed a stray lock of hair from my forehead, locked the car and went inside. The entrance hall with its bare walls and curved marble staircase was like a scene from an old black-and-white movie.

"Thea." William's voice echoed slightly as he hurried down the stairs to greet me. "Darling, I was getting worried."

My next move was to melt into his embrace while the music rose to a crescendo and the credits rolled. Still in role, I offered him my cheek to kiss and said, "I'll run and get changed."

"Don't take too long." Catching hold of my arm he drew me close. "God, I've missed you. You've only been gone a few days and already it feels like weeks."

"For me too." As soon as I spoke I knew it was true. Much of what was going on in number fifteen was in my head. I was giving air and shadow a substance they didn't possess. Being here with William, with someone who loved and wanted me, was what mattered.

"Wear your hair up tonight, darling. And the white dress." He twisted a wayward curl around his finger. "The one with the lacing down the back."

The one that Sadie always said made me look like a parcel. I bit back the words. I could make up my own mind about what to wear and would have made a point of doing just that, except that the white dress was to hand and putting it on would buy me a little extra time.

"William tugged gently at my hair then let it go. "Come down as soon as you're ready. I'll pour you a drink."

At the top of the stairs I leaned over the ebony banister, checked that he couldn't see me, and ran along the landing to the room I used as my study. I stuffed the laptop into its bag and hurried back to our bedroom, cursing as I heard a car sweep up the drive. The first of our guests had arrived. I wasn't ready and William would want me at his side.

A quick shower and I was sitting at the dressing table fastening my damp hair with an armoury of clips. I was too pale and there were shadows like bruises under my eyes. A swish of blusher, a dash of eyeliner, and I was done. The dress William had chosen had somehow expanded and hung loosely from my shoulders making me look like a little girl dressing up in her mother's clothes. Even the precariously high-heeled sandals felt too big.

Car doors opened and shut. Voices floated up to the half-open windows. I swore silently and reached for my engagement ring, the diamond weighing heavily on my finger.

The ridiculous shoes swamped my feet and the only way to stop them from falling off was to splay out my toes. William was always telling me that he loved his "pocket-sized Thea" and that I might be "vertically challenged" but everything was "in perfect working order". So why did I feel the need for such restrictive footwear? Unless it was to make myself taller, to show that I too had status.

Switching on a smile I walked tentatively into the hall. From my vantage point I saw that the house was already filling with guests. As the day faded into a soft twilight the lamps had been lit. A murmur of voices, a clink of glasses, the occasional snort of laughter or cry of surprise rose into the air. The people who'd been invited were mostly from the office; there were some business acquaintances and one or two of William's old friends. There was no one I'd known before I had gone to work for Martindale and Grey. That part of my life had gone and with it my small group of friends. When Sadie had died they'd sent messages and flowers but William had discouraged them from visiting and, locked in my grief, I hadn't cared whether they came or not. This party had been a chance to reconnect but I hadn't invited them, nor had William suggested that we should. Had I slipped so seamlessly into the life he wanted for me that I no longer needed anyone else but him?

I'd always been the less sociable twin. Sadie had loved being the centre of attention. From early childhood any party we'd gone to had ended up revolving around her while I was content to stay on the margins and observe. It was my way of taking care of us, keeping us safe by making sure that Sadie didn't do anything too outrageous.

Tonight, whether I wanted it or not, this party was

about William and me.

In the room below me groups formed and reformed as people assessed each other, chatting to those they found compatible and moving swiftly away from those they didn't. In the centre of this ebb and flow, William, glass in hand, moved effortlessly among his guests.

Keeping him in sight I started down the stairs, placing each foot carefully, my free hand skimming the banister rail. In the movie I was scripting in my head he would know I was there. His glance would meet mine and hand-in-hand we'd greet our guests. In real life, he was too busy playing the host to notice me and I was tempted to back up the stairs, one step at a time, my white dress merging into the white walls until I was absorbed into the shadows at the top of the landing.

I might have made my escape if it hadn't been for the woman watching me from the other side of the hall. The last time I'd seen her was at Aunt Jane's funeral. On that occasion she'd been dressed discreetly in black; tonight, in a metallic robe, copper bands around her wrists, her skin blue-black, her curls tight against her skull. She was a deco sculpture of a warrior princess.

At The Grand the intensity of her connection with Sadie had shot through me like an electric charge. This time her focus was on me, her glance challenging and dangerous. I made myself look away and as I did William saw me.

He was at the bottom of the staircase before I reached the final step. With his arm around my waist he gestured to a passing waitress, took a glass of white wine from her tray and put it in my hand. The Sauvignon was greenish, its bouquet sharp. I took a sip and lifting my head once again met the woman's eyes.

"Who's that?"

"Minerva Beckford. A friend of Martin's. Do you want me to introduce you?"

"Later. There's other people I should talk to first. Love you." I freed myself from his grasp and walked towards some of the younger members of the firm. We talked for a while about work then drifted away. I sipped my wine; the alcohol sliding through my veins, my head light, almost disassociated from my body. Fragments of conversation washed around me, snagged on my consciousness, then floated away before I was expected to engage.

"Lovely party."

"Beautiful house. So stylish, so deco, William has great taste."

"Congratulations on the engagement."

"When's the wedding?"

"I hear you're planning to..."

I am? As far as I know, apart from the venue, the file marked "Wedding" is empty. I gave what could be interpreted as an enigmatic smile and wandered through the connecting doors into the dining room where tables had been spread with white linen and laden with food. Sushi curled on sea-green platters, crostini were displayed on thin slabs of slate. There were heaps of carefully arranged samosas, rolls of smoked salmon and Thai fish cakes with tiny bowls of brightly coloured dip. Mousses trembled, terrines were topped with slivers of citrus and baskets of napkin-covered toast stood beside earthenware dishes of pâté. Pomegranate seeds glowed like jewels in rice salads, slices of beef spread on wooden boards, legs of chicken nestled in baskets.

Plucking a leaf of lettuce from a glass bowl I fled into the garden. The French windows in the drawing room were open and people stood on the terrace, drinks in their hands, their shadows spiked and elongated by the lights that hung from the trees closest to the house. Beyond them the half-acre of lawn was dark, the line of conifers at its boundary black shapes against the night sky. Jazz played softly in the background, a murmur of syncopation followed by the haunting wail of a sax.

The heels of my sandals dug into the ground as I stepped onto the lawn. Kicking off my shoes, I spread my toes relishing the soft dampness of the grass. Away from the house the moonlight was sharp and bright; the air cooler, easier to breathe, and I drifted towards the resinous scent of pine trees.

"Hi there." The voice was warm and deep. "Can you give me a minute?" Minerva Beckford had followed me into the garden. Like a rebellious child I took another step but years of training and a horror of appearing rude wouldn't let me go any further. "I was hoping to speak with you tonight. I'm Min." She held out her hand and her grip was firm and purposeful. "I can't tell you how sorry I am about Sadie."

"Yes well…" The words stuck in my throat. Unwilling to meet the other woman's gaze, I jerked my head to one side and caught a glimpse of a girl in a white dress, her feet bare. My other self. For a moment, she stood there watching, then she was gone.

Sadie. I wrenched my hand free, started forward then stopped, pressed my palms against the side of my head, counted my breaths. Like fog rising from the river the familiar numbness seeped through my senses.

"Are you okay?" Min's voice was muffled,

distorted. Dropping my hands I attempted a smile. "You saw something. There by those trees. I got a sensation, but I don't often see. I'm not very gifted in that way."

But you knew she was here. My breath juddered in short gasps. Up until now everything I had seen, with the exception of the red-haired woman at Aunt Jane's funeral, had been centred around the house, but now Sadie was reaching out to tell me that I should go back to where I belonged, back to Belvedere Crescent.

"I've had too much to drink and not enough to eat. If you'll excuse me." I began to back away. "I have to go."

I'll make some excuse. I'll call a cab. At this time of night I'll be home in less than fifteen minutes. Please, please get out of my way. If you don't I think I'll have to hit you.

"Of course. I didn't mean to intrude but I'd so appreciate it if you could spare me some time to talk to you about your great-aunt's work. Not now but if we could make a date for some time soon. I don't want to press you, but Sadie was going to collaborate with me before she died. She said—"

My body was melting, I was falling, dissolving, becoming one with the myriad of atoms that whirled through the universe.

"Hey." Something heavy and warm was holding me back, forcing me to breathe and open my eyes as house and trees regained their solidity. "You need to sit down." Min's arm was around my shoulders, propping me upright.

"I need to go home."

Min raised an eyebrow. "Sure. Let me help you into the house."

The light from the terrace blurred the edges of the

lawn; the hard surface of the stone jarred on my bare feet; and I was caught up by the hum of voices, the throb of music, and press of bodies.

"I was a bit faint. I'll be all right now. Thank you."

"Shall I get your shoes? You left them on the grass."

"They don't matter."

Nothing mattered. It might be our engagement party, the night we made our formal announcement that from now on we were a couple, but the need to be back in Belvedere Crescent was so powerful that, ignoring the pain and embarrassment I was about to cause, all I could think about was how I was going to escape.

Manoeuvring my way through the guests I did my best to avoid the hands that stretched out to me, the yips and cries and shrieks that vied for my attention, but as I hurried past the gaggle of women surrounding William I was caught by a girl with a thick blonde fringe.

"Thea, we were just saying. You and William, you're so lucky to have this amazing house. Will you live here or will you sell after you get married?"

I hesitated, my thoughts with Sadie and the overriding compulsion to be back in Belvedere Crescent and, in that brief pause, William answered for me.

"Oh, we're selling." He rested his hand lightly on my hip. "We're putting both this house and the one that Thea's great-aunt left her on the market. It's the logical thing to do. What we make on both properties will mean we can buy, or even build, a house that will be ours. No history. No baggage." He smiled down at me, the cologne he wore, the heat of his body, cloying and sickly.

"I don't think so." Anger surged, stinging my

throat.

"Darling, it makes sense. It's what we've agreed." His hand moved to my elbow, his fingers pressing into my flesh.

"I've changed my mind. I'm not selling Belvedere Crescent." My voice was clear and cold, lancing through the babble that surrounded us so there was a moment when everyone fell silent, followed almost immediately by a surge of voices as our guests blotted out the embarrassment of witnessing my outburst.

"Thea." There was a note of warning in William's voice. "I know you haven't been feeling very well and you've probably had a bit too much to drink."

"It's nothing to do with the wine. I'm not selling." His grip tightened but I shook him off. Turning away I stumbled against a table. Pain shot through my side and I blinked furiously to keep back my tears.

"Now you've hurt yourself." His voice was full of warmth. He wasn't blaming me for the scene I was making. He probably thought it was grief that was driving me and I should go and calm down until I was ready to re-join the party. A few days ago I'd have let him make my apologies while I hid in our bedroom and waited for him to come and see how I was. William would have been in control and I would have taken my lead from him.

Not tonight. I raced upstairs and rang the taxi firm.

"Pick up," I hissed as the number rang and rang then clicked off. "Shit." I flung the phone onto the bed and the door opened.

"Can I come in?" Minerva Beckford filled the doorway, her presence oddly reassuring.

"Fucking taxi firm, they won't pick up."

"Then I'll take you." Without asking any questions

she handed me my discarded sandals. "Get your bag and we'll go."

CHAPTER FOURTEEN

Minerva drove quickly and competently through the sleeping streets. She didn't ask why I had to leave in such a hurry nor made any comment about what had happened at the party. Parking her yellow Citroen in my space, she unfolded her long limbs and slipped into the darkness of the overhanging trees.

One with the shadows, she was waiting for me to invite her into the house and let her loose among the secrets coiled among Aunt Jane's papers. Sadie might have trusted her. I was more wary. All I knew about Minerva Beckford was the strength of her connection with my sister; as for the source of the energy that flowed between them, I had no idea where it came from and it was not something I wanted to explore.

"Thanks for the lift." I scrambled out of the car. Laptop under my arm, I hurried across the road but Min was at my shoulder, her robe glittering in the light of the streetlamp, her eyes hungry.

"Are you okay?"

I jabbed my key into the lock and kept my voice as light as I could. "I'm fine. At least I am now that I'm home. I'm not too good with crowds. You know how it is. I've been ill." I trotted out the excuse that everyone else would give for my behaviour, gave a semi-apologetic shrug and pushing the door open let the gathered warmth of the house draw me inside.

"If you need anything..." Min was saying as the door began to close. Thick and strong, it would hold back any intruder. "Here." Long fingers held out a card slipping it through the narrowing crack. The door closed with a dull thud and her last words were cut short. I was finally alone.

The cat had not come to greet me and there was no sign of it in the kitchen or in the bedroom. *Perhaps,* I thought, *it's finally gone back to where it belongs.* But as I pulled off my clothes and fell into bed I missed its furry body curled up on the eiderdown. I'd become used to its company, to its yellow stare that brought me back to the ordinary things of life, like fresh cat food, or a sun-warmed windowsill.

It was the midmorning sun sneaking beneath the blind that woke me the following day. My skin was tight, my mouth tasted of stale wine, but I felt rested and lighter. The decision I'd made the night before about not selling the house had been weighing me down, but until I'd come out with it I'd had no idea that I hadn't made up my mind.

A yowl outside the bedroom door told me that the cat had not abandoned me and it wanted its breakfast, which reminded me that I also needed to eat if only to stave off an incipient hangover. My phone bleeped and I deleted the message from William without bothering to read it. He'd either be angry or understanding or both and I wasn't ready to deal with what he was feeling. Nor did I want to face the social fallout that would come from running away from my own engagement party.

There was no food in the kitchen and the cat's cries were becoming more and more urgent, but having left my car at William's a trip to the supermarket for supplies was not possible.

"Okay. This is what we'll do." I stepped out of reach of the cat, who was threatening to attack my ankles. "I don't need to go out to feed you. I'll do a Waitrose order. I'll say it's an emergency, that there's a starving animal here and if they don't deliver immediately I'll report them to the RSPCA."

Unimpressed, the cat stared at me as I logged on. I ordered a couple of boxes of cat food plus tins of tuna and salmon in case of emergency, a loaf of bread and a carton of milk. I added the strawberries, raspberries, peaches, nectarines, grapes, and a watermelon that I lusted after. Tomatoes, lettuce, cucumber, peppers followed. Then biscuits, dripping with dark chocolate, crinkly with nuts, mellow with ginger, a rich blend of ground coffee, and a packet of Ceylon tea.

There was something unbalanced about the list. I was conscious that William wouldn't approve but it would do to keep us fed while we stayed secure in our private world, enclosed in the safety of the house where no one could bother us.

I pressed send, deleted more messages from William and a text from Min. While I was waiting for the delivery I decided to start the search for my family. Logging into a genealogy site, I typed in our names and date of birth, but all that came up was that we were the adopted daughters of Jane Gordon. I gazed blankly at the information then flushed with embarrassment at my stupidity. My brain must be fuddled from lack of sleep. If I wanted to know the truth about our parentage I had to find the adoption agency and start the process of looking for our birth mother.

My self-recrimination was interrupted by the doorbell, but since it was too soon for the Waitrose van I didn't move. My visitor, however, did not give up. The bell rang again and again until, finally, a set of keys was posted through the letterbox.

I've left your car outside. Min texted.

Ignoring the message, I logged on to Adoption

Support Services. What puzzled me was why Aunt Jane had kept this a secret. In 1985 an unmarried woman having children was no great scandal. Our aunt was a successful professional, too old to have her own babies, and so it was not beyond the realms of possibility that she had adopted a pair of twins to fulfil a need for children.

She didn't like babies. She hated children. She didn't love you, came the voice. I swung around and the abrupt movement sent my head spinning. Sink, dresser, crockery all swirl together like pieces in a kaleidoscope.

<center>~~~</center>

Light wavers and blurs. A square of grey sky, bisected by the railings at the top of the basement yard, fills the window. Rain bounces from puddles and seeps in under the kitchen door, the circle of water widening as The Poet opens it. A girl stands on the threshold. She holds a Moses basket in one hand. With the other she pushes back a strand of hair. The red-gold curls flattening like worms on her skull drip water down her back. Her flimsy jacket and long dress cling to her thin body revealing the curve of her belly.

"I've come to see Professor Gordon," she says. The Poet looks bemused then his face lightens in recognition and he holds out his arms in greeting. The girl walks past him. She puts the basket on the table. "Will you go and get her?" Her voice is hard.

The Poet shakes his head. He looks younger, smarter and sadder than I remember. "She won't come down. She says she won't see you. I've done my best but she's very angry. I've never seen her so furious, so cold and closed up. You shouldn't have come. There's nothing I can do for you."

"Shit."

"I'm sorry. There's got to be places, people, the father..." He trails off ineffectually.

"If I knew where he was."

"Your family then."

"Mum's dead. The only family I have now is here. You know that. That's why I came. But—" she lifts her chin "—we'll manage. You can tell her that from me. On the other hand, don't bother. Oh well—" She glances at the babies. "It's us three against the world. I don't suppose you want to see them, do you?"

"I don't." The Poet clears his throat apologetically. "I don't know anything about babies."

"There's nothing to know. They eat, they shit, they sleep and sometimes they cry. Quite a lot actually – most of the time, if you want to know. Which you don't."

The Poet nods absently and peers hesitantly into the basket.

"They're very small."

"They're very new." The girl sways, the colour draining from her face. "Sorry, I'm feeling a bit strange."

"Quick. Sit down." The Poet moves to catch her but she crumples to the ground. "Jane," he yells. "Come down here. I don't know what to do."

That's us. That's me and Sadie. We really did arrive in a basket, like Sadie always said.

~~~

I started forward but the room was fading, everything was going dark. Ears ringing, I clutched the back of a chair and by the time I had steadied myself the ringing had transformed itself into the dull note of the doorbell.

"I thought there was no one in," the delivery man said. "It sometimes happens, you know," he added
~~~

conversationally as he carried in the groceries. "They say they'll be there. They book the slot and then when you turn up—" he pulled a face and shook his head "—there's no one in. Happens more times than you'd believe. Is this where you want us to come next time? The basement flat is it?"

"Yes." I wasn't going to explain that the house was probably the only one in the terrace that hadn't been converted into separate apartments. "That would be good."

"Right then, my lover, no substitutes. You're in luck. We had everything you wanted today. I'll be seeing you again, most likely. This is my run most days."

I gave him a smile and a wave as he went up the steps to his van, then locked the kitchen door, sliding the bolts across and hanging the key on a hook on the dresser before pulling the curtains halfway across the window so no one could see inside. The yellow-checked gingham was worn and thin. To be invisible to passers-by I would have to replace it with a blind.

The cat jumped on the draining board and meowed loudly.

"I've got you the premium stuff," I told it as I squeezed the contents of a pouch into a dish. "You'd better like it." Ignoring me, the cat settled down to the serious business of eating while I stored the rest of the shopping in the larder, setting it out so that the shelves looked full. Later, I would stock up on staples, pasta and rice, baked beans and tomatoes, and fill the freezer with meat and vegetables to provision myself against the need to shop. Another order, a really big one this time, would do us for a month.

"Shower gel, shampoo, kitchen roll, toilet roll…" I

scribbled on a scrap of paper. "Washing powder..." A sudden bang sent my pen skittering wildly. It was followed by a thud and the sound of nails being hammered into wood. The cat scooted for cover as I rushed to the door. I turned the handle and tugged but the key was on its hook on the dresser and the bolts were drawn.

The last nail had been hammered into place and the van driven away before I was at the top of the basement steps. A scarlet *For Sale* sign had been fixed to the railings: thick white letters on a black background revealing the number of bedrooms, the almost self-contained flat in the attic, stripping the house of its privacy.

How dare they? Shaking with rage I tore at the ties that bound the wooden stake to the iron work. Unable to loosen them I pulled and tugged, cursing and swearing, my hair tumbling over my face as the letters swam and merged into one swirling mass.

"Is everything all right?" A middle-aged woman was looking at me in concern.

"They can't do this to my house. I won't let them."

"Should I—" The woman backed away.

"No. Thank you. I—" Suddenly aware of the eccentricity of my behaviour I held up my hands and keeping my eyes on the ground slunk back into the basement. The cat gave me a quizzical look, but I couldn't meet its glance. The thought of how I, Thea Gordon, had turned into a sweating swearing madwoman made me hot with embarrassment. I never behaved like this. It was Sadie who threw temper tantrums. When we were children I was the calm reasonable twin, the one the adults turned to for advice when they didn't know what to do with my sister.

In the office I was known for my ability to stay

cool under pressure, so why had the sight of that board tipped me over into a frenzy of uncontrollable fury? It was almost as if I'd been possessed. An image of a red-haired woman in a black dress slid into my mind. A distant echo of laughter, malicious, triumphant. To banish it I ran the tap and splashed water on my face, letting it drip down onto my chest until the top half of my dress was soaked.

There was no mystery about why I was so angry. I'd told William that I wasn't going to sell and he'd ignored me and put the house on the market. Or had he? It was completely out of character for someone who was usually so considerate and careful about finding out what I wanted. Could it be, was it possible that I'd done it myself? The three of us had agreed at the meeting in The Lemon Tree to sell. Had I in the weeks after Sadie's death gone ahead with our plan?

I searched my memory but had no recollection of getting in touch with the estate agent. I couldn't even recall which of the many Bristol firms we'd chosen to deal with the sale.

Whoever it was I'd tell them there had been some mistake. Or perhaps it would be better to say that I'd changed my mind. That way if I'd set the sale in motion first place I wouldn't appear to be totally stupid.

Of course it wasn't you. Why would it be? You're staying here.

"I am," I told the cat, who was nowhere to be seen. "All I've got to do is get the name and number off the board and phone them." But that meant going out into the street where anyone could see me. Apart from the woman who'd asked if I was alright there had been no one else around, but the way I'd been yelling and screaming the neighbours must have heard what was going on. It would be all around the crescent by now that Thea Gordon had gone mad. As soon as I showed my face they would be at their windows, their kids pointing me out, making faces, shouting insults. No doubt the whole thing had been filmed and was already out on social media.

You'd better stay in then. It was the unknown voice again. *You can go out when it's dark. If you keep out of sight they'll forget. People always do. No scandal lasts for long.*

"Sadie?" There was no reply. "Please," I whispered. "Help me."

~~~

I'm running. Sadie is ahead of me holding up the pen she's snatched from my hand. It's my pen. It's got pink and purple feathers on the end of it and I bought it with my pocket money. She darts around the table. I do the same and then we're chasing each other. Round and round we race until I bang into a corner and send a plate crashing to the ground. Blue-and-white shards scatter over the tiles. We both skitter to a halt and I sense rather than see Sadie coming to stand beside me. My side hurts. I rub my hip and try not to cry.

"*Jesus Kochany.*" Mrs K turns from the sink, her arms swathed in bubbles. "Thea, how many times have I told you, no running in the house? You are so clumsy."

I press my fist against my mouth. It's not fair. Sadie started it but experience has taught me that Mrs K will take no excuses. I'm the one who broke the plate so I must be punished.

"It was my fault." Sadie looks defiantly at the housekeeper. Their eyes lock. I bite my lip. Sadie's hand slips into mine. There is a tickle of feathers. "I took her pen. I've given it back. Sorry."
~~~

Knowing how hard it is for Sadie to apologise, I squeeze her fingers. Mrs K clicks her tongue. There is a storm in her face and any minute now it will break, swamping us in a torrent of anger.

"Aie, aie, aie. What am I going to do with the pair of you?" Mrs K shakes her head reproachfully. The storm has abated. It will be no more than a strong wind because Sadie has owned up. "You have to learn to behave. This is not your playground. You want to play? You go outside. Look at you. You lucky children, you have the run of the gardens."

It's raining. I nudge Sadie before she can speak. Sadie pulls a face, but stays silent.

Mrs K sighs heavily, "Sadie, you can fetch the brush and pan and sweep up the pieces. Every little bit, mind you, and be careful. I don't want any splinters in your knees." She turns back to her washing up.

I stand beside her with a tea towel in my hand. I reach out to take a plate but it recedes from my grasp, the room grows dim. Mrs K is a rounded shape against the grey square of the window. Bristles scrap against the tiles, the sound filling my head as I am sucked back into darkness.

~~~

Fire glows in a black-leaded range. A girl in a cap and pinafore stirs a large pot. A red-haired woman, her hair scraped back from her sharp white face, takes the ladle, lifts it to her lips and shakes her head. The girl mumbles and is sent to fetch something from the larder. When she has gone the woman fills a bowl with soup, sets it on a tray and carries it out of the room.

~~~

I'm on the stairs. The door to the study is open. A girl in a black dress is sitting with her hands in her lap. An older man is speaking to her,

"The provisions of your father's will make you a very wealthy young woman."

From the landing above comes the sound of coughing. The sweetish cloying smell of a sickroom where the windows are never opened, and a fire burns day and night. A servant girl hurries up the stairs. She is carrying a basin covered with a cloth.

~~~

"It's okay, you're not too late. She's not dead yet. The nurse says it could happen any time. She's with her now." Sadie jerks her head towards the staircase. "We don't have to go up straight away."

The hand on the grandfather clock lurches past the minute and strikes.

~~~

"Your great-aunt was a wealthy woman and a very astute one when it came to caring for her dependents. There was a lot more money in her estate than one would have expected."

~~~

"If you didn't live here, where would you live?" Sadie sits on the closed lid of the toilet, filing her toenails.

"I don't know." I sink deeper into the bathwater.

"You never know anything." Sadie looks up. "When I'm a famous actress, I'm going to live in LA and you can come and visit if you like."

You mean we won't live together, the thought flickers between us.

I open my mouth, but the voices are filling my head and I can't speak.

Pair of peas in a pod.

Twins share certain attributes.

You can't do this, Jane.

No one will get hurt. I'm not irresponsible.

Remember the questions?
~~~

Thea, Sadie she is not like you. You are a good girl.

~~~

The voices were coming closer, demanding, hectoring, pressing in from all sides. Images slid past at such a speed that I could no longer distinguish one from another. Everything was blurring in a whirl of colour and sound. The blood was thudding in my head, that cruel mocking laughter echoing around me, bringing with it a paralysing fear that held me even though I tried to claw my way out to breathe in air that was free of nightmare and dread.

"I am not going to faint," I said.

"Then put your head between your knees." There was a hand on my shoulder. Surfacing through swathes of darkness that gradually lightened into mellow sunlight, I was aware that there was someone standing over me. When my eyes finally focussed and the pounding in my head had subsided, I looked up and saw a fair-haired stranger.

"Who are you?"

"I'm sorry. I didn't know anyone was here," he said.

"What are you doing in my house?"

"It's okay. I didn't break in. I'm not a burglar. I've got a key."

"A key! Who the hell gave you a key?" Struggling to my feet I felt the hall floor sliding, the blackness returning. A hand on my arm steadied me. I was led to the stairs and made to sit on the bottom step.

"Are you still feeling faint? Do you want me to get you some water?"

"No. Go away."

"I will as soon as I'm sure you're all right. I couldn't leave you unconscious on the floor."
~~~

"I'm not unconscious and I never was. I might have been a bit faint but I'm fine now. I'm talking to you and I am perfectly rational." I gripped the banister rail and pulled myself to my feet. "So please go"

"Look, there's obviously been some mistake. I was told by the agent the house was unoccupied."

"Shit."

"Yes, I know. Highly embarrassing for both of us. You are the owner, aren't you? Not just another viewer who's been taken ill?"

"I told you it's my house and it's not on the market."

"What about the sign? The one that's attached to the railings?"

"There's been some mistake. They came and put it up this morning."

"I knew it wasn't there last night," he said ruefully. "At least Min didn't say anything about it."

"Min!"

"She brought you home. Min's a friend of mine and Ed's. She asked me to go with her to pick up your car from where you left it at the party and drop it off here. Then by pure coincidence I was browsing some properties when your house came up and it looked a good prospect, so here I am."

"You want to buy it?"

"Sure. There's a lot of demand for properties like this."

"It's a big house for one person."

"I wasn't thinking of living in it. We'd convert it into flats – or rather apartments. Call them that and their price goes up."

"You're not doing that to my house."

"Okay." His hand was on the doorknob. "Just let Hydes know. You don't want anyone else walking in like I did."

"I'll ring them as soon as you're gone. It must have been a shock for you, finding me like that."

"I was thinking I'd have to call the paramedics. I was about to check you over when you came too. In case you're wondering, I am a doctor. Ben Appleton." He put out his hand. It was warm and firm and in any other context reassuring, but he wanted my house so I remained wary.

"You said you were going to convert the house into flats."

"Yes, that's what I do with my brother. Ed's a medic like me. We're twins. We inherited some money from our grandmother when we were students. We used it to buy a house, did it up, sold it on, did it again, made more money, and we've been doing it ever since."

"He didn't come with you?"

"He's on call. It makes no difference which of us sees the property, we pretty well know what the other one's going to think."

"It was like that with me and Sadie. At least some of the time." Envy so fierce that my insides twisted made me look away.

"Min told me, you're a twin."

"Yes. No. I mean..." I trailed off. "It's so difficult. Am I still a twin now that Sadie's dead?"

"I'd say you are." Ben sat on the step below me. Hands loose between his thighs, staring straight at the door, he said softly, "I can't imagine being without Ed. I think it would feel as if part of you isn't there anymore."

"It does, sort of and yet..."

I'm still bloody here. Sadie was standing at the top of the stairs. Ben's shoulders stiffened but he didn't turn around.

"I can see why you don't want to sell," he said, getting to his feet. "Some houses have a feel about them."

"Good or bad?"

"It's different for each one. Ed's better at this than I am. He picks up the vibes. I don't." Then with a quick change of subject, he went on: "If you're feeling all right, I'll go." He held out his hand. "Good to meet you, Thea Gordon."

Our eyes met and there was something in his glance that told me that whatever he might say about his lack of sensitivity, I was certain he'd heard Sadie, or at least sensed her presence. I was about to take the risk and tell him about her when his phone rang.

He pulled an apologetic face, waved a hand and left. I stood on the step and watched him go out into the afternoon.

CHAPTER FIFTEEN

The house settled around me, wrapping me in a sleepy stillness. The voices were absent, the rooms silent. The cat appeared at the top of the stairs and, holding its tale in a characteristic question mark, strolled into the kitchen where the low ceiling had kept in the heat, trapping the lingering traces of long-ago meals.

I opened the window and the cat jumped up and stretched out on the sill, one black paw dangling over the edge of the Belfast sink. A copper-stained tap dripped onto the white porcelain.

Going to the fridge I took out lettuce, cucumber and tomato, and put them on a plate. I wished I had some salad cream. Legs passed by the window. There was a burble of chatter in a language I didn't recognise. I nibbled a tomato. A car drove into the crescent. Doors opened; children's voices floated down into the kitchen.

"Bye."

"See you tomorrow."

"Text me."

While I was being battered by voices that may or may not exist, in the streets above nothing had changed. Kids had been picked up by mothers on the school run, or were strolling home after clubs or sports fixtures, bags bumping on their backs, phones in their hands.

I had only to walk out of the door and I'd be in that world, where disembodied voices came through devices and the dead did not speak. It wouldn't be the same without Sadie but I'd had enough of the fear and uncertainty in this house. My lack of control over the estate agent's sign had scared me. I wanted my life to be normal, to go to work in the morning and come home to someone who cared about me. I'd been so close to throwing it all away because of an obsession with Belvedere Crescent but, if I was lucky, William would understand.

I tipped the rest of my salad into the bin and checked my phone. William had rung, texted, emailed, left voice message after message. He'd done everything but bang on the door, demanding to be let in. If I didn't reply soon he'd come to make sure I'd not done anything stupid.

As if you would. Sadie's voice was in my ear, but remembering that moment on the roof and the almost overwhelming temptation to step over the edge, I was not so sure. If I'd given in then it would all be over, the endless years without Sadie, the struggle to live like everyone else when inside I was numb with grief.

There was also a part of me that wanted William to suffer as I'd done, to be told that one day he would come to terms with his loss and move on with the rest of his life. While he was waiting for that mythical day to arrive he could spend endless and expensive hours talking to Dr Radik, none of which would make the slightest difference to the way he was feeling.

When Sadie had died the doctors had made of point of telling me that no one could have predicted what was going to happen. There had been no symptoms, no way of knowing that the aneurism in her brain could burst at any moment, so there was nothing anyone could or should have done, and I was not to blame myself.

If I'd taken that step out beyond the roof tiles William would be haunted forever by the thought that he might have been able to do something to stop me. He'd tried his best and instead of being grateful I'd walked out of the sanctuary he had created, running away from our engagement party and retreating to the chaos that was my childhood home.

He'd given me the space I needed and even though I was still furious with him for going ahead with the house sale, if I wanted our relationship to survive it was time for us to talk.

If he grovels will you go back to being happily engaged? Sadie came straight to the point.

I don't know. I'm not there yet.

He won't wait for ever, she reminded me. *Which just goes to show.*

Go away Sadie. I pressed my palms against my ears until all I could hear was the beat of blood in my head. Gradually I loosened the pressure and picked up the phone.

Thea, can we talk? Please. It was that last word that swayed me. William hated to ask because it made him vulnerable and that scared him. If he was going to open up to me, the least I could do was to hear him out.

I've been a cow. He's put up with so much from me.

Don't let him change your mind. Sadie was back. *Stick with what you want. Whatever it is...*

I will. I'm going to deal with all this rationally and calmly.

Yeah. Keep it calm, sis. Don't lose it.

So now you're dealing out relationship advice.

So now I'm watching your back.

I'm okay. The phone was in my hand. William's message on the screen.

Can I see you this evening? I can be there about eight.

Nothing around me stirred or moved or spoke. There were no voices, no laughter.

Okay, I sent back.

I'll bring food x

There was no anger, no recriminations for ruining our party. It was more than I deserved. Alone in the house, except for the cat, I had been driven by grief. The memories Sadie and I shared had been so vivid I'd been sure they were real. William had been right to be afraid for me. Much longer and I would have tipped over into some sort of craziness. What I needed was another human being, someone who existed in the here and now. When Ben had inadvertently walked in the voices had gone. It was as if he'd tilted everything back into balance. William's cool common sense would keep it that way.

You want to be rid of me too.

Never. I could never do that. It's just that sometimes it's so hard. One minute you're here then you're not. And never knowing when it's going to happen.

Did I feel a hand on my shoulder? A faint flutter of air on my cheek? The kitchen was empty. Even the cat had disappeared.

~~~

At eight o'clock there was a knock on the basement door. William stood on the threshold, his figure blocking the evening light so that all I could see was a dark shape before it stepped forward and became William. Solid and reassuring, he put his arms around me and I tipped my face upwards for a fleeting kiss. He held me for a long time and when he finally let go he kept hold of my hand.

"I've got food and wine in the car." He moved towards the door taking me with him. Sunlight
~~~

splashed on the top of the basement steps; beneath them the shadows were deep, above them the line of railings spiked like a stockade.

"I'll set the table." I withdrew my hand. "We'll use the best knives and forks and plates, though they won't match. We were always losing bits from the cutlery sets. The silver is in the dining room and it's hell to clean..."

"Thea." He held up his hand and my burble of words petered out. "I'll be back in a minute. I've parked right outside. There was a space behind yours."

Bumper to bumper. A big fish guarding its young. His hair shone like white gold, his figure elongated as it moved out of view.

On the table I put a white linen tablecloth, cutlery that could almost be from the same set, and a pair of Spode Italian plates. The glasses were from a supermarket, the candles from the cache Mrs K kept under the sink in case of a power cut.

"Thai curry," William announced. "Green for you, as usual, and a red curry for me. Jasmine and sticky rice, because I wasn't sure which I was in the mood for."

I don't want either. I don't want anything. I clenched my teeth as William unpacked the foil cartons.

"I'll need two serving dishes."

And serving spoons and napkins. All those things I didn't think of. The table settings that had seemed so romantic were now a clumsy jumble of mismatched things put together by a child playing house.

"We can warm them through in the microwave. You do have a microwave don't you, Thea?"

"Mrs K wouldn't have one in the house. She had

this theory that the rays poisoned your food and that's why everyone was getting cancer."

"So you don't have one." Not even a twitch of the lips betrayed his irritation.

"Yes, of course we do. We got one for Aunt Jane after Mrs K retired."

"I've got something else for you. I couldn't carry it all."

I should have gone with you. But I didn't want to. Or you couldn't.

That's stupid. I can go out any time I want.

"Can I help?" My throat was dry and my voice so quiet that William didn't hear me. I tried again but he was already going up the steps and I decided to leave things as they were.

He returned with a bunch of flowers. Packed tight, the white roses were a cloud of blossom. Once unwrapped and put into water each bloom stood stiffly in the blue-and-white jug, and in the flickering light of the candles the roses, with their deep-green leaves and waxen petals, looked as if they'd been fashioned out of plastic and wire.

We sat with our hands touching as William poured chilled white wine.

"To us." He raised his glass.

"You and me." The wine blurred the edges. The setting sun drew the light from the room, leaving us marooned in a circle of candlelight.

"Eat up. Before it gets cold. " William spooned food onto my plate. I lifted my fork to my lips and the aromatic scent of the spices awakened my appetite. Each mouthful strengthened and warmed my blood.

"This was a good idea of yours." I'd been right to see him. He was what I needed.

"I wanted to make it up to you. I know you were

upset and it wasn't what I intended. I was trying to help, to make things easier. Poor darling, you've had so much to deal with recently. You've been very brave but I should have seen that you weren't ready for our party. You were still too fragile to cope."

I took a swig of wine and put down my glass. "It wasn't that. I was bloody furious because you didn't let me speak for myself. 1 want to make my own decisions in my own time."

"Are you still angry with me?"

"About the house, yes."

"I can understand that."

His words, intended to be soothing, prickled like burrs. What made me even more angry was that instead of having a row he was smothering me with his concern. I couldn't say what I really felt but was trapped by his acceptance of my increasingly erratic behaviour.

"I shouldn't have interfered." He reached over and took my hand. His fingers played with the diamond on my fourth finger. "The past forty-eight hours have been hell."

"For me too. It all got really weird." A montage of pictures and voices spiralled through my brain and I couldn't suppress a shudder.

"You shouldn't be on your own. You do know that, don't you?" William got up and put his hands on my shoulders. I turned around and he pulled me gently to my feet.

You're right. I don't do alone. I don't know how. I need to be with someone.

Anyone?

"William," I murmured. Was there an echo of mocking laughter? To shut it out I moved closer. My body soft against his, I wound my arms around his neck. And kissed him. Gently at first, tasting the feel of his lips, relishing the way he held back, letting me take the lead. The laughter grew louder – and I slid my tongue into his mouth, conscious of nothing but the straining of my breasts, the quickening of my breath, the loosening of my limbs. He was pressing against me, his hands on my buttocks, pulling me in to him.

My legs parted. I was going to have him take me now, here.

In full view of the kitchen ghosts.

The room swum back into focus. "No." I pushed at his chest. He let me go and I took his hand. "We've got to go upstairs."

CHAPTER SIXTEEN

In the hazy moment that is half sleep and half waking, I yawn and stretch out my hand to touch William, curl myself around him and feel his skin warm against mine, but his side of the bed is cold, the sheet as smooth as if no one has slept there. As I move, my feet tangle in a swathe of material.

I push back the covers and stare at the nightdress that encases me from head to foot. Last night we stripped off our clothes, leaving them on the floor as we fell onto my bed. The sex had been good. Bodies slicked with sweat. Salty and hot, not sweet with the scent of lavender as in this dream.

I sit up and look around me. I appear to be in Aunt Jane's room, in a time before the walls were stained sepia by tobacco smoke, so the colours are sharper and clearer, the flowers on the wallpaper bright and newly printed. Instead of an old tartan blanket and tired pillows, the ones at my back are plump with feathers. The satin coverlet is deep pink, as is the velvet-covered chair by the fireplace. On the table beside it is a collection of miniature china boxes and a vase of silk flowers. There is a marble sink set into a washstand with brass taps on one wall. Daylight filters in under lace-trimmed blinds; the mulberry-coloured curtains have a shiny new gloss. Silver-framed photographs and a small gilt clock stand on the mantelpiece, and the furniture gleams with polish.

The reflection in the wardrobe mirror is of a girl with sleep-tangled hair. She's wearing an elaborate nightgown. Its tucks and laces echo the wedding dress that hangs half-glimpsed through the open cupboard door.

This, I reason, must be the trigger for my dream and though I don't understand why I should be in this bedroom rather than my own, I see it as a sign that everything is all right between us again. I lean back against the pillows and wriggle my shoulders. The vividness of the detail around me suggests that what I am experiencing is a lucid dream. Pleasant enough in itself, but I want to be awake, to put an end to the strangeness of the past few days and get on with the next stage in my life.

Somewhere, I have read that to move from lucid dreaming to full consciousness I have to slip back into deeper sleep, so I slide down into the bed, pull up the covers and shut my eyes. The sunlight is gold and orange against my lids, the mattress too thin and the elaborate nightdress twists awkwardly around my legs. Kicking my limbs free, I open my eyes. I'm still in the big mahogany bed.

This is taking longer it should. Perhaps I should dream myself awake. I take a deep breath, hold it for a count of three and exhale. I relax and visualise William lying next to me, his head on the pillow, his skin warm. I turn. The other side of the bed is empty.

A flicker of unease shoots through my veins. Waking is harder than I thought but if I stay calm, close my eyes, let my limbs fall loose, the next time I look he'll be there beside me.

A quick rap at the door tells me the dream is over. William is bringing me a cup of tea. I'm back in reality.

"Amelia? Are you awake?" The voice is both familiar and unexpected. I've heard it cajoling, prompting, mocking, and now she's here on the other side of the door.

"Shit." My hand flies to my mouth. Across the room the girl in the mirror stares back with shocked eyes. I lower my arm. Repeat the action. With the same result. I'm dreaming I'm Amelia, the girl whose dress I'm going to wear for my wedding.

The door opens and a red-haired woman enters carrying a tray set with fine linen and delicate china. Between the teapot and the cup there is a single white rose in a crystal vase.

"Hortense. How kind of you, but you shouldn't have bothered. I could have rung for Eliza." The words fall from my lips as if someone else was speaking – and my mind whirls as I try to work out what's going on. When I've seen and heard things that have happened in the past I've always been myself, standing apart and observing. This time it's different.

Am I in the middle of a past life regression? If I am, how has it happened? I can't be in a session with Dr Radik because William and I haven't left the house since last night. Or have we? Has my mind splintered and I'm sitting in the psychologist's consulting room allowing myself to be taken back to a life I've already lived?

No, I tell myself. *That's not right. I don't believe in any of that stuff.*

The woman with the red hair is familiar because I have seen her on the stairs, in the cemetery and in the kitchen, and I realise that in my dream she is treating me as if I'm Amelia Victoria Edwards, the little girl I've seen grow from a child who read *Alice* with her father to the young woman glowing with happiness on her wedding day.

Hortense puts the tray down on the table in front of the fire. "I thought you might want to have breakfast in your own room this morning." Her glance flickers over the unruffled sheet next to me. "Louis and I will be eating downstairs. Will you join us or shall I bring you something? Would you like bacon and eggs, or maybe kedgeree, or a couple of chops?"

My first thought is to refuse their food because if I eat I might be trapped in this time, like Persephone in Hades. I try to shake my head but find myself saying, "I'd like eggs and toast with marmalade, please."

"Drink your tea first. You don't want it to get cold." Hortense pulls the pink chair up to the table, then pours milk into the cup, followed by a clear stream of tea, and as she does so I realise that my bladder is full. I throw back my covers desperate to get to the toilet.

Hortense anticipates my need and holds out a chamber pot. I can't wait. My need is too urgent. Squatting down, I'm sure I'll wake in a wet bed, but even that humiliation will be worth having escaped this dream. A hot wet smell rises around me. I'm expecting to feel a damp sheet. Instead there's the smooth edge of porcelain against my thighs.

Wake up. I dig my nails into my palms. Nothing changes. I'm aware of Hortense at the side of the room but I won't look at her. Finally, since it seems that there is more dream to be lived through, I get up and smooth down my nightdress. In one swift movement Hortense covers the pot with a linen napkin, drapes a shawl around my shoulders, then manoeuvres me into the chair and hands me a cup. Embarrassed, unable to meet the other woman's eyes, I take a sip of tea.

Hortense leaves the room, taking the brimming chamber pot. As soon as she has shut the door I run over to the window and pull up the blind. In the bright summer morning the street is empty. From somewhere, not too far away, comes a steady clip-clop of hooves, the rumble of wheels, the churn of a motor engine. A bicycle bell rings and a delivery boy turns into the crescent, his basket piled high with brown-paper packages. Peddling fast to gain speed, he takes his hands off the handlebars, sits back in the saddle and coasts. A door opens; a maid comes out with bucket and scrubbing brush. Hand on hip, she grins at him. The boy touches his cap and rides away whistling.

It's like watching a film yet the smell of the room, the feel of the windowsill beneath my hands, are solid and real. Pulling the cord I lower the blind. My throat is dry as if I'd slept with my mouth open, and I pour myself another cup of tea. It's lukewarm and there's a sour tang to the milk. I pour it away into the washstand basin and run the tap. The teapot is almost empty. Lifting the lid I mash the leaves, squeezing out the rest of the liquid. In the half-filled cup it's the colour of melting toffee. I swirl it around and the way it hides then reveals the whiteness of the china sweeps into another image.

~~~

Amelia is seven years old. Her father is holding her hand and they're walking along the quayside on a dank November afternoon. The masts of the sailing ships, with their furled sails, and the solid funnels of steamships, reach up into the grey sky. A faint mist dampens her coat and Tam O'Shanter, and she's taking care to avoid the puddles that gleam with traces of oil. The harbour side smells of mud, river water, tar and tobacco. Men shout orders, some in languages she doesn't recognise, their faces brown as autumn leaves. Others hurry past carrying sacks of grain, or trundle trollies packed with
~~~

wooden boxes.

Warehouse windows blaze with light. Through the open door of an office she sees clerks labouring over leather-bound ledgers. She tugs at her father's hand and he stops and smiles at her as she looks up and reads the names engraved in the stonework. *Edwards and Bailey.*

"That is us, Daddy."

"It was, my dear, but it's not our business now. It's been quite some time since our family was in trade so your mother has no need to fret." There's a sharpness in his tone that could spoil their time together and she hurries to ask the question she knows will please him.

"Tell me about the ships and about the wine that comes from across the sea."

"The wines we imported came from Spain and Portugal. We'll find those countries on your globe when we go home."

~~~

Sherry. I force my attention back to the cup in my hand. Like the tea, it is brown, but sweet, too sweet. The other names, the ones on the tip of my memory, I can google. My laptop is in my room on the next floor. I turn towards the door, but my head begins to pound and there is a darkness behind my eyes that threatens to close over me. I take a deep breath and as I struggle to fill my lungs the walls billow and swell. Nothing is stable. The very fabric of the house is changing.

The nightdress coils around my legs. I stagger and half-fall onto the bed. None of this is real. Reality lies on the other side of waking. I must keep a grip on who I am and where I come from. I am not Amelia. I am...

Images slide through my mind: two little girls
~~~

with dark hair, one a finer copy of the other; a plump elderly woman who smells of vanilla; a thin hawk-nosed aunt with yellowed fingers; a rambling, shambling figure of a man with a kind but slightly absent smile. They are my family. This is my house. I concentrate on my room: the black cat on the bed, the yellow shift thrown over the back of the chair, my blue-green dress drying in the bathroom, my laptop...

"There." The hand on my forehead is cool and steadying. A cloth dipped in lavender water wipes the sweat from my face and neck. "What bad luck to have been taken ill on your wedding day. The best thing for you to do now is to sleep."

I fight to stay awake but I am sliding into darkness and uncertainty. The dream, if indeed it is a dream, is no longer under my control.

"Am I dying?"

Or am I dead? Is this the Purgatory the nuns at St Cecilia's promised those of us who died without being in a state of grace?

It's very different from the penitential place we'd been taught to expect, but the feeling of dread is overwhelming. I may be sitting in bed, propped up by a pile of pillows, but I've no idea what I'm doing here – and what is worse I can't find a way out. All I know is that I shouldn't be here. Beyond the bedroom door is another life, another world, and that's where I belong.

"Dying? What a question." Hortense smiles. Her teeth are a little too big for her mouth. "Of course not. You are not very well, that's all. There's nothing to be concerned about, Amelia dear. I'm here now and I'll look after you. After both of you."

Both of us? Is Sadie here in this dream too? If she is then it won't be so bad.

"Louis knows you need to rest."

"Louis?" Searching my memory I recall a boy with golden hair. He was kind that day in the garden, when he rescued Amelia from his spiteful sister.

"Oh dear," Hortense shakes her head. A lock of hair escapes from its pins and curls around her neck. She pushes it back and there's a glint of gold from the ring on her finger that prompts me to look down at the wedding band on my left hand.

Is it possible that William and I are already married? If we are, then why is my last memory of the night I decided we would start again? To have forgotten our wedding makes no sense. William has booked Coombe Magna Manor as our wedding venue because he claims it has some family connection. Though whether it's his family, or mine, I can't recall. I'm going to wear the dress I found in Aunt Jane's wardrobe. That stunning Edwardian dress— My jumbled recollections come to a halt. The dress. Is that the link? Does that dress have such a powerful resonance that I'm dreaming of myself as that bride?

"You're still half asleep." Hortense smiles and her fingers close around mine. Her grip is a little too hard for comfort and her thumbnail digs into my palm. The pressure lasts only for a moment. I've scarcely registered it before it's gone, but the hint of menace remains.

"Rest now. You're such a frail little thing. So like your mother. Poor Aunt Eugenie suffered with her lungs, so we must take great care of you."

My mother was a student at Bristol University.

I struggle to retain the image of the girl with the twins in the Moses basket, but however hard I try it is superseded by that of the emaciated grey-faced woman who is Amelia's mother. Her eyes are sunk into her head, her chest heaves and gasps for air. She coughs and there is blood on her lips.

"I am afraid there is nothing more that can be done." The doctor shakes his head.

"What if I take her to a sanatorium in Switzerland, won't the mountain air will help her?"

"It is too late for that," the doctor murmurs and Eugenie closes her eyes.

Antibiotics. That's what she needs, my twenty-first century brain screams.

Then I remember, I'm back in a time before they were discovered and there will be no such powerful drugs for Amelia if she also falls ill. The only way to keep her healthy is to avoid infection and make sure she has plenty of good food, fresh air and exercise. I know I'm not Amelia but something tells me that I have to nurture this body for my own survival.

"I'm getting up," I tell Hortense.

"Not now. Maybe tomorrow, when you're feeling a little bit stronger." Hortense is rearranging my pillows, pushing me gently back into the enfolding softness and I am so very tired. Keeping myself focussed on who I am is taking all my energy.

"Darling?"

It is hard to open my eyes and the face looking down at me is vague and indistinct. All I can make out is the brightness of his hair and the relief is overwhelming. Then my vision clears and I realise that it's not William who is sitting on the bed stroking my hand. This man's features are softer, his hair not William's white blonde but the soft gold curls of the little boy in the garden.

I don't want to say his name. I'm gripped by the chilling conviction that the moment I do I will be trapped in this time and place forever, that if I surrender to the dream I'll never find a way back to reality. But my lips are already moving.

"Louis." It's more of a sigh than a word.

"I've come to see how you are. Hortense says you slept well. You have to get better, Amelia." His small pink mouth purses into a pout. "Everyone is dying. Your mother, my mother." He clutches my fingers like a frightened child. "We're all alone. Except for Hortense, of course. But you mustn't worry. She'll take care of both of us."

I don't need taking care of. There's nothing wrong with me.

My hand reaches up to my neck. The cross and chain are missing, but the memory of them is comforting. It brings with it a dose of Mrs K's common sense and her insistence on the beneficial effects of a good breakfast. I'm swept by a sudden desire for porridge cooked with a pinch of salt and served with a knob of butter.

"I think I could manage some toast." Once again the voice that speaks is not mine.

"Coddled eggs, toast and tea. Perfect invalid food." Louis clasps his hands. "I'll get Hortense to bring it for you."

"There's no need." I attempt to sit up. "Eliza will do it."

"Eliza?"

"The maid." Layers of memory threaten to engulf me and I fight to clear my mind.

"Oh." Louis looks puzzled then his face clears. "She's not here anymore."

"Why?"

"Hortense has made some changes to the staff."

"What has she done? Why did no one tell me?" I'm getting angry. My head is thudding. "This is my house." My voice wavers and rises. Louis shrugs and holds out his hands.

"Hortense didn't want to worry you. When you get better, and you will get better, she'll hand back the keys."

But I, or rather Amelia, have only been ill for a day. Or has it been longer? How much time have I spent in this bed? How long ago since we got married and why don't I know?

The door opens. Louis jumps to his feet and takes the tray from Hortense. "Capital," he says. "You've brought tea. I can certainly do with a cup. It's so hot and stuffy in here. I'm parched."

"It's not for you. You've had your breakfast." Hortense smiles and taps him playfully on the arm.

"Which is why you've only brought the cup. How stupid of me." Their eyes meet and there's a tension between them as if she has a hold over him, or is it that he has a hold over her? After a beat or two longer than would be usual, he turns to me. "And to my shame, rather selfish too."

"Momentarily thoughtless maybe, selfish never," Hortense is quick to reply. "I'm sure Amelia agrees. Though of course she hasn't known you as long as I have." She pours a cup of tea and hands it to me. "I've asked Dr Reynolds to call."

"I don't want to see a doctor." Being treated as an invalid puts in me in the power of this woman. I remember the aura of hatred and menace that emanated from her at Aunt Jane's funeral and know I must not trust her. What I have to work out is why. What is it that Hortense has against me, or is it Amelia she hates, or both of us?

When I concentrate hard I can think clearly as Thea, but when I lose focus I drown in the memories, fears and emotions that make me Amelia. I'm imprisoned in the mind and body of another woman and to survive as myself I have to find a way of breaking free.

I know where I am, the question is when. Judging by the clothes Louis and Hortense are wearing, the furniture and the plumbed-in washstand, we are somewhere at the start of the twentieth century. There's no calendar in the room and if I ask what the date is they might think that Amelia, or I, or whichever of the two of us it is, has lost her mind. To be considered insane will only make me more helpless than I am already.

My heart begins to race, my head spins, and I have to shut my eyes against a sudden flare of scarlet. It laps against the walls. It washes over the furniture, dying it a blood red that pulses and throbs like the pain in my temples. Has a blood vessel burst in my brain, as it did in Sadie's? I lie still and wait.

Although my head aches and my vision is blurred my body still functions and I can hear clearly as Hortense says, "Amelia, you mustn't take any risks with your health. Dr Reynolds will be here this afternoon." She looks at Louis. "Amelia will want to wash and change before the doctor calls."

"In that case I'll leave you." He bends and kisses me on the forehead and I catch hold of his hand.

"Don't go. Please, I want you to stay," I whisper.

Hortense clicks her tongue. "That wouldn't be proper."

"She's my wife," Louis argues.

Then stay here and protect me. Make sure nothing terrible happens. I don't know why, but I feel safer with you.

"Yes?" There is a question in Hortense's voice that makes me wonder if there's some doubt about the marriage. What it might be I've no idea. The snippets of memory I get from Amelia are random and disjointed.

"I think you'd both find it rather awkward if Louis was present." Hortense lowers her eyes as if what she's about to say is going to embarrass us all. "There are certain female matters that are best left to us women."

I blush. To my horror I blush. My embarrassment is followed by a burst of anger against the pale-faced young man who should be helping me but who seems totally under the control of his sister. If my head wasn't so muzzy and my lips not so thick I'd call him back. As it is, he's gone and Hortense is sponging my face and hands with lavender water. She helps me change my nightdress and asks if I want to use the chamber pot, or whether I could manage, with her help, to walk to the toilet. Needing neither, I shake my head and ask her to open the window, a request Hortense either does not hear or chooses to ignore. Instead, she pulls down the blinds so that the raw redness of the room becomes a gentler pink.

Perhaps I am ill after all and I, or Amelia, am having hallucinations caused by a high fever. But there are no shivers, no aches and pains, and my skin is cool, my pulse regular. I shut my eyes and tell myself that when I open them again the pink that suffuses everything will have faded away and I'll see colours again.

~~~

"Mrs Latimer." A raven has perched on the bedrail. "I'm sorry to see you unwell and so soon after your wedding." The bird's beak melts and softens into a face. The skin is grooved and lined, the lips are thin and disapproving.

I liked you better as a bird.

"I want to examine you, if you will permit me," the
~~~

doctor says.

"I don't want anyone to touch me," I say slowly and clearly.

"Come, come, Mrs Latimer. How else am I to help you?"

By leaving me alone. I close my eyes and cross my arms over my chest.

The doctor turns to Hortense. "From my observation and from everything you have told me I would diagnose a case of hysteria. If I am correct the best you can do for your sister-in-law is to let her rest. Let nothing disturb her. I prescribe total seclusion and in a few weeks you should see an improvement. It is—" he lowers his voice, so that I have to strain to hear what he's saying "—not uncommon when a young woman who has led a rather sheltered life enters into the state of matrimony."

"Bollocks!" The word explodes around the room, bounces off the vermilion walls, coming to rest in a blob of jelly at the doctor's feet. "What I need is to get out of this bloody bed and have some proper food. All this lying down is sapping my strength. That's all that's wrong with me." I throw back the covers and swing my legs over the side of the bed.

A hand on my chest pushes me down and I collapse onto the pillows.

"What you need is a sedative to calm you down." A spoon is thrust between my lips. Thick black syrup slides down my throat. "She will sleep now and I will call again tomorrow," the raven squawks, and flies out of the door.

I beat uselessly against the covers. There is something in the room upstairs that I have to find, but it's difficult to recall what it is. The voices rising and falling around me are making it almost impossible to think.

"Oh Louis, it's far worse than we feared," a head with red spikes is saying.

I shut out the image and concentrate on delving deep into my consciousness.

Phone. I have to find my phone. That was the word I was searching for. As soon as they've gone I'll get up and...

CHAPTER SEVENTEEN

I wake in the middle of the night. In the dark, the redness of the room is muted but my mind is clearer and I remember what I have to do to free myself from this nightmare. I have to get to my old bedroom on the next floor and if William is not there then I can phone or message him. Once I'm with him then all this will fade into the past where it belongs.

I sit up carefully, wait for the expected vertigo, and when it doesn't come I turn so that my legs dangle over the side of the bed. To get to my feet I push with my arms but there's no strength in them; they give way and I slump awkwardly back onto the mattress.

Shuffling to the top of the bed, I grasp the mahogany bedhead. The wood is curved and polished but it gives me purchase and I haul myself upright. Resting my hand on the bedside table, I manage a few steps before lurching forward and grabbing hold of a chest of drawers. I rest against the polished wood, gasping for breath. Only a little further and I'll reach the door handle, it'll turn, and I'll step out into the corridor. Before I reach it the door opens.

"Amelia, darling. What are you doing out of bed?"

"Louis." I collapse against him. He puts his arms around me and I rest my head on his chest. He smells of clean skin and fresh air as if he's been out walking. He pulls me close and strokes my hair, and some other part of me that is not Thea wants to cry with relief because he still loves her in spite of this wasting sickness.

Don't. I draw back. *Don't give in to this. If you*

become Amelia you'll be lost.

"Let me take you back to bed." Louis's hand moves to my waist. A shiver of desire stirs through me but there's no response from him. He holds me gently and there is affection but no passion in his touch. I could be a friend in distress, a small child or animal needing comfort. Anything but a wife. There's no sexual tension between us and the spark of attraction I felt for him has gone. Maybe he's gay and doesn't know it, or is supressing it because he sees it as a sin and against the law. Or it could be that he is asexual or inexperienced and is afraid of what he might be asked to do. Whatever the reason, I have to convince him that it doesn't matter to me. All I want is his support. As I search for the right words I realise that while Thea knows what to say, Amelia does not. I have to be careful not to shock him. If I tell him I love him, will that be enough to persuade him to help me?

He bends his head and kisses my hair. I smell brandy on his lips and turn my face away. "What is it? Have I hurt you?"

"It's not you. It's..." My stomach cramps. The alcohol has made me think of food. "I'm hungry. I haven't eaten for so long."

"Hungry?" His face lights up with a school-boy grin.

"Starving."

"Then you shall eat. We'll have a midnight feast."

"Just the two of us?"

"Of course. Hortense would never allow it. Can you manage the stairs or shall I go on a raid?"

"I'm coming with you." However weak I feel I can't miss the chance to escape. Louis guides me to the door. He opens it and I catch a glimpse of shabby wallpaper, the incongruously modern radiator. It's all so close. One step and I'll be back in my own time, but my feet won't move.

"Shh... We must be very quiet." Louis' breath tickles my ear.

We cross the threshold. For a flicker of a second I feel the threadbare carpet beneath my feet, see the electric light hanging from the ceiling; then the snapshot vision of the twenty-first century is gone.

"Wait here," Louis murmurs.

Defeated, I slump against the wall. I'd been so sure that all I had to do was to step outside the room and I'd be free but whatever holds me here is stronger than I'd thought. "Don't leave me," I whisper but he is swallowed by the darkness. Minutes pass. My heart is racing; my mouth tastes sour. Then a flare of light dances over the walls, grotesque figures jag and posture, coiling back into the wainscoting, and Louis is back, his hand cupped around the candle flame. His face is white, disembodied, his eyes bright with mischief.

"I brought a candle. Didn't want to light the gas in case she caught us. Come on." Louis half-carries me along the corridor.

At the top of the stairs we stop and I grab hold of the banister rail. If I trip and fall I might break my neck. If I die in this time will I be dead in my own? Or will that death free my spirit to return to my own body? My grip tightens on the polished wood, as does Louis's around my waist.

"It is all right. I'll take care of you," he murmurs and step by step we make our way down the stairs.

When we reach the ground floor where the gas light has been left burning in the hall; no doubt Hortense was expecting her brother to come in late and I pray that she's not waiting up for him. My legs are trembling with exhaustion and there's still another flight to negotiate before we reach the kitchen. Willing myself to stay upright, I take Louis's hand. On the basement stairs we jostle for space. Louis goes in front and I follow him into the underworld.

The kitchen table is scrubbed, the pots and pans gleam and there's a faint glow from the embers in the range. Louis looks around him in bemusement as if he expected his supper to be laid out ready.

"The bread and cheese will be in the larder," I tell him.

"Well, I'll be damned." Louis tugs at the handle. "It appears to be locked."

"I don't have my keys. Your sister's got them."

"To spare you the bother." Louis is quick to excuse Hortense and I look away to hide my anger at the fact that she has walked into the house and taken over as if she, not I, were mistress here. "It looks as if our plan will come to nothing." Louis shrugs apologetically.

I stay silent, fighting to hide my growing fear. Leaving Aunt Jane's bedroom has not brought me back to my own time. I glance across the room to the wall where Mrs K's icon should hang.

~~~

She is standing by the range heating milk in a red-enamel pan. The strip lighting is harsh bringing the scene into sharp focus. "Hot chocolate. Then upstairs, my angels. Wash your teeth and say your prayers before you get into bed."

"It's cold in our room." Sadie pulls a face.

"The chocolate will warm you."

"Kneeling on the floor hurts my knees."

There is a sharp indrawing of breath. "Never forget that Our Lord died for us on the cross." The milk fizzes and boils over. Mrs K whips the pan off
~~~

the heat.

My hand goes to my neck where my cross should be.

~~~

The scarlet glow that covers everything intensifies. Louis stands silhouetted against it. A demon among flames, his face narrows, his expression becomes threatening, then shifts again to a puzzled concern.

"Are you all right? You're looking awfully strange. Shall I call Hortense?"

"No."

"I won't be a moment. Stay there and I'll be back."

The room shudders. Walls melt. Streaks of crimson seep from the plaster. I grasp the edge of the table but the wood crumbles beneath my fingers and I'm rocked from side to side. My feet are no longer on the ground. My body has no contact with anything solid. I am spinning in a vortex. Disintegrating.

~~~

Vomit rose in my throat. I staggered to the sink and was hideously and violently sick.

Better? Sadie was at my side.

You could have helped me.

I wasn't there. I didn't see. I didn't know. I'm sorry, sis, I didn't know it was going to be like this for you.

Well it was shit. Utterly terrifying shit.

I turned on the tap and let it flow at full power and when the sink was rinsed clean I poured myself a glass of water and drank it slowly to soothe the rawness in my throat.

The kitchen was not quite in focus; familiar shapes fuzzed and blurred as if seen through a fog. I blinked and rubbed my eyes. The warm glow of an electric streetlamp shone through the top of the window. Louis had gone. Everything looked the same as it did when William and I had left it the night before. The roses stood on the table, stiff and white in their vase, their scent mingling with the smell of coriander, lemon grass, garlic and coconut milk from the empty cartons on the draining board.

A wash of pink swept across the sky. The streetlamps went out. I filled the kettle and put teabags in the pot but remembering the last cup I'd had I couldn't bring myself to drink it.

Lace it with brandy, for the shock.

I hate brandy. You know I do. Sadie, what's going on? What's happening to me?

There was no reply. The room was empty.

Fuck you.

If that was all the help Sadie was going to be then I'd work this out for myself. I forced the first sip down my throat. It was fresh and hot with no taint of rancid milk. Had it been the tea that Hortense had given Amelia that had made her feel so ill? Milk that had gone off wouldn't have had such a violent an effect. Her stomach might have been upset; she might even have been sick, but she wouldn't have experienced those hallucinations: the raven on the bed rail, the disembodied head with red spikes, the crimson staining on the walls.

Thinking about what I, or rather Amelia, had seen made me wonder if, unlikely though it seemed, the whole episode had been a hallucination caused by the spices in our Thai takeaway. But we'd had food from The Giggling Squid before and never experienced anything like this. My next thought was whether someone could have slipped something into my food. An idea I quickly dismissed. I hadn't been anywhere and while William could be overbearing at times with his ideas of what was and wasn't good for me, he hated drugs or anything that threatened his self-control – I'd never seen him drunk and he disapproved when I'd had more than I should. To dose me without my permission would be to go against everything he believed in.

The other argument against it being all in my mind was that I'd gone to sleep in my own room and woken up in Aunt Jane's. Then I'd come down to the kitchen with Louis. Where I was now.

Sadie and I had never walked in our sleep, which left me with the only other explanation. I, like Sadie, had gone back in time, because in this house time was fluid and there were no boundaries between one century and another. Was this what Aunt Jane was working on? Was this the basis of her experiments with Sadie? Or on Sadie? Was that why my sister hadn't told me what was going on, because what was happening to her was so terrifying that she wanted to shield me from it?

All my life I had thought that I was the more grownup of the two of us. Had I been wrong? Was it Sadie who was the strong one? Was she the one who protected me rather than the other way round? When I'd first seen Hortense, she'd come racing back and she was there on the roof to stop me from throwing myself over the edge.

And now I needed her help to face Hortense.

The kitchen door opened. Not knowing who or what I was going to see I braced my feet against the floor, my forearms on the table anchoring myself to this time and place.

"Thea, darling, what are you doing down here?"

"William?" For a moment I couldn't think what he was doing in my house at this time of morning. His hair was rumpled, his feet were bare, and he was wearing nothing but a pair of jeans.

"I woke up and you weren't there."

"When? When did you wake up?" Had I spent the whole night in my own bed and what I'd taken to be a time slip was no more than an intensely vivid dream?

"Just now. Why?"

"I don't know. It's nothing." My instinct told me to hold back, but if I didn't share this with William it would become barrier between us. "I mean…"

"I'll make us some coffee, shall I?"

Couldn't he see how shaken and upset I was?

"Yes. And then…"

For God's sake sit down and let me talk to you.

He doesn't want to listen. He doesn't want to hear what you have to say.

"Shut up, Sadie."

"What did you say?" William turned round.

"Nothing."

Go away Sadie. Leave me alone.

Yeah, well. The sound of Sadie's laughter filled the kitchen. William, a spoonful of coffee in his hand, froze. It was only the briefest fraction of a second but long enough for me to ask, "Did you hear that?" If he'd sensed Sadie's presence this was my opening. I'd tell him everything and he'd look at it in his clear logical way and together we'd work out what we should do.

"Hear what?"

"Why are you lying?" I sprang to my feet. "I saw you. You stopped what you were doing. You know she's here."

William poured boiling water onto the coffee. "Thea—" his voice was reasonable, his manner calm "—it's your grief. You want to see her so much that you imagine she's here."

"I knew you'd say that but it isn't true. The

grieving is but I am not conjuring Sadie up to make myself feel better. Most of the time she's saying things I don't want to hear."

"That's to be expected. Remember the stages of bereavement: after shock comes denial, then anger and guilt."

"Is that how you felt when your parents died? Did you go through all the stages neatly one by one?"

"That was different."

"One rule for you then and one for me. And if I don't do it properly there's something wrong with me?"

"You could certainly do with another session with Dr Radik."

"No I bloody couldn't. He doesn't know what's going on any more than I do. It isn't just Sadie, it's the others, it's the house."

"Then move out. Sell. As we agreed."

"You think that would solve it? That moving away would be the end of it? If only. I saw her in the cemetery and she was laughing."

"Surely not. Not even Sadie would laugh at a funeral."

"I don't mean Sadie. I'm talking about Hortense. You're not listening to me. I'm trying to tell you something really important and you're not listening."

"Thea, darling." He put his left hand on my arm, his touch firm and cool on my bare flesh. "Shh." He pressed his right forefinger against my lips. "You're getting muddled and confused. It might be that you need some medication. You really have to see Dr Radik again, if only to get yourself back to a place where you can think logically. I'll make you an appointment." William's voice took on that familiar hypnotic quality which used to calm me down but now only roused me to contempt.

"Don't bother. If I want an appointment, I'll make it myself, thank you." I wrenched myself free. "I'd hoped we could talk. I wanted to tell you so we could do this together but you don't want to know."

"Thea, you're sick. I didn't want to say it. I thought you'd come through the breakdown but it looks as if you've had a relapse. There's no shame in that. You just need some more treatment."

"I'm not ill and I'm not crazy."

"You're not going to admit it? You do realise that until you accept that you need help you'll never get better."

"I told you what I think. I told you what I need and you can't, or you won't, do it. All I wanted from you, William, was to listen to me."

"I've listened. I've listened to this for months. I thought you were making progress and we could finally move forward and have a life of our own."

"Without Sadie. Yes, that would suit you. You were always jealous of the link we had."

"I love you, Thea. I really do, but this..."

"This is more than you can deal with?"

"I'm not saying that."

"That's what you mean. You can't deal with this crazy madwoman any longer."

"I love you, Thea."

"I know." My anger seeped away into sadness.

How can I tell him that I can't live with him? I can't be the woman he wants. He's not right for me, either. If it hadn't been for Sadie dying we wouldn't have stayed together. We're too different. I'm not pliable and submissive. I don't need a man to complete me. What I want from my partner is for him to understand where I'm coming from and to support me in what I want to do. What William does is caring and keeping me safe. He's no good at letting me stand on my own two feet—

He has to be in control and that will never change. Sadie's voice broke through my thoughts.

William and I stood and looked at each other; the silence between us burdened with all the things that should and should not have been said. The cat padded into the kitchen and wound itself around my legs.

"I can't do this anymore," William said stiffly. Not wanting to see the pain in his eyes I bent to stroke the cat. "If you get help," he added, "we might stand a chance."

I straightened up. "No we don't. We never did. We're too different. At one time I thought we might make it but now I know we can't."

"Don't say that. We complement each other. Like you and Sadie. That's what you're looking for, isn't it?"

"It might have been once, but not anymore."

"Thea, I know that's how you feel at the moment, but please don't make any hasty decisions. Give us both time to think things through. If you go and see Dr Radik..."

I shook my head. The cat butted at my legs and as I went to fetch its dish the kitchen door opened then shut, and William was gone.

I ripped open the pouch of cat food and watched as the cat devoured its breakfast, its sharp white teeth tearing at the lumps of meat.

The sun slanted in through the window. The air, cleansed by a night almost free of fumes, was fresh and hopeful. I felt no regret, rather a sense of relief tinged with a little sadness. I'd not wanted to hurt William but it was better to break up now than later. As things stood I could simply walk away. I had my own life, a house and a job, though that would have to change as I could hardly stay in the firm where my ex-fiancé was a senior partner.

How different it was for Amelia. That bright interested little girl who had wanted to be a doctor or an explorer had grown up to fall in love with a man who kept her prisoner in her own room. How had that happened? She must have believed that he loved her. She had been so happy on her wedding day but as soon as they were married everything had changed.

The light shifted. The sun was directly on my face and as I squinted to shut out the glare there was a red and orange afterglow.

Whatever had caused Amelia's condition, seeing everything in scarlet had been one of the consequences. I didn't know of any disease that would cause that sort of hallucination but taking drugs might well have that effect. It was unlikely that a young wealthy middle-class girl would be using, in which case it had to be the medicine she had been given.

Without stopping to eat or to clear away the previous night's dishes, I found my laptop, cleared a space on the kitchen table and began my research. Amelia might have taken any number of substances in the medicine her doctor prescribed for quite minor conditions such as coughs or colds, but none of these would produce the visual disturbances I'd experienced. The other possibility was that she'd exceeded the dose. I rested my elbows on the table, cupped my chin in my hands and tried to remember the sequence of events. I'd woken up feeling ill. Or had I? It was later, when everyone around me was insisting that I was unwell, that the headaches, nausea and visions began. I wasn't taking any medicine then, so whatever was making me sick had to be in what I was eating or drinking, and the person who had brought me my breakfast was Hortense. If she'd wanted to rid herself of an inconvenient sister-in-law she'd wasted no time. The question was whether Louis knew what she was doing.

I shifted in my chair. Dressed only in the t-shirt in which I'd slept, my smell rose around me, hot and salty. The undeniable trace of sex. Which had not been there when I had woken as Amelia. Louis had not slept with his wife. Had his concern for her fragile health kept him from making love to her? Or was it the lack of interest I had sensed in him. If that is what he felt then why did they marry? Unless it was for money.

Amelia was rich. She'd inherited the family fortune, and as her husband Louis had a very comfortable life, as did his sister. Ultimately, however, the money was Amelia's and Louis would only gain control of it on her death and not even then if they had children. But what if he needed it now? It would be easy enough to hasten his wife's death. No one would question it, especially if her mother had a history of consumption and her father had died relatively young. The thought was chilling but even though it made sense I was not convinced by the idea of Louis as a murderer. His sister on the other hand...

"They're not going to beat me," I told the cat. It gave me a look, then jumped onto the windowsill.

I went back to my laptop, occasionally getting up to walk to the door and back, or refill my glass of water. Moving helped me think. It also put off the moment when I'd have to leave the safety of the kitchen and face the rest of the house. The thought of stepping back into Amelia's life scared me but I couldn't stay down here, half-dressed and rank as a bag lady, nor could I run away. Even if I rang William and asked him to bring me some clothes Hortense's spirit was not confined to this house. She could follow me wherever I went. The only way of freeing myself was to face whatever was waiting for me and put an end to it, forever.

My fate, it appeared, was linked to Amelia's. If I was right about that then, since the only family that had lived at number fifteen were the Gordons, there must be a biological connection between her and the woman who had adopted us.

I told you, we were left in a basket on the doorstep

Why this doorstep? There must be a reason. And why should an older single woman with a good career want to take in a pair of twins?

I don't know. I could almost see Sadie shrug.

"You don't know anything," I said out loud.

None of us do.

I slammed my elbows on the table. Sadie might retreat into ignorance, but I was the one that was being threatened by the malign presence that had manifested itself in my life.

Hortense wants her little brother for herself. She always has done.

Once the thought had occurred to me it seemed so obvious. The evidence was in the way Hortense looked at Louis, how quick she was to use the excuse of Amelia's so-called illness to separate the newly married couple, her determination to keep them apart. Had she succeeded?

If I could discover what had happened to Amelia and her husband I might find a way forward. Once again I logged on to the ancestry site. I stared at the screen but the letters danced and dissolved into a red tide that spilled out over the table, lapping at my hands. The cat meowled, its cry echoing down a distant tunnel, receding further and further away until all that was left was a dark silence.

My body folded in on itself. I was being dragged backwards, my joints being pulled out of sockets. All sensation disintegrating.

CHAPTER EIGHTEEN

The hand on my shoulder brings me to my senses. I look up into blue eyes and a brow furrowed with concern.

"You're very pale. You look as if you're going to faint."

"Louis?"

"It's all right, I told you I'd be back. I've found provisions. Come with me." He puts his arm around my waist and forces me to my feet. I try to resist. I'm reluctant to leave the kitchen because it's here that I'd gone back to my own life. But I'm given no choice. Buoyed up by daring to defy his sister, Louis is too strong for me in my weakened state, and gently but firmly steers me up the stairs.

His courage doesn't run deep. Every few steps he stops and listens for any sign of Hortense.

"Good thing she sleeps like a log or we'd never get away with it," Louis whispers when we finally reach the hall. Steady on." He gasps as my legs give way and I have to grab hold of him to stop myself from falling. "We're nearly there. Can you manage a few more steps or shall I carry you?" His face falls. "I should have carried you over the threshold when we got back from the church for the wedding breakfast, but Hortense said that was rubbish since the house was already yours and all we were doing was coming home."

"It doesn't matter. I can manage. I'm stronger than I look." I try to convince myself.

"That's capital." He tightens his hold and manoeuvres me towards the door of my father's study. With his free hand, Louis turns the handle.

As the door opens I shrink back from the inferno. Walls, carpet, ceiling, are all lit by the hellish crimson light that emanates from the glowing embers in the hearth. "Come on, old girl. You can't give up now. Not when our quarry is in sight." Louis pulls me into the room. "See!" he says triumphantly. "A meat pie, bread, cheese and half a bottle of port. Wasn't I a good boy not to eat it all? Hortense always leaves supper out for me for when I come in late. It's not what I'd planned for our feast. I'm afraid I've already demolished more than my fair share but, since my sister was so mean as to lock us out of our own larder, we'll have to make the best of what we've got."

"This," I breathe, "is perfect." I stumble into one of the wing chairs that stand on either side of the hearth. If I keep my eyes half closed the redness is almost bearable. Louis takes the knife and hacks at the squat loaf of crimson bread, cuts me a slice of vermilion cheese and a chunk of the red rawness of the meat pie and hands me the plate. To avoid looking at the food I feel for it with my fingers, breaking off small pieces which I cram into my mouth.

My throat is dry making it hard to swallow and I force down the food, fearful of being discovered. I know it has not been tampered with because Hortense would never hurt her beloved brother. Besides, I need to eat, to gather as much strength as I can to face my enemy.

Louis hands me a glass and I drink, relishing the smoothness of the port as it slides down my throat. He's standing over me and I risk a quick glance from under my lashes. "You look better already. There's some colour in your cheeks. You were as pale as death. You know you really had me worried. I thought, when I came back into the kitchen—" his voice falters and he turns his head away "—for one terrible moment that you were gone. That I'd lost you just as I'd lost Mother. You were so white and strange."

"I felt faint. That's all. I needed this." I lift the glass to my lips and savour the way the alcohol runs through my veins, dulling some of the fear that beats at the edge of my consciousness. "Thank you, Louis."

"You should drink to us. We should drink to us." Delighted, he brings another glass and fills it to the brim. Crimson liquid in carnelian glass. I can't bear to look at it and concentrate on holding his gaze as we solemnly toast each other. "As soon as you're stronger we must go on our honeymoon."

"That would make me very happy. You and I in…" I have no memory of where we were planning to spend our honeymoon.

"The Italian Lakes. Hortense says they are very beautiful at this time of year as the weather is not too hot. Though how she would know since she's never been there I've no idea. She was to have arranged it all. Don't you remember?"

"I do recall something…" I smile up at him.

Was his sister really going to come with us on our honeymoon? Was that usual? Was Amelia never to be free of her? Or was Hortense planning to wait until her sister-in-law had succumbed to whatever disease the doctor would diagnose before taking the grieving widower away from the scene of his loss.

"To be alone in Italy, just you and me, would be so romantic. I've always wanted to go to Rome and Florence too," I murmur.

"Hortense said…"

"Shh." I stand up and put my finger on his lips.

This is my chance to convince him that Hortense has no place in our marriage, or if that is too much to ask of my young husband then I'll argue that his sister can run the household and leave me to be his wife. "Hortense has been very kind to me. I know how deeply she cares about you but—" I lean towards him, parting my lips and winding my arms around his neck. He bends his head and I half-close my eyes, but even as I wait for his kiss he is pulling away, distracted by the pad of slippered feet.

There is a sharp click of tongue and Hortense has me by the elbow. "Louis, whatever are you thinking of? This is very inconsiderate of you. You know what the doctor said. Come on, Amelia, you must have your rest. Let this silly boy of ours finish his supper. Such food is far too rich for your delicate stomach."

"We were – Amelia was hungry – I thought—" Louis stammers.

"You're behaving like a pair of children, a pair of naughty children." Hortense smiles playfully, her fingers digging into my arm as she attempts to steer me towards the door.

"Aren't we just." I dig my feet in and jerking my shoulder free myself from her vicious grip. "It was too bad of me." Playing the part of the innocent ingénue, I cock my head to one side. "Please don't blame Louis. He was only doing what I wanted because I said I was hungry. Which must be a sign that I'm getting better."

"For which we should all be grateful." Hortense looks at Louis.

"Quite right too," he replies. Hoping for his support I take a step towards him, but he makes no move to close the gap between us. "Which was why I—"

"Why you fed the poor girl game pie and cheddar

cheese. I only hope she'll not suffer for it."

Louis flushes and looks down at his feet.

"I shall be fine in the morning." I try to catch his eye but he doesn't look up.

"So we must hope," Hortense says tartly. "In the meantime let me bring you a milky drink to help you sleep."

"I don't want to put you out," I say quickly.

"Oh, it'll be no trouble. No trouble at all. Louis take your wife to her room."

I try to tell him that I can manage without his help but my head feels as if it's floating slightly above my body. The muscles in my thighs are trembling uncontrollably and when Louis obediently takes my arm I cannot stop myself from leaning against him.

"Steady on," he whispers as the room spins. My feet tangle and I stumble against the desk. "We can make it, old girl, and if you can't I'll damn well carry you up the stairs."

"Thank you." I smile at Louis. His face is stained by the redness that colours everything I see, but there's a grim determination in his expression that fills me with hope. He will not abandon me completely. Whatever hold his sister might have over him he has some feeling for his wife. If only I could look directly at him but the redness of his eyes, the unnatural colour of his skin, is too much to bear.

"You can hardly stand." Hortense is at my side. "Louis, you are not strong enough to manage her on your own. Let me help you."

"That's good of you but we'll do it. When we get to the stairs Amelia will have something to hold on to and we can stop to take a breather whenever she wants."

"As you wish." Hortense's lips twist into a bitter smile. Her nostrils flare, and the crimson hue of her skin gives her the aspect of a demon that has been thrown out of its domain and pitched into a world it does not understand. With a sharp toss of her head she stands aside, brushing back the skirt of her dressing gown as we pass.

"Up the wooden mountain," Louis says as I grip hold of the banister.

The gas light in the hall burns with an unnaturally red flame; our shadows creep painfully behind us. When we reach the top of the stairs Louis stops to catch his breath. Two of the doors along the corridor stand open. The light spills out from Hortense's room. Aunt Jane's is dark, and from the stairs above there is the glow of a lamp to guide Louis to his solitary bed. Or is it my way back? I'm so sure that Sadie is waiting for me in the old nursery that I start forward. The sudden movement is too much, my legs buckle and only Louis's swift action saves me from sprawling on the carpet.

"Hey, where are you going?" he chides gently. "What's the rush? You have to wait for me. It's not far to go now, we're almost there."

"I don't want..." My limbs shake violently.

"If you don't want to be ill then you have to do what everyone says."

"Everyone—" my breath comes in hard gasps as I choke out the words "—is not right. Sometimes you have to go with what you feel."

For a moment everything hangs in the balance. Louis' embrace stiffens, becomes awkward, as if he's supporting a stranger who has suffered a fainting fit in the street. If he denies what I've said then I am lost.

~~~

"I've brought you some hot milk. It'll help you sleep." Hortense stands in the doorway holding a tray; on it
~~~

is a glass covered by a lace-trimmed cap.

"No milk." I clutch Louis's hand. He sits on the bed like a visitor in a sickroom. "Please no." My lips are dry and cracked, my throat parched, but I won't drink anything Hortense gives me.

"Nonsense." My sister-in-law flushes a deeper shade of scarlet. Her hair, plaited for the night, hangs like a rope over her shoulder. She puts down the tray, takes the glass and advances. Her shadow looms above me, a gnarled and hunched shape hovering over the ceiling. I clamp my lips together. It's childish and pathetic but short of knocking the glass from the woman's hand there's nothing I can do.

"Leave it, Hortense. Can't you see she doesn't want it?" Louis turns to his sister.

Hortense puts down the glass. "I'm doing my best for you. I'm doing my best for you both." Her voice shakes.

"We appreciate it. We do." Louis slides his hand from under mine. "You've been so good to us." He gets up and puts his arm around his sister's shoulders. "You've been working so hard and you must be tired. It's very late. Why don't you go back to your room?"

"But..." Hortense glances at the milk.

"I'll make sure Amelia drinks it and if she doesn't I'll drink it myself."

"Not after that supper you won't. It won't do your digestion any good. I won't have you being bilious even though it'll be a terrible waste of food." Hortense glares at me. "No doubt that doesn't matter to you since you've never gone without." She picks up the tray and sails out of the room.

"You mustn't mind what she says." Louis's eyes are on the door. "Hortense can't forget what it was like for those years after Father died. We were so poor and it was such a struggle for Mother. Sometimes all we had to eat was bread and milk." He wanders over to the fireplace. "I might be Uncle George's heir but there still isn't very much money." He picks up a china candlestick, examines the mark on the bottom as if he's valuing it and puts it down. "Hortense has always hoped that one day we'll take our rightful place at Coombe Magna as lord and lady of the manor. But as for me—" Louis comes back to the bed "—I don't know whether or not I care. After all, who wants to live in a draughty old manor house, when one can have all the delights of being in town?"

What about me? What about Amelia, your wife? Where do I fit into this picture?

I wait for him to mention me, but he doesn't. Is there no place for me in his future? In spite of all his reassurances, deep down does he think I'm going to die? What does he mean by "the delights of being in town"? Is there some hidden meaning there I can't access? Somewhere in my memory there are snatches of conversation, fleeting images, fragments of a whole that I'm too tired to put together.

I close my eyes and his hand on my forehead is cool and soothing. I want him to stay with me but it's too soon to ask him to spend the night in my bed. It would upset the fragile balance of our relationship and I'd risk losing my only ally in the battle with Hortense.

"I'll see you in the morning." His lips skim my cheek. Then I'm alone in this wide bed in a scarlet room. In spite of my exhaustion, I don't want to sleep because there have been too many times when I've woken up in Amelia's body when I'd expected to be back in my own.

There are places like the kitchen where it seems I can return to being myself. I lift my head from the pillow and push against the mattress but whatever I've been taking makes me so tired that I can't find the energy to sit up let alone go down two flights of stairs to the basement without any help. I'll have to rest and wait until the poison Hortense has been feeding me has passed through my system. If it ever does. What I'm going to do if it's irreversible ... I'm not going to think about.

Logic tells me that if Thea Gordon is alive in the twenty-first century then I can't die in the early years of the twentieth. In spite of that I toss and turn for the rest of the night and it's not until the first light of dawn creeps beneath the blinds that I drift into a doze.

The wheels of the milkman's cart rumble along the street. A door opens and closes. I tense. If this is Hortense I don't want her to find me flat on my back unable to move. Keeping my head straight to avoid another attack of vertigo I slide myself up onto my pillows.

"Amelia, you're awake. How are you feeling this morning? I let you sleep, because I thought after last night you'd be exhausted and need your rest." Hortense bustles across the room.

There are so many answer I could give to this question but only one that will give me an advantage and I have to think carefully before speaking. "I'm not well. Not at all well." I put a quiver into my voice and half-shut my eyes. "My head..." I wave my hand and let it fall limply onto the covers. "Hortense, I have to..." Anxiety sharpens my tone and I find it difficult to gage whether I'm overdoing it or not. I can't read the mask that is my sister-in-law's face and have no way of knowing whether I've convinced her or whether she's guessed that I'm playing a game. "I have to see Doctor—" for a moment the name will not come, then I remember "—Reynolds. Please send for him. Tell him to come as soon as he can."

"Of course, if that's what you want, but he was only here the other day."

"I feel worse. There are things I have to tell him." I press my lips together. "I was too... It was difficult but now... Oh, Hortense, I'm afraid."

"What is it? You were so much better, yesterday." Louis coming into the room strides across to the bed. He takes my hand. His fingers tremble but he meets his sister's eyes. "If that is what Amelia wants then we will send for the doctor immediately. It's not as if there would be any difficulty paying his bills."

Hortense flushes. Her head jerks up and she draws in her breath as if she's been insulted.

"I'll see to it. I'll send the maid with a note."

I sigh and briefly squeeze Louis's hand, then let it drop for it has to look as if I'm sinking fast. If Hortense thinks I'm dying then she won't feed me any more poison.

"Stay with me Louis," I mouth and to my relief he understands.

"Go now, Hortense. Don't wait. Please."

"Oh Louis, oh my dear, I had no idea. She should never have left her bed last night." Hortense hurries from the room.

I shut my eyes and concentrate on stilling my breathing. Louis brings a chair and sits at the side of the bed. He looks miserable, probably consumed with guilt for feeding me all that rich food last night. I know it's done me nothing but good but I can't tell him. For my plan to work he has to believe that I've not got long to live.

After a while Louis gets up and begins to pace up and down the room. From time to time he glances out of the window. "It won't be long, my darling," he reassures me, or is it himself? I moan softly and he rushes to my side, sits on the bed, and taking my hand raises it to his lips.

The doorbell rings. There's the sound of muffled voices followed by footsteps coming up the stairs.

"Doctor Reynolds, at last." Louis hurries to greet him. "Thank God you're here."

"My sister-in-law's condition appears to have worsened overnight. We're very concerned," Hortense says.

"She's lost all her strength. She can hardly lift her head from the pillow." Louis sounds distraught.

"I'm afraid the rich food she had for supper last night has done the damage," his sister adds.

"Indeed? What have you been eating?" Dr Reynolds is leaning over me, his fingers on my pulse.

"Bread and cheese. And some meat pie." The tremble in Louis's voice betrays his guilt.

"Mm." The doctor appears to reflect.

Tell them that's good. That I need nourishing food: fat and protein for my muscles, carbs for energy.

"My brother meant it for the best. He was worried because Amelia has no appetite. A little tea and toast is all she can manage," Hortense says quickly.

The doctor turns to her. "If you would help her sit up, Miss Latimer, I will examine her." Hortense starts forward but Louis gets there first, sliding his arm under my shoulders and holding me as the doctor opens his bag.

"I am going to listen to your chest." The stethoscope is cold, the doctor's face impassive. I dare not look at the others in case my expression betrays me and keep my eyes lowered.

"Her lungs are clear. There is no need to worry on that score," the doctor announces.

"Thank God," Louis breathes.

"As for the weakness and general debility, I will prescribe a tonic. In the meantime, Mrs Latimer, you must do your very best to take some nourishment. I suggest beef tea and gruel to which you may, if you wish, add a dash of brandy to fortify the blood. I am sure Miss Latimer is conversant with food appropriate for the sickroom." He is packing away his stethoscope. He will leave and I'll have lost my chance.

"I... I..." I stammer. My throat is parched, my tongue swollen. "There is something I have to ... in private."

"Ah." The doctor nods in understanding. "Mr Latimer, if you would leave us."

Louis relinquishes his hold and kisses me quickly on the forehead. He leaves but Hortense shows no sign of going with him. I shake my head weakly and the doctor dismisses her with a glance. She gives a barely perceptible sniff and follows her brother out of the room.

"Now..." The doctor clears his throat. "What is it you wish to say to me?"

I push myself up against the pillows and make myself look in the doctor's eyes. To my horror the words I've so carefully prepared tumble out in an almost incomprehensible babble. "I can't eat their food. She's poisoning me. I know she is. Please, you must believe me." I grasp his hand. "You're my only hope."

Dr Reynolds purses his lips. He gently frees himself from my grip, draws himself up and looks down at me. "Mrs Latimer, how long have you suffered from this delusion?"

"I'm not making it up. It's the truth. Everything looks—"

He holds up his hand to stop me. "Mrs Latimer, I have made a study of cases such as yours. In my opinion you are very young to have embarked on marriage and sometimes—" he coughs "—the demands made by an active husband on an inexperienced wife can be, how can one put it, rather too taxing."

It's not the sex. I don't think there's been any.

"Louis, my husband, he doesn't..." For once I am grateful for the uncharacteristic flush of embarrassment.

"I see. The difficulty then is on his side and you in consequence are suffering from a mild case, and I repeat mild, of hysteria, complicated by nervous exhaustion."

"I'm not imagining it."

"Of course you are not. Hysteria is a genuine complaint. There's no need to worry, it will pass. Together, you and your husband will come to an accommodation. Treat him with gentleness and patience and all will be well. In the meantime, rest is the best remedy. I will call on you tomorrow to see how you are progressing." At the door he stops. "I leave you in good hands."

I want to call him back and tell him about the changes in my vision but I'm afraid that would be seen as another symptom of my hysterical state. In a final attempt to communicate more than I've already said, I hold his glance.

A slight frown gives me hope that he's understood, then he shakes his head and leaves the room.

My attempt to win him over to my side has failed. Apart from Louis, who's an uncertain ally, there's no one I can turn to. This is the first time in my life I have been totally alone. Until the accident there was always Sadie. We'd had our fights and there were times when we hadn't got on, but when the need arose we were always there for each other. Even after her death she's looked after me, cutting through my grief that day on the roof when I was so tempted to jump, racing back to the house to save me when I first encountered Hortense. It's only here in this time she can't reach me.

Is this my punishment? We were so closely linked that at the deepest of levels I must have known there was something wrong with her and if I'd said something she could have had treatment. The doctors can say what they like about the condition having no symptoms. They don't understand about twins and wouldn't believe me if I told them about the pain in my head the day Sadie died.

If only I hadn't been so focussed on my own life. My engagement to William and my job had come between us. I should have taken Sadie to that audition but I put a meeting with a client before the needs of my twin. And now I am trapped in some sort of Purgatory where I am neither Amelia Latimer nor Thea Gordon, but some strange mixture of the two. This is why I cannot escape. I have to serve my time until I have expiated my guilt.

Bollocks! Why am I thinking like this? Wallowing in guilt will drain me and I have to stay strong to defeat Hortense.

Voices drift through the door the doctor has left ajar.

"How is my wife? If you could spare me a moment I'd like to speak to you without my sister present."

"Of course. I quite understand. The matter is delicate. Is there anything in particular you wish to tell me about? I can assure you of my complete discretion." There is a pause. "Mr Latimer?"

"I'm afraid that she is dying."

Does that mean he is on my side? That he has finally seen what Hortense has been doing? Or is he faking concern as a cover for his part in their plan? How can I tell?

"Not at all, my dear man. I must admit that the situation, as I see it, is complex. However, I do believe that there is nothing wrong with Mrs Latimer that cannot be cured by rest and good nursing and I'm sure your admirable sister can provide the latter."

Louis clears his throat. "The trouble is, Amelia seems to have taken against her."

"Which of course complicates matters. Tell me, does your wife appear to be suffering from hallucinations?"

"I..." he hesitates and another voice joins the conversation.

"Forgive me, doctor, I was on my way with some tea to tempt Amelia and I couldn't help overhearing your last question. My brother may not be aware of it but there is a history of mental instability in my sister-in-law's family."

"I didn't know that," Louis says.

"Of course you didn't. You were only a child but I do remember Mother talking about her sister, Amelia's mother, suffering with her nerves. I think with good care and a loving husband Aunt Eugenie outgrew her affliction, although it may have returned after his death." She pauses. "It would certainly explain why she and Mother had such a terrible falling out. It is a great sadness to us all that we saw nothing of our aunt in her final illness. It was not until after her funeral that we were able to do anything for our cousin. It's something I'll never be able to forgive myself for. What makes it worse, doctor, is that Louis and Amelia were childhood sweethearts and it was only her mother's intransigence that kept them apart."

Why was my mother so against the match? In many ways Louis was the perfect choice.

I half-smile at the memory of the golden-haired boy in the garden who had stood up for me against his spiteful sister. The young man, in shabby mourning clothes, who had called on me after my mother's death, his brightness lighting up the room, his touch on my hand sending a jolt through my veins. His kindness and gentleness was in such contrast to Mother's cold snobbery and Father's dry wit, no wonder I'd fallen heedlessly in love, abandoning all plans to further my education and make a life as a woman of independent means.

You were an idiot, I berate the part of myself that is Amelia. *Falling for the first man who paid you any attention, the first man who'd come into your life. Your only excuse is that you were lonely. You'd lost your both your parents and death is the greatest of aphrodisiacs.*

Dr Reynolds exhales sharply and I listen intently, willing him not to believe Hortense's lies as she spins the story that will exonerate her if the doctor discovers the poison in my system. She wants me to be diagnosed as insane so that when I die everyone will think I killed myself. By confiding in the doctor I may have made things worse.

"My diagnosis stands and so does my prescription. To make things easier and take some of the burden off your shoulders, Miss Latimer, I am going to send for Nurse O'Halloran. She is very experienced and comes highly recommended. If anyone can nurse your sister-in-law back to health, it is she. However, not even Nurse O' Halloran is infallible and if Mrs Latimer has not improved significantly in a few weeks' time then I am very much afraid that we will be left with no choice."

"What do you mean?" Louis asks.

"Your wife will have to be consigned to Bradwell Grange. It is, I can assure you, a very select establishment. Our patients are given the best care and the most up-to-date treatments. Some have benefitted from a short stay, others will, sadly, never leave; but you may be reassured that while they are with us their every need is being met."

"Amelia will be put in an asylum!" Louis sounds shocked.

"That may be our only option," the doctor says smoothly.

Hortense is quick to add, "It will be for the best, Louis, and you know that's what we both want for Amelia."

So failing murder that's her plan. I'll be locked away in an institution for the rest of my life. I've read how people with mental illnesses were treated in those days. Once committed, there was no appeal and they could spend years wasting away behind barred windows and locked doors, inexorably losing all sense of self. Is this what's going to happen to Amelia?

CHAPTER NINETEEN

"Mrs Latimer, if you would just let me make you more comfortable." A large red-faced woman in a starched cap and apron is bending over me. Before I can reply I'm being gently but firmly settled into a sitting position. A washcloth is dipped into a bowl of warm water and the nurse is sponging my face and hands.

"There you are now. I do like my patients to be presentable at all times. We may be unwell but we can look our best. A lovely corpse is a thing of great beauty, don't you know." She looks appraisingly at me then her face breaks into a smile. "I see you share my sense of humour. 'Tis a blessing that is, to be sure. Some of my ladies, let me tell you, have been so po-faced I've not known where to put myself. But you and I, young Mrs L, are going to get on famously."

"Thank God," I whisper.

Nurse O'Halloran puts her hands on her hips. "I do not stand for profanities. Not even in extremis are we to take the name of the Lord in vain."

"I was—" I croak hastily "—sincerely giving thanks."

"Now that is good to hear. A little prayer never comes amiss. What is needed next is to have ourselves a little maid to be emptying the slops, but seeing as the girl seems to have given her notice I'll have to be doing it myself." She balances the basin against her hip. "When I come back you'll be having your breakfast."

I begin to speak.

The nurse shakes her head. "There's no need to

concern yourself. I prepare all my patients' food myself. It is one of my rules and the lady of the house, or the mother, or grandmother, has to abide by it. Relatives of the invalid, bless them, often think they know what they are doing but—" she clicks her tongue "—they don't have the years of experience that I have in running a sick room."

As the door shuts behind Nurse O' Halloran, I suffer my first pangs of hunger. For days I've resisted thinking about food in case I was tempted to eat what Hortense gave me and now I'm swamped by images of bacon baps –the bacon crisply fried, juices merging with the taste of brown sauce and melting butter that seeps into the soft white bread – washed down with builders' tea, strong and brown, the tannin jolting energy through my body.

"Here we are." Nurse O'Halloran returns with a bowl of thin grey porridge-like substance and to my shame my eyes fill with tears. "Open up." The nurse dips the spoon into the gruel. "Be like a little baby bird. No? Very well then." She sighs heavily and I'm afraid that she'll wrench my mouth open and force the disgusting stuff down my throat. "It doesn't look very appetising, I can see that. But my dear Mrs L, it is made to my own recipe and is full of goodness. See—" she lifts the spoon to her own lips and takes a mouthful "—I think I've got it right this time though it could do with a little more seasoning." She puts down the bowl, reaches into the pocket of her apron and takes out a small brown bottle.

"No medicine, please."

"Now why would I be giving you that?" The nurse takes a gulp from the bottle. "If you want to be strengthened, like a good Irish girl, then you want a dose of whiskey. It will set you up for the rest of the day, I promise." She wipes the lip of the bottle and dribbles a little into the bowl.

"I can feed myself." I take the spoon and the nurse beams as I start to eat. Laced with whiskey, the gruel tastes surprisingly good.

"That's the way." Nurse O'Halloran nods with satisfaction. "When you've cleared your bowl like a good little missus, then we shall have some tea."

There are two cups on the tray and the tea has been left to stand for so long that it is a thick brown sludge-like liquid with a sharp kick, which is only partly masked by the spoonfulls of sugar that Nurse O'Halloran stirs into our cups. We drink in companionable silence, the nurse sitting in the button-backed bedroom chair, legs spread wide, apron dipping between her knees.

"That's that then," she sighs when the last drop has been drained from the pot. "I'll be setting the room to rights and then we'll have a short nap." She heaves herself to her feet and reaching into her bag takes out a cloth and proceeds to dust every polished surface in the room. When she reaches the mantelpiece she moves the French gilt clock and the photographs to one side and, in pride of place, she sets a small enamel plaque. Surrounded by an elaborate frame of turquoise, green and violet cur-licues, the image of the Sacred Heart of Jesus has been printed onto a background of pale but lurid green. His robe is bright red, his heart emits beams of gold, and he is entwined by the ring of thorns that symbolize his suffering. His expression, however, is bland, his right hand raised in a limp blessing.

"A present from one of my ladies. A small object of devotion. I trust you have no objections." There's a belligerent tone to the nurse's words that I am quick to assuage.

"Not at all," I tell her. Hideous though it is, there

is some comfort in the picture because I'm reminded of me and Sadie with Mrs K in the basement kitchen, where we felt warm and safe from whatever was going on in the rest of the house.

"I've been known to give notice in houses where I've not been appreciated." There's a pause as I search my befuddled brain for a soothing reply. "I've never been short of a position. Dr Reynolds has every faith in me."

"I am sure he has." I'm overwhelmed by an enormous yawn. The whiskey has taken effect and, much as I want to stay awake, it's getting harder and harder to fight off the waves of sleep.

"Now we'll have a little nap." Nurse O' Halloran takes another bottle from her bag. A slim flask with fluted edges.

"No, please, no sedatives. I don't need them. I'm tired enough as it is. I'm sure I'll sleep."

"Humph." The nurse snorts. The genial comradeship of the past hours is sliding into truculence. She strokes the edge of the bottle with a bloated finger and there is an avid look in her eyes.

She wants it. Or rather she needs it and I don't. I have to keep my head clear.

"You've been so good to me that I feel as comfortable and easy—" my glance strays to the picture on the mantelpiece for inspiration "—as I did when I was a little girl. My nanny, who was from Ireland, used to sit by me and say the rosary. The sound of her prayers was like a lullaby. It may be too much to ask but I'd be so grateful if you'd..."

"Of course," Nurse O'Halloran's voice is brisk. "Not everyone would approve but between you and me these matters will be kept confidential." She taps her nose in a gesture straight from pantomime.

"I won't breathe a word."

The nurse's expression changes. She sits down in her chair and spreads out her skirts, smoothing down her apron, eking out the last moments before uncorking the laudanum and taking a swig. "For the pain in my side and the ache in my feet." The rhythm of words segues into, "In the name of the Father and of the Son and the Holy Ghost..."

Eventually the patter of prayer is replaced by the inhaling and exhaling of breath, punctuated by snores and grunts as the nurse's head sinks onto her chest.

I, on the other hand, fight the urge to sleep. No longer gnawed by hunger I've won my first victory. If the poison hasn't done too much damage to my system, under Nurse O'Halloran's regime I'll grow stronger, my mind clearer.

The clock ticks and the sounds of the street drift in through the window: a child calls out, a car stutters past, followed some time later by the ring of the delivery boy's bicycle bell. Along the corridor a door opens then shuts. Footsteps approach, the door handle rattles. I tense then take a deep breath. I have to look as if I'm asleep. The handle turns but the door doesn't open. There's a slight thud as if someone is pushing against it followed by a brief impatient tap. Nurse O'Halloran gulps noisily startling herself into wakefulness. The knocking comes again.

"Open the door Nurse and let me in."

"I'm sorry, sir." Nurse O'Halloran heaves herself to her feet. "I won't have my patient disturbed."

"I want to see my wife."

The nurse looks at the bed.

"I am afraid that won't be possible."

"I want to see how she is..." Louis's voice trails away.

"I'm..." I start but the nurse interrupts.

"She doesn't want to see you, sir. Not as she is. It wouldn't be right." Nurse O'Halloran winks at me. "Men," she mutters, "the problems they cause. Apart from Our Blessed Lord, that is, and the dear priests and Dr Reynolds, of course. There's no need to worry yourself, my dear Mrs L, I won't let him near you until you're are quite well again."

"But..."

"It's what the doctor ordered." Nurse O'Halloran is firm. "If you want to get better then we must do as he says. That's right, isn't it?"

"Yes," I agree, reminding myself that this woman is the only person in the house that stands between me and Hortense.

"After all that excitement I think we could be doing with another pot of tea." The nurse rings the bell and after a little time there is a tap at the door.

"Please Nurse, you rang?" the child's voice is unfamiliar.

"Wait a moment will you and I'll open the door."

A girl of about twelve stands in the corridor. Her face is broad and cheerful, her nose generously sprinkled with freckles.

"I'm Biddy, the new maid," she says looking directly at me.

I want to say something to welcome her into my household but before I can find the words the nurse sends her off to fetch the tea.

~~~

She returns with the tea tray, her bottom lip caught in her teeth as she concentrates on not spilling the milk or rattling the teacups. Beside the teapot is a posy of roses. Biddy picks them up and holds them out to me.

"The master said these are for you."
~~~

"Did he now? And what does he mean by sending poor Mrs Latimer a bunch of flowers. Hasn't he been told that she must have complete rest?"

"I don't know. I'm just doing what I was told and anyway what's the harm?"

"Take them away. At once."

Biddy raises her eyebrows, then before the nurse can react scuttles away.

Have I got an ally? Will Biddy help me if I ask her? She brought me roses from Louis, so she's prepared to be a go-between. I wish I knew what it all meant. In Edwardian times flowers were supposed to have their own meaning, so if I knew the significance of that particular shade of pink I might have some idea about where Louis is coming from.

I stare at the tray where the roses had been and realise I can see colours again. My vision is returning to normal which must mean the poison is leaving my system.

We drink our tea and then Nurse O'Halloran says I must rest. I lie down obediently, half-close my eyes and wait until she's settled in her chair. After a while her head begins to droop. Her bosom rises and falls. When her breathing deepens I get up and move cautiously towards the sleeping woman.

A sudden gasping influx of breath and I freeze, then the nurse's head falls back against the chair, her mouth opens slightly and her hands fall to her side. I tiptoe closer, lean forward, slip my hand into her apron pocket and pull out the key.

The metal is warm in my fingers. The key turns easily in the lock. I bite my lip but Nurse O'Halloran doesn't stir as I open the door.

On one side is the staircase to the nursery floor, on the other is the way to the outside world where my car will be parked at the side of the road and all

I have to do is get in and drive away. The image of the Fiat, the shine of its bodywork muted by summer dust, is so vivid that I'm convinced it's there waiting for me. All I have to do is run down the stairs, pick up the keys, and walk across the road.

Concentrate, I tell myself. *Visualise it and it will happen.*

Whether it's the force of my will or having escaped from Amelia's bedroom, but the house is changing. I can see the worn carpet, the faded green wallpaper, the electric light hanging over the stairwell.

Then Louis comes up the stairs.

"Amelia," he cries.

My hands fly to my mouth. I was so close. A few more moments and I'd have been gone.

"You've escaped the dragon. Well done, my darling." Louis bounds towards me, his hair shining like a halo.

I put my finger to my lips. "Shh," I whisper. "She'll hear us. I'm supposed to be in bed resting."

"Then, shouldn't you?" Louis looks worried.

"I'm not going back, not yet. I can't stand it. I feel like a prisoner in my own house."

"Doctor Reynolds says you need peace and quiet."

"What does he know? What does anyone know? What I want is some fresh air. Then I'll feel better."

"We'll go out, I promise. As soon as you're well again."

"You mean it?"

"Of course." His eyes don't meet mine and I'm afraid I can't trust him. That he'll do whatever Hortense wants regardless of the consequence for me ... for Amelia. Yet there was a time when he stood up for her. Maybe I can trigger that response again. I touch his arm.

"Do you remember that day when we were sent

out to play in the gardens? You were so kind to me then."

"And my sister was so beastly. Hortense—" he begins then stops.

"Yes," I prompt.

"Hortense means everything for the best," Louis says awkwardly. "She looks out for me. She's all I had after Mother died."

"Now you have me."

He says nothing, making it obvious that Hortense is the most important person in his life. Amelia scarcely counts. It's his sister who has manipulated the whole situation and is keeping the two of them apart. If I'm right and Louis is afraid of making love to his wife, allowing Amelia to be imprisoned in her room and treated as if she's ill or mad, delays the moment when he has to be her lover.

How am I going to deal with this one? I stink. I desperately need a shower. I spend most of the day locked in my room guarded by an opium addict. All I have to work with is the body of a girl who's as inexperienced as the man she has to seduce. I almost laugh. If the Amelia he knows takes the initiative Louis will be repulsed. If I do nothing I'll be stuck here forever. I have to take things very slowly and gently, be tactful and understanding, never make any demands he can't meet.

"I do love you," Louis says unexpectedly. "It's just that Hortense says we have to do what the doctor says. When you're better I will take you away. It might not be to the Italian Lakes, at least not straight off, but we could start by taking the tram to the Zoological Gardens to see the lions. Just the two of us."

"I'd love that. It'll be like when we—" I search desperately for Amelia's memories and by some mercy they flood back "—we met again and—" I lower my head "—I fell so in love with you that all I wanted..."

He takes my hand. The part of me that is Amelia yearns for him. Her emotion sweeps through me and I find myself wanting to protect him, to save him from his sister and help him grow into the person he could be. To do that I'll have to stay, and now that Sadie's gone and I've broken up with William there's nothing for me in the twenty-first century.

The bedroom door flies open.

"Mrs Latimer, what on earth is going on?" Nurse O'Halloran cries.

I move closer to Louis, hoping he'll defend me, but he drops my hand and steps aside.

"I'm sorry," he says.

"Saying sorry is all well and good but it won't repair the damage you've done. Just look at the colour in the dear missus' face. She's got herself overexcited again and Doctor Reynolds warned us over and over again as to where that might lead. Come along now—" she takes my elbow "—back to bed with you."

I cast a despairing glance at Louis but the door is already shutting and he's making no effort to intervene.

Nurse O' Halloran pulls the bedclothes so tightly around me that I can't move my legs. When she's sure I can't escape she puts her hand on my forehead.

"Hum!" She blows down her nose, then feels my pulse. Another snort and she drops my hand. With a great sigh she says, "And I thought we got on so well."

"We do," I hasten to reassure her. "I'm much better now and it's all because of you."

"That's as maybe, but I can't stay in a house where my methods are not respected. My patients have to do what they are told. Doctor Reynolds expects it of me."

"You can't go. You can't leave me. I'll do whatever you want. I promise. Only stay. I beg you, please"

You're the only thing that stands between me and Hortense.

"It's too late for that. You've a strong head on you and won't be taking my instructions, which is what I'll be telling the doctor."

"I'm not mad."

"You're of a nervous disposition and Mr Latimer isn't helping."

"But I need you. I thought you felt comfortable here." I look over her shoulder at the picture of the Sacred Heart, hoping that will sway her.

"It's too late. I've made up my mind." Nurse O'Halloran purses her lips. "It's not been an easy house. Right from the very start Miss Latimer made it plain that she doesn't approve of my regime. And as if that wasn't enough you and Mr Latimer have been behaving like a pair of children. There are other families, Mrs L, where they'll be grateful to have me. And that, I'm afraid, is my last word on the matter."

~~~

In the night, footsteps come and go along the corridor and I listen, trying to make out what's being said by the hushed voices on the other side of the door. Nurse O'Halloran sleeps soundly, her belly rising and falling, her snuffles and snores too loud for me to hear the voices clearly. I wonder about getting up, creeping past the nurse's truckle bed and pressing my ear to the door, then decide it's not worth the risk. If I'm caught Hortense will use it as more evidence against me. It'll be better to wait until
~~~

morning and see what happens then.

~~~

"The master was taken sick last night." There's a note of triumph in the nurse's voice as she brings in the breakfast tray. "But what would you expect of young men and their wild oats?" She tuts in delighted disapproval as she pours the tea.

Her view of Louis as a debauched young buck is nothing to do with the man I'm getting to know. I've smelled brandy on his breath but I've never seen him drunk. Hortense wouldn't allow it. His sickness, on the other hand, I can use to my advantage.

"If my husband it ill—" I pause "—it is my Christian duty to go and how he is."

Nurse O'Halloran's eyes turn to the picture of the Sacred Heart as if seeking divine guidance and even though I no longer believe in a compassionate God I murmur a swift prayer under my breath. "Whatever you please. I've told Miss Latimer what I think and I've given my notice. I'll be leaving today."

It might be a good idea to tell her I'll miss her and thank her for all she's done but the words stick in my throat. By not following her rules I've annoyed her and she's taking out her anger on me. "Fuck you," I mutter under my breath. The words that Amelia would never use are empowering. I watch without a qualm as Nurse O'Halloran packs her bag. She is quick and efficient. The picture of the Sacred Heart is removed, the gilt clock put in its place, and the nurse is gone.

The sun is bright with the mellow warmth of late summer that is merging into autumn. The light still carries a slight tinge of pink but the harsh scarlets and crimsons that suffused everything have gone, flushed away with the poison that was seeping through my body. I realise how much Nurse
~~~

O'Halloran has done for me and how vulnerable I'm going to be without her.

There's a tap at the door and Biddy enters. "I've come to see if you need anything, miss, I mean ma'am." She looks around the room, her gaze lingering on the mantelpiece where the picture of the Scared Heart had been. "I'm glad that thing's gone. Having a miserable face like that starin' down noon and night wasn't going to help no one. Whoops—" she puts her hand to her mouth "—I shouldn't have said that."

"It's quite all right, I agree with you," I say. *I'm glad it's gone. Along with its owner. This girl, young though she is, might be much more help.* "Now Biddy – isn't it? – I'm going to get up so you can help me dress."

"Oh yes, ma'am. If you say so ma'am. Only I've got to get Mr Latimer's bread and milk to him first. He's not been at all well in the night and Miss Latimer says it's the only thing he'll take. If it's all right with you I'll run down to the kitchen then up to the old nursery as fast as I can, but Mr Latimer's up on the next floor so it'll take me a minute. Then I'll be straight back."

"Take your time. I'll go and see him when I'm dressed."

"Ma'am, you can't. I shouldn't have said anything." Biddy chews her lip. "Miss Latimer said I mustn't tell because you mustn't be distressed in case you got worse again."

Giving her an excuse to send me away. No wonder she told a twelve-year-old skivvy to keep her mouth shut. She knew the child would blurt it out sooner or later.

"It's all right, Biddy, I won't say that you told me."

"Oh, thank you, ma'am. You see I do want to keep

my place here. I like it with Cook and you and—"
She stopped.

"Don't worry. I'm not getting rid of anyone. This
is my house and I'll be back to running things very
soon."

Or at least Amelia will.

As soon as the girl has left the room I slide out of
bed. The door is open, the corridor empty. It would
take a little effort to go upstairs to Louis' room.
Hortense has put him on the next floor to make it
more difficult for us to reach each other but I'm
feeling stronger. A flight of stairs is not going to stop
me. Before I can get going, however, the sound of the
basement door opening and shutting sends me back
into my room. If I want to reassert my authority I
can't have the servants catching me creeping
around in my nightdress, and I certainly don't want
a confrontation with my sister-in-law.

The footsteps pass by and the door remains
closed. Hortense, I'm sure of it, on her way to see
Louis. He didn't look well the last time I saw him and
it's possible that he's caught a fever – but there
could be another more sinister explanation. His
sister, sensing that we're getting closer, is dosing
him with something to keep him out of the way. Or
is she so obsessed with her little brother that if she
can't have him no one will? If I'm right, then we're
both in danger.

I pull on my stockings, slide my chemise over my
head, step into my knickers, fasten my petticoats
and am buttoning my corset when Biddy reappears,
face flushed and cap askew from running up and
down the stairs.

"I'll wear my—" *Jeans, trainers, t-shirt.* The words
swirl in my brain. I scrabble for an image but
everything is blank. I've no idea what dress Amelia

would choose – or what she's feeling. It's as if she's disappearing, taking her past with her, leaving me stranded.

"You've gone very white, ma'am. Can I do something?"

"I don't know." There is a blackness behind my eyes that ebbs and flows and I feel as if I'm falling. Am I leaving, going back to being Thea? I try to give into the sensation but a sharp acrid smell brings me back to my senses. Biddy is leaning over me, holding a small glass bottle to my nose. I inhale and my mind clears.

"That's better. Thank you." I stare at the girl in the wardrobe mirror who both is, and is not, me.

"Your dress, ma'am?" Biddy prompts.

"The blue one." The words come without thinking. Biddy fetches it from the wardrobe. She brushes my hair and pins it up on the top of my head.

"You look very pretty, ma'am." Biddy steps back from the dressing table. I look at my reflection and suppress a shudder. The picture is complete. I am Amelia and it is Thea Gordon who is fading.

I step out into the corridor where sunlight pours through the stained glass at the top of the stairs. It splashes scarlet, emerald and gold across the walls and carpet – and falls on Hortense, giving a sickly yellow hue to her face and hands as she advances towards me.

"Amelia, I didn't expect to see you up." Hortense's voice is clear and sharp.

"Pardon me, Miss Latimer." Biddy stands awkwardly in the doorway. Her hands twisting in her apron as she glances from one of us to the other. "I should be getting on."

"So you should." Hortense's smile and tone are artificially warm. "Run along now."

Biddy bobs us both a curtsy and hurries away.

"A promising child. Can I tell her to bring you anything?"

"I'm going to see Louis. I hear he is unwell." I turn my back on my sister-in-law.

"No, my dear, that would not be wise." Hortense's hand is on my arm. "Nurse O'Halloran made it perfectly clear that you were not to be upset in any way."

"Nurse O'Halloran has given notice."

"That was unfortunate. Apparently her methods were being disregarded."

We stare at each other. The nurse's defection plays into Hortense's hand. She can tell Doctor Reynolds that I've been totally unreasonable. I've refused to do what I was told and by blatantly going against his instructions have displayed another symptom of my insanity. I try to come up with a good reply, but all I can manage is, "Since she's no longer in charge, I'm not obliged to follow her advice. She herself says I'm so much better."

"The advice, as you know, came from Dr Reynolds." Hortense's fingers tighten. Her nails dig into the fabric of my dress, her knuckles are white with the pressure. To free myself I'll either have to prise each finger loose or knock her arm away. Whatever I do it'll be reported to Reynolds as hysterical violence.

"Yes of course. What was I thinking?" I smile at her.

In reply Hortense's voice is sickly sweet. "There's no need to worry about Louis. I'm taking care of him myself."

"I'm sure you're doing an excellent job, as always. Let me know when he's feeling better and I'll come and see him."

Not that I am going to wait for that. As soon as you're out of the way, I'm going to warn him. Before it's too late – for both of us.

CHAPTER TWENTY

I go to the window and look out at the street. Opposite the house is the space where I park. I stare at the line of railings hoping that, if I visualise it, my car will appear. I conjure up its sleek shape and navy paintwork but even as it develops the image runs together like watercolours that are too liquid, and all I can see are hard black lines and beyond them the trees and shrubs of the communal garden.

Breathe. Take deep breaths. Centre yourself and concentrate. I am Thea Gordon. I am thirty-two years old. I was born in 1985. I have a twin sister Sadie. We were adopted by Aunt Jane. Who is, who was...

The thoughts splinter and jag. Images shuffle and blur. A hawk nosed woman, the smell of cigarettes, a plump body and kind arms, another black-haired green-eyed girl. A boy with long golden curls, taking my hand and leading me out of a garden towards the red-haired girl who waits at the gate, her face pinched with disdain.

She doesn't like me. The thought surprises and scares me.

An only child, educated at home, I've never had much experience with children of my own age. I try to think what I might have done to upset her, but there is nothing. Then we are running across the road, up the steps of number fifteen, and Hortense is smiling and chatting as if we're the best of friends.

"She's always been jealous of you because you had everything she wanted," I tell the part of me that is Amelia. "And now she hates you because you have Louis, who's the only person she's ever loved."

I press my forehead against the windowpane.

Below me people come and go. If I call out will they hear me? If I scream will someone send for the police, or will the passers-by continue about their business, eyes averted, ears deaf to such a vulgar display? Perhaps they already know that the newly married Mrs Latimer is unwell, the balance of her mind disturbed. Servants' gossip travels fast in the crescent. Eliza had always been a good source of information about what was going on. I remember as a child coming down the stairs to the kitchen and hearing snippets of conversation, brief giggles and gasps that were quickly suppressed when I entered.

There will be no help from outside. Whatever I do will be up to me.

"I've brought your lunch, ma'am." Biddy coming in with a tray interrupts my thoughts. "Bouillon—" the girl's tongue trips over the unfamiliar word "— and fish pie. There's apple crumble and custard for pudding. Miss Latimer says it's your favourite."

My mouth goes dry. "I'm not hungry."

"Oh ma'am. It looks so tasty. Couldn't you bring yourself to take just a teeny bit?"

"No!" I throw up my hands. "Take it away."

"Miss Latimer says you must eat something."

The girl's face twists as if her job depends on my appetite, yet I know that I can't let a morsel of food that Hortense has been near to pass my lips. "Tell Miss Latimer that I was resting." I look straight into Biddy's eyes, willing the child to understand.

"Resting," Biddy replies brightly. "Yes ma'am, I will. Shall I take the tray downstairs?"

"No, leave it. Who knows, I might take a fancy to the fish pie." I pull a face and Biddy grins and nods.

The bouillon is easy. I tip it into the washbasin and turn on the taps. The fish pie is more of a problem. I cover the plate with the napkin and carry it to the toilet, where I scrape half the contents into the pan and flush them away. The rest I move around with my fork, so that it will look as if I've eaten a little.

My hands shake as I put the plate back on the tray. Now that I have started eating again my appetite is back and I'm hungry. Surely one mouthful followed by a little of the apple crumble wouldn't do too much harm? I reach for the fork then put it back. My body has only just cleared itself of the poison. I can't risk ingesting any more. But I have to eat.

"Oh ma'am, you managed a little," Biddy says when she comes back for the dishes. "Miss Latimer will be ever so pleased. She'll be sure to ask how you've done when she comes back. She's been so concerned." The girl's voice falters at the expression on my face. "Don't you want me to tell her? Being as you haven't eaten it all."

"Miss Latimer has gone out?" I have to make sure.

"Yes ma'am."

"Then I'll have bread and cheese and I'll come down to the kitchen to fetch it."

"Oh ma'am, you can't. I mean…"

"Of course I can. It's my house and if I want to see how things are going in the kitchen then I will."

Biddy chews her lip but she knows her place and follows me obediently down the stairs.

Hand on the basement door. Eyes shut. Breathe in the rich smell of Mrs K's soup. Winter soup, thick with vegetables and pearl barley— That's the wrong memory, the wrong time. To get back to my life I need the scent of white wine and Thai takeaway.

I inhale but it's too late. Biddy coughs discretely and I can't stand there any longer. The stairway is dark and there's a murmur of voices coming from the kitchen. Cook sits at the table chatting to the char woman who comes to scrub and clean. They're drinking tea and there's a loaf of bread and a slab of cheese in front of them.

"Well bless me, Miss Amelia – Mrs Latimer I mean." Cook rises to her feet. "We were just saying, Joyce and me, that it's a poorly start you've had, you and Mr Louis."

"I'm much better now. It must be your delicious fish pie."

"Humph," Cook snorts. "Plain food for invalids that's what I was always taught but no, she must go fiddling about with it, adding a bit of this and a pinch of that. I don't wish to speak ill of any relation of yours, Miss Amelia, but I don't brook no interfering in my kitchen. First that Nurse O'Halloran was throwing her weight around, making comments where they're not wanted, and Miss Latimer also takes it upon herself to tell me what to do. I won't have it, I really won't."

"Quite right too." This proves what I've suspected and feared.

"If it goes on I'll be giving in my notice," Cook continues.

"No, please don't do that." My mouth is dry. "I don't know what we'd do without you." Cook may not realise what's going on but she doesn't like Hortense any more than I do and she's known me since I was a little girl. Put to the test, her loyalty will be with me. "You've been with me such a long time you're part of the family. Oh!" I put my hand up to my head as if I was feeling faint.

"Are you all right, miss?"

"I just have to sit down and perhaps a cup of tea and a ... a slice of that bread and cheese?"

"You've a fancy for it?" Cook winks at Joyce who

nods and gives her a knowing look in return.

"New girl, whatever your name is, pull out a chair for Miss Amelia and fetch her a clean cup."

Biddy hastens to do as she's told and I'm poured stewed tea. I cut a hunk of rough brown bread and a piece of salty Cheddar cheese. Cook rests her hands in her lap, watches me eat and nods with satisfaction. "It takes some ladies that way," she says. Biddy grins.

"Better than puking up your innards, which is what I did with mine. All five of them and it never got no better. Don't know how I got through it. I really don't," Joyce adds.

The caffeine in the tea has heightened my senses. Sunlight dazzles on the brass taps; the draining boards on either side of the sink are bleached of colour. A faint haze of coal dust hangs above the scuttle next to the range. A drawer in the dresser is out of line. Inside, a bunch of keys lies on a pile of neatly folded cloths. Cook shifts her buttocks. Biddy sticks her finger out as she holds her cup to her lips and slurps delicately.

We sit together contentedly but the moment doesn't last. Already there's a stirring of unease, a feeling that this is not the right place for the lady of the house. Biddy shifts awkwardly on her chair. Cook sighs and prepares to heave herself to her feet. I have be the one to make the move, I have to appear to be in control.

"That was lovely." My voice sounds artificially bright. "Just what I wanted. Biddy, you can bring me some more bread and cheese for supper." Maid and cook exchange glances. "I've such a fancy for it."

"If that's what you want, Miss Amelia, that's what you'll have."

"My ma says you've got to give in to the cravings.

It's best for the—" Biddy begins.

"Don't you worry. Miss Latimer can say what she likes but I know what's right." Cutting across her, Cook turns to me. "I'll send Biddy up with the bread and cheese before supper. Then if you're not hungry for what she says you've got to have you can send it right back and we'll have it straight in the bin."

Relieved and grateful I return to my room where the rest of the day stretches interminably in front of me. I've nothing to do but wait until the servants have gone to bed. When the house is asleep I can creep down to the kitchen and let myself out with Cook's keys – if she's been careless enough to leave them in the drawer. To help the time pass I look for something to read. The only book I can see is on the mantelpiece where the picture of the Sacred Heart had stood. I pick it up and almost laugh at the irony of the title. Amelia is reading *The Time Machine* by H G Wells. The ornately tasselled marker is on the chapter where the Traveller meets the Eloi girl in some far-distant future.

Is there some cosmic synchronicity in her choice? Has Amelia travelled forward as I've travelled backwards? Is it her way of escaping Hortense and her sham of a marriage? If so, how? Is there some mechanism that I can make use of to bring me back to the twenty-first century? Or is this another false hope?

~~~

Candlelight throws a wild shadow which follows me along the corridor. With my shoulders hunched, it hangs over me then shrinks as my hand curls around the sputtering flame. It's past midnight and I'm the only one in the house still awake.

Except for the ghosts. Of which I am one. I shake the thought from my head and go down the
~~~

basement stairs.

In the kitchen, the open drawer I'd noticed that afternoon has been pushed into place. If Cook has done what she should and taken the keys to her room then I've lost my chance. If she's hasn't...

Please, I pray, *let them be there.* I pull open the drawer. The keys lie on a pile of newly washed and starched cloths. All I have to do is find the one that opens the back door.

"Amelia!"

Dear God, does the woman never sleep? My hand shakes, candlelight wavers, and shadows caper and prance over walls and ceiling. Hortense glides towards me. Her candle is steady in her hand; her face, the hair pulled back into a tight plait, is an impenetrable mask.

"What are you doing?"

Take the key and run. The door is only a few steps away and although we are evenly matched in height and weight Hortense is not as desperate as I am. I spin around. Push forward. But with a sharp upward swipe the candle is knocked from my grasp. The keys clatter to the floor.

~~~

"I found her in the kitchen, doctor. She had the key to the basement door and was muttering something about a wedding. When I tried to reason with her she became violent and struck me." Hortense's hand goes to her cheek. Broken blood vessels stain purple beneath the white skin.

Dr Reynolds leans over the bed. His fingers are cold on my wrist as he feels my pulse.

"I am afraid that she's becoming demented. She says such terrible things." Hortense's voice trembles.

The doctor straightens up. I try to speak. I have
~~~

to tell him what really happened, that Hortense is lying, but my tongue has grown too big for my mouth and won't form the words. As he turns away I will him to look at me but his eyes are on Hortense. "She has become over excited again," he says stiffly.

"It's my fault." Hortense lowers her head. "I didn't keep a close enough eye on her. When Louis went down with this sickness I was so worried about losing him that I'm afraid I let Amelia do as she wanted. She insisted she was well enough to go back to her duties, but obviously she was wrong."

"Your brother is making a good recovery which is more than I can say for his wife. You should have spared her the worry of her husband's illness, as I advised you to do. The harm, however, has been done and she can no longer be nursed at home. I will put the arrangements into place. In the meantime I have given her an opiate and she will sleep."

No. I must not shut my eyes. I must not let them do this to me but whatever the doctor has given me is sliding through my veins. My eyelids are heavy, my breathing slows.

"There is no other way. She will have the best treatment." The doctor pats my hand as if I was a child. "I will send my assistants for her within a day, perhaps two."

~~~

"A day, at the most two." The words bang and thump in my head. This is all the time I have left before they come to take me away. If they lock me up in Bradwell Grange will I ever return either to this house – or to my own time?

Night is on the cusp of dawn when I struggle out of my drugged sleep. A pale light seeps in under the blind turning the room into a sea of shadows, the furniture's grey shapes lurching out of the mist. Not
~~~

even the servants are up at this hour and the house is silent as I creep up the stairs to the room where my husband sleeps. I push the door open a crack and peer inside. If Hortense has decided to sit up with her brother then my last hope will have gone but to my relief the chair beside the bed is empty.

Louis lies curled up like a child, knees to chin. I bend over him and whisper. "Wake up. You've got to wake up."

He stirs and stretches out his limbs. His eyelids flutter.

"Louis."

"Mm." He is slipping back into sleep and it occurs to me that he might have been given a sedative. I take him by the shoulder and shake him. He flings out an arm to throw me off. "Go away, Hortense. Let me sleep."

"It's me, Louis. Amelia. Your wife. You have to help me. They're going to lock me up and you're the only person that can stop them. You're my husband. They have to do what you say."

He sits up, staring at me, his eyes unfocussed. And I realise how stupid I've been. It would have been better to have crept in under the covers and woken him gently before warning him of the danger we are in.

"Amelia?" Louis is returning to consciousness. Footsteps are hurrying along the corridor. Hortense sweeps into the room.

"Oh my dear." Her eyes are on her brother.

"What's happening?" he asks plaintively.

I take my husband's hand. "Listen to me. I am not mad. I'm not ill. Neither are you. It's Hortense..."

"Stop this. Stop this at once." The slap across my cheek throws me off balance. No one has ever hit me before and the shock renders me speechless.

"I'm taking her back to her room." Hortense advances towards me.

"I'm not going. I'm staying here. Don't come near me." My voice rises and Louis pulls the covers up to his chin. "I'm perfectly sane. It's what she put in the food that's caused it. She's poisoned you too Louis. She's evil, she's—"

"Miss Amelia?" Cook appears in the doorway.

"Louis look at me." I focus my attention on him but he shrinks away, terrified by what he sees as madness.

"I'm afraid Mrs Latimer has suffered a complete nervous collapse. We must get her back to her room. Don't worry Louis, everything is going to be all right. Amelia is going away for a rest."

"What's happening?" Biddy joins Cook.

"Come on, Miss Amelia, let me help you." Cook's hand is on my arm. Hortense takes the other while Biddy stands at the door, her face white as she watches them lead me away.

There's nothing I can do. There are too many of them and any further outbursts will only make things worse. I drag my feet along the carpet but it's a token gesture. Before the door closes behind me I hear Biddy stifle a sob.

"I'm so sorry, miss. And we thought we might be expecting a happy event." Cook wipes her eyes on the sleeve of her nightdress as she helps Hortense manoeuvre me into a chair.

"Mrs Latimer will be going away today. The doctor says she needs the rest," my sister-in-law says briskly.

"You know I'm not mad." I look the old servant in the eyes. "You've known me since I was a baby so why won't you believe me?" I want to get her alone to make her admit that she's seen Hortense tampering with my food but Cook is a good servant. She's used to deferring to authority and Hortense has been running the household for weeks. If she takes my side against her she runs the risk of losing her job. Eliza has already been dismissed and at Cook's age and without a reference it will be hard to find another position. Besides, what I have to say sounds like a story out of a cheap magazine and it is easier for her to believe that I've lost my mind.

"It is time Amelia is dressed. The carriage will be coming for her shortly." Hortense takes charge.

They're going to be rid of me by morning. I'll be moved out of the house under the cover of darkness, so none of the neighbours will know, and scandal can be avoided.

"Shall I..." Cook wavers, uncertain whether she should offer to help me or to leave.

"I can manage," I say quickly. "It will be easier though if you allow Biddy to do my hair." The two women exchange glances. "I won't hurt or frighten her and you'll be outside to make sure no harm is done."

"I suppose it's all right." Cook takes the initiative. "I'll get her, miss."

Biddy's nightdress is too short, her ankles and wrists look thin and brittle, but there's an edge about her and she waits until we are alone before she says, "Is there anything I can do for you, ma'am?"

I nod and put my finger to my lips in case Hortense is listening, then look around for something to write on but there are no pens or paper.

"Ma'am?" Biddy glances at the door.

"Tell Louis I need his help," I mouth. There are voices in the corridor. Cook is tearful. Hortense is sharp and business-like.

"Your clothes?" Biddy prompts and with her help I scramble into my underwear and pull on my dress. In the street outside, a carriage draws up in front of the house. My hands curl into fists and my heart thumps beneath my corset. The doorbell rings.

"I must go," Biddy says. I want to cling to this child, to anchor myself to the room, but Biddy has no power. She might be the only person who believes me but she can't delay the inevitable. "I'll be back." She jerks her head in the direction of Louis's room.

She's understood. She'll go to him. There's still a chance, albeit very faint one, that Louis will realise that I've been telling the truth, that we're both victim of Hortense's scheming. Even if he does, will he have the courage to come to me and assert his right as my husband to stop them taking me away?

I wait. The minute hand on the clock doesn't move. I hold my breath. Time stretches.

Voices rise from the ground floor.

"The lady is in the front bedroom."

"Is she calm?"

There is a muttered conference then one of the men says, "It won't bother us one way or the other, Miss Latimer. We've brought the restraints though we'd prefer not to use them during the transfer. It can be very upsetting for all concerned, as I'm sure you understand."

"You must do whatever is necessary. My sister-in-law is in a highly volatile state. The sooner she's removed to a place of refuge the better."

There's a moment of fear so intense that I'm almost blinded by terror, then the door opens and two men in white jackets enter. The younger one is carrying a stiff bundle under his arm.

"Madam," the older of the two addresses me. "If you're ready."

I hold my head high and keep my shoulders straight. I have to appear totally compliant. If they so much as suspect anything they'll truss me up in a straitjacket and I'll be robbed of that brief moment of opportunity, those few seconds before I'm bundled into the carriage. That's when I'm going to run for my life. If I'm right and leaving the house is my way home then before my captors can react I will have disappeared.

There's still a faint possibility that Louis will change his mind and come to my rescue so I walk as slowly as I can down the stairs. One attendant in front, the other behind me, my hand on the banister rail, my ears straining for the sound of Louis's voice.

When the first man gets to the bottom he turns and holds out his hand. I ignore the gesture and take time to look around me as if saying goodbye to my home. There's no sign of movement on the upper floor.

Hortense comes to open the door.

"We'll be quick," the older man says. "Our business is to be discrete." Hortense nods and stands aside to let us pass.

A faint line of pink edges the rooftops. The last trace of a fingernail moon lingers in the sky. The air is damp, the road slicked by a mist of fine rain. A carriage, its windows blacked out, is waiting for me. One of the horses raises its head, snorts into the early morning air and droplets sparkle in the light of the gas lamp.

It's going to be harder than I thought. Hortense stands on the top step supervising as Doctor Reynold's men usher me towards the carriage. One of them opens the door and bends to pull down the steps. Before he can turn to help me inside I'm away, slipping round the side of the vehicle and running, running as fast as I can along the crescent.

"Wait!" It's Louis. "Wait Amelia, wait."

Will he save me or will he bring me back, push me into the carriage and watch with Hortense as they drive me away? I don't stop. I'm at the end of the crescent where the road slopes down into Hensman's Hill. Louis is gaining on me, the two attendants behind him.

A thunder of hooves, a rumble of wheels. A delivery wagon hurtling towards me. A whip cracks, a man shouts at me to get out of the way.

"Amelia!" Louis reaches out. I flatten myself against the wall and his foot slips on the wet pavement. There's a thud. The lead horse rears, the wagon sways violently. Louis lies sprawled at my feet. His eyes are open, blood trickles from his nose and mouth. He's not breathing.

Hortense screams, throws herself on her knees and cradles her brother in her arms.

Don't move him. Call an ambulance. That's what I want to say but I can't.

Hortense raises her head. Her face is white, her eyes glitter and there's so much venom in that look that I shrink back. The rain on my face and hair falls like tears down my cheeks. People come running. I'm aware of voices, the sound of boots on paving stones, a hand on my arm guiding me gently back into the crescent.

CHAPTER TWENTY-ONE

"Thea are you okay?" I had to blink a couple of times before his face came into focus.

"Ben Appleton?"

"Let me get you inside."

"Into the house? No, I'm not going back in there."

"I don't think you can go anywhere else dressed like that."

The pavement was cold beneath my bare feet and I was wearing nothing but an oversized t-shirt.

"I don't know…"

"You don't know what happened?"

"No," I lied. "I look as if I've just got out of bed."

"Do you walk in your sleep?" His arm around me, he was leading me up the steps to the front door.

I could tell him that I did, explain why I was out in the middle of the road wearing very little. Would it prevent his questions? I decided to risk the truth.

"I'm not sure you're going to believe this," I began.

"Trust me, I'm a doctor." His tone was light and jokey but there was concern in his eyes. "Look, you really can tell me things. You don't have to if you don't want to but if it'll help, I'll listen."

He was opening the door and we were about to go in. I held back, afraid that once I crossed the threshold it would start again, that Hortense was waiting for me in the shadows that lurked in the hallway.

"It would help to talk. Even if you think I'm—" I stopped, reluctant to use the word that had condemned Amelia to the asylum.

"I won't judge. I promise. But if you're staying out here you should put some clothes on."

"You're right. The trouble is I don't want to be on my own just now. Will you come upstairs with me?"

"Sure. I'll wait outside the door while you dress. You can leave it ajar if you want."

"I can't do that." A door could be the barrier that would allow me to slip back into being Amelia. "I need you stay with me. I'll explain but please…"

"Okay and I won't look."

"Thanks."

That's quick work. Sadie's voice was in my ear. *I like him. He's so much better than the other one.*

I knew you never liked William.

He controlled you. Or tried to. Welcome back, sis.

Ben gave me a puzzled look and I smiled at him but didn't try to explain. We went up to the second floor and as we neared the old nursery my footsteps faltered.

"Do you want me to go in first?" Ben sensed my unease. I nodded then changed my mind.

"No. This is something I have to do for myself," I said and flung open the door.

The duvet had been pushed back. My bag was on the floor, my makeup on the chest of drawers. The room smelled of sleep, my deodorant, and a trace of William's cologne. Ben walked over to the window and raised the blind. The half-drawn curtains held back the morning sun. He looked down into the street as I pulled on knickers and jeans, a pair of sandals, then fastened my bra underneath my t-shirt before discarding it and putting on a clean one.

"Thanks. I feel more human." I tied my hair clear of my neck. "More myself."

"Do you have any coffee?" Ben said.

"Is that what I need?"

"I don't know about you—" he grinned "—but I could do with one. Are you ready to go downstairs?"

"Yes."

"I'll stay till you're okay. Unless there's someone you can call."

"No... Sadie's dead and there isn't anyone else." I walked to the door, stopped and looked down the corridor. The worn carpet, the grubby wallpaper, the line of dirt along the skirting board: the house was its familiar shabby self. There were no gas mantles, no taint of coal dust. I smelled sunlight on Ben's clothes and beneath it the slightly sweet scent of fabric softener – and was seized by an urge to bury my face in his shirt and breathe in the twenty-first century.

"Everything okay?"

"Just checking." I tried to keep my voice light.

"We can wait a bit longer."

"I'm fine."

It was like wading into warm water but instead of my body adjusting to the temperature, with each step the heat increased. As I passed Aunt Jane's room I was sweating, my hands slippery, my t-shirt clinging to my chest, and by the time we stood at the top of the stairs I felt as if my limbs were melting.

Not a good look. Sadie was laughing. She was sitting on the banister rail, head back, breasts thrust out, swinging her legs in a parody of fifties womanhood.

"If you're not careful, you'll fall." Ben gripped my elbow and pulled me back.

"It's okay. I wasn't going to jump or anything."

"I know you weren't." He was talking to me but his eyes were on the space where Sadie had been. "Can we get out of here?"

"You saw her, didn't you?" I waited until we were on the ground floor before I asked.

"I saw something," he said carefully.

"You saw my twin. You saw Sadie."

"She looked like you."

"Except her hair is – I mean was – different. She won't hurt you. She's positively harmless."

Humph! Sadie snorted indignantly. Ben and I exchanged glances.

"You can hear her too, can't you?"

"Yeah. I can. It's... Hey, this has never happened to me before. It's Ed who's the psychic one, not me."

"That's what I thought about me and Sadie. She was the one that had the link with the past. Then when she died I kind of inherited it. No wait. There was the time before that, when I first saw Hortense..." I shuddered. "Can we not talk about that here? Let's go out for that coffee."

"You're sure?"

"Oh, I am." Nothing was going to stop me walking out of the house and leaving behind whatever was holding me there. "I'm going out." The words were not for Ben but he nodded and I reached into the brass pot and took out the key. It was lighter than I'd expected and made of yellowish metal with the word *Yale* inscribed on the rounded head.

"We changed the locks. Why did we do that?" I mused.

"To keep intruders out?"

"Or to keep things in."

"This is getting too weird for me. Do you want me to open the door?" Ben held out his hand.

I shook my head. Since I'd come back to number fifteen, the house had held me in its grip. If I wanted to return to a life of my own I had to break free but leaving wasn't going to be easy. My skin prickled as I lifted my arm to put the key in the lock. Voices babbled in my ears.

Stay, don't go. You're safe here. Here with Sadie.

"Pants!" The expletive, childish though it was, sent the demons flying, the sunlight flooding in.

After the dimness of the interior the outside was too intense. The morning dazzled and danced. Framed by the door, Belvedere Crescent curved into a symmetrical terrace of houses, windows dark against golden stone, doors bright with new paint. Cars were neatly parked along the kerb, my Fiat on the opposite side of the road. Not having been driven for a while its windscreen was smudged by a sticky layer of pollen that had fallen from the overhanging trees. Their shadows stretched across the flat greyness of the road, petering out into tendrils as they neared the edge of the pavement. A car accelerated up the hill, its engine impossibly loud to my heightened senses. The cat leapt down from the wall leading up to the front door and twisted around my legs, its purr trembling with electricity.

"I could do with sunglasses and earplugs." I screwed up my eyes and put my hands over my ears.

"Is it too much? Do you want to go back inside?"

The cat butted against my calves then slinking between us it sat down in front of the door blocking our return.

"What I want is coffee." My hand closed around the octagonal handle, feeling the heaviness and warmth of the metal as I pulled the door shut. A curl of black paint floated to the ground, its underside sickly white against the slate of the step. The cat lifted one leg and began to clean itself.

Walking felt odd, my legs curiously free, sandaled feet obscenely bare. The sun was hot and I reached up to adjust my hat to shield my complexion, then hastily dropped my hand as I realised what I was doing, and lengthened my stride to keep pace with Ben and banish the last vestiges of Amelia.

In the café the coffee machine hissed, cutlery and crockery clattered, voices rose and fell. The leather chair was deep and comfortable and I leaned my head back and breathed in my surroundings.

"Cappuccino, double espresso. Croissants with jam and butter." The waitress put down our tray.

"I thought you should eat. There were times on the way here when you looked as if you were going to pass out on me," Ben said.

"That's because everything was so strange. It was as if I'd never seen it before and at the same time I knew every detail – the dust on the leaves, the old bits of moss where the pavement never gets any sun." I took a sip of coffee, drinking in the sweetness of the chocolate topping, the frothiness of the milk, the bitterness of the liquid beneath.

"Where I was before..." A ray of sunlight slanted across the table and my attention was caught by black flecks of grain in the wood, thin paper napkins folded into small squares, and the edge of brown along the rim of my cup.

"Thea."

"Sorry." I focussed on the man in front of me. "If you hadn't seen Sadie I wouldn't be telling you this. It sounds crazy but it seems I can go back in time, and what's even more weird and disturbing, when I'm there I become someone else. A girl called Amelia who lived in our house some time before the First World War. That's it."

"Okay."

"It was as if I was possessed. Except it wasn't. I was her, I had her memories, her view of life, but at the same time I was me and I still had a twentieth-first century perspective on things. Right at the beginning, Louis was afraid that I, or rather Amelia, would die of TB like her mother, which scared me because I knew it was too early for the antibiotics that could have saved her life and mine too. That's when I was thinking like Thea. At the same time I could remember being Amelia as a child and going for walks with her father and seeing the sailing ships in the harbour.

"I don't understand how this can happen. Not this dual personality thing anyway. It was different for Sadie. She used to see things and I think, from something Amelia said, she might even have travelled back in time, but Sadie wouldn't talk about it. It was the one thing we never shared. Aunt Jane had sworn her to silence and for about the only time in her life Sadie did as she was told."

"Do you think your aunt did something to trigger this?"

"Not deliberately. She was genuinely surprised when I told her about Sadie."

"You told her?"

"It was supposed to get Sadie out of trouble. Instead it led to all this."

"You can't be sure."

"I'm not sure about anything. First it was Sadie then it was me, but before I went back to her time I actually saw Hortense. She was in the house when Aunt Jane died and then I saw her again at the funeral. She was in the cemetery and ghosts don't travel, or do they?"

"Don't ask me. I'm no expert, but—"

"What?"

"There are a number of things that could have happened."

"I imagined it all? Great! That's what William thinks. That it's all part of another breakdown."

"Time doesn't exist, at least not as we understand it." Ben ignored my interruption. "I'm sure you know about that, it's the stuff of science fiction and fantasy but based on genuine research into quantum physics. There's also a theory that memory can be passed through the DNA, that we inherit memories as well as physical characteristics. You've lived in that house all your life. The house belonged to your aunt and has been passed down through your family. That would make sense, especially if what you were remembering or living through was a traumatic event."

The thud of a body on the cobbles, the crush of heavy wheels over flesh and bone. Hortense screaming and screaming.

"That would work on one level but the problem is, that as babies Sadie and I were dropped off in a basket on the doorstep. Well, not exactly. The basket was put on the kitchen table."

"And you were taken in? Then there must have been some family connection. Your aunt wouldn't have been allowed to adopt you otherwise."

"That's what I thought and I was working on it when all this started."

"So it is significant."

"It must be. It's all so complicated. I don't know where to begin. What you said makes sense – but then there's Hortense." I lifted my head and leaned towards him and as I did so the room receded. Faces blurred, sounds faded and I was being pulled backwards.

CHAPTER TWENTY-TWO

"Thea, stay with me. Thea." Someone was calling my name. A hand reached out and seized mine. The sensation of falling backwards subsided. My head spun, my ears throbbed, but my vision cleared and his face came into focus. Brown eyes, fair hair; not William or Louis. Confused I shrank back but his grip was firm and I couldn't pull free.

"Thea," he said again.

"Ben?"

He nodded. "You're back. For a moment there I thought..."

"You were going to lose me?" *Or I was losing myself. Not again. Please don't let it be that.*

"Not exactly, you still had a pulse. I did think you might be having a seizure. It's the one thing we didn't consider. You could do with being checked over, to eliminate the possibility that there's something physically wrong."

"I'm not ill."

"I didn't say you were."

"I see my dead sister and so did you. If I'm hallucinating then you are too."

"I told you. I don't have a handle on this but as with any other diagnosis we have to look at all the options, starting with the most mundane."

"That there's something wrong with my brain?" Even as I spoke a great weariness spread over me. Ben, like William, didn't believe me. "They tested me after Sadie died. I'm okay." I got up. "Thanks for breakfast."

"You haven't eaten anything."

"I'm not hungry."

"Thea." He was on his feet now. "Please. Sit down."

"William wanted me to see a psychiatrist. You want me to have a brain scan. Why can't either of you listen to what I'm actually saying?"

Ben held up his hands. "I'm listening and so—" he warned "—is everyone else."

I glanced around the café and people's eyes shifted to their laptops, tablets or phones. The man at the next table hid behind his newspaper. No one was looking but even the baristas had stopped their chatter. I could flounce out and provide them with more drama but where would I go? Back to Belvedere Crescent? Would Sadie be there, teasing, provoking, laughing? Or would it be Hortense who was waiting for me?

I sat down and the café readjusted itself as customers settled back into their own concerns. To give myself time to think I drank some coffee. My croissant was still slightly warm and I watched the butter soak into the pastry, heaped on a spoonful of raspberry jam and took a bite. Flakes of pastry speckled my t-shirt and I brushed them away with a growing sense that things were returning to normal. My mind was not scrambled and as an intelligent woman and a lawyer I was used to solving problems.

"I'm going to look at this logically."

Ben nodded. "Discounting physical causes, what about the grieving process?"

"That would be a consideration – if I was the only person who'd seen Sadie."

"Okay, since I've seen her too we can cross that one off the list. Which leaves us with some sort of supernatural explanation." He gave a wry grin.

"That's the way we have to go." I waited for Ben to

object but he was nodding in agreement.

"It's been going on since we were children and escalated when Aunt Jane died. Then after Sadie was gone I started thinking, wondering..."

"Did you get anywhere?"

"No. It was as if I was being smothered. I don't mean literally but time became so fluid that I didn't know when or where or even who I was. The last time was the worst. I thought I was never going to be me again. I'd got so entwined with Amelia that there were times I didn't know which of us was which."

"That could be the crux of it." Ben was following my train of thought.

"Who I am?"

"More specifically, where the person you are comes from. We've got to look at your family history."

"That's going back to your genetic theory?"

"Sort of. As a doctor I know that family history can be a crucial clue to a patient's illness." He held up a hand to cut off my reaction. "I'm not saying you're ill, just that events in the past might explain what's happening to you now."

"That's what I was trying to research. Then everything went crazy." I helped myself to the second croissant. "Trouble is, I don't want to go back to the house. Ever."

"Sell it to me then," Ben said lightly.

"No." My hands clenched, my muscles tensed. "I can't."

"So?"

"Don't. Don't do that counselling bit with me. I had enough of that with Dr Radik."

"I won't if you don't want me to but you have to decide where you're going right now and I—" he glanced at his watch "—have to be at work soon so time is limited. By the way, what made you change your mind?"

"About?"

"About not selling the house. One minute it's on the market, the next you tell me it's not. Then this morning, first thing, I get a text saying the sale is on again and I've got first refusal if I want it."

"You got a text? From me?"

"Sure." Ben scrolled down his messages. "That's why I came. I was free this morning so I came over."

"I didn't send you a text."

"You must have done. It's here somewhere." He frowned at the screen.

"I didn't. I couldn't have. I wasn't even thinking about the house. William came round last night. He brought a takeaway and we had supper and then—" the colour flared in my cheeks but I held Ben's gaze "—we went to bed. In the morning we had a row and he left. After that I was Amelia. I was another woman in another time. I couldn't get back here, not until I escaped from the house and..." I didn't want to talk about Louis's death. "That's when you found me. I didn't have my phone on me."

"That's odd. I can't find the message. It must have got deleted by accident."

We looked at each other.

"There's another possibility," I said. "If it wasn't me then it was Sadie. I don't know how it worked but you were there when I needed you."

"If that's right then we need someone who's an expert on the paranormal."

"You mean Min? Minerva Beckford?"

"Well, we both know her."

"I've only met her a couple of times."

"I know you're worried and it's only sensible to be

cautious. Ed and I can vouch for her as friends. She's not some flaky clairvoyant. She's worked at various universities and has got quite an academic reputation."

"Which was why she was so keen to get a look at Aunt Jane's papers."

"So you want to pass on that idea."

"No. Someone or something in the house was warning me against her. They didn't want her there. Maybe they knew she was a threat."

"That she could exorcise them?"

"Can she?"

"I don't know."

"If I was sure Hortense was never coming back, that I was rid of her for ever, then—" I shook my head.

"Then you'd never sell."

"I don't know about that but I'd feel better about everything."

"Okay. Do you want me to get in touch with Min?"

My fingers grasped the chain around my neck. "I think Mrs K would prefer a priest but let's go for it."

"Right. I'll text her. Then I've got to go. Sorry. Or do you want me to walk you back?"

"Thanks but I can manage the street. As for the rest of it, whatever's going in in that house, I've had enough of it. I'm going to sort it once and for all."

The cat was waiting for me on the doorstep. It moved to one side to allow me to go in then followed, twisting around my legs and purring loudly as I went to fetch my car keys and then escorting me back to the door. Tail in the air, it watched me run down the steps but when I looked back it had gone.

~~~

"Miss Gordon." The receptionist glanced up from her computer screen. "I didn't think you were visiting
~~~

today.”

“I came on impulse.” I switched on a smile. “It’s such a lovely day and I was in the area.”

“I’m sure Mrs Kowalska will be delighted.”

Would she? The last time I was here our old housekeeper had skilfully managed to avoid answering my questions. Was she protecting me or herself? Whichever it was, this time I was not going to let her get away with it.

Mrs K sat on the sofa by the window, eyes closed, head bowed, murmuring the words of the prayer as she slid the rosary beads between her fingers. The rhythmic cadences flowed through me, filling me with a sense of peace.

“*Wimie ojca, syna i ducha sweitego.*” Mrs K completed the final mystery and made the sign of the cross. I walked over and gave her a kiss. She smiled and put her hand on my arm. “Thea, it is so good of you to come and see me.”

“It’s good to be here.” Determined for answers I pulled over a chair. A fleeting frown crossed the old woman’s face. “There’s something I’ve got to ask you,” I said.

Mrs K leaned back and laced her hands over the top of her stomach.

“Please—” I looked straight at her “—don’t put me off this time. I have to find out who our birth mother was. It’s really important that I do. All I know is that she left us with Great-Aunt Jane, but I don’t know why or how we came to be adopted. The adoption agency would help but the process takes time and it’s urgent. So I came to you.”

“Ah.”

“Believe me. Everything hinges on this. My sanity for a start.”

“Humph.” Mrs K blew down her nose. “I always

feared no good would come of it. Bringing two innocent babies into that house." She lifted her hand and made the sign of the cross to ward off some ancient evil. "Your Aunt Jane, she was a strange woman. She didn't like children. Babies she detested."

"Then why if she hated kids did she take us in? Wasn't there anywhere else we could go?"

"Families." Mrs K sighed. "So complicated. Always."

"So we are related. Sadie and I thought we must be. That was why we called her Great-Aunt Jane and not Mum or Gran. What was her connection to our birth mother? Why didn't she tell us? By the eighties everyone was open about adoption. There was no shame to it."

"Thea, gift of God, Sadie, princess, look at the names your aunt gave you. In spite of her ways she did love you. She wanted you to do well. She had plans for you."

"I'm not sure she meant us much good."

"No harm came to you."

"That's where you came in. That's why you didn't leave us."

"Not until you were old enough to be safe."

I reached over and squeezed the old woman's hand. I would always be grateful for what Mrs K had done, how she had been there for us throughout our childhood.

"Oh Thea, there can be no harm in telling you now. Your mother Marigold was Jane's niece. Not long after you were born she came to the house with both of you. That is when it happened." Mrs K crossed herself again. "Poor Marigold collapsed and died, and Mr Trevelyan, he said adopting you was the right thing to do. In those early days, when I first came, they would talk about it, not thinking that an old Polish woman understood every word they said."

"Why didn't you tell us about our mum?"

"What would have be the good of that? As I told you, she died. I said prayers for her soul and your aunt said I was never to mention her. It was her place to tell you not mine." Mrs K's chin trembled, her face puckered as if she was going to cry. We had meant so much to her; she had no children of her own and had been our surrogate mother from when we were only a few weeks old.

"Of course it was. You did the right thing," I reassured her. "I suppose no one thought it mattered. Our birth mother was dead and at least we had a secure home. You were so good to Sadie and me. I don't know what we would have done without you." I got up and kissed the old house-keeper on the forehead.

"My Thea—" Mrs K beamed "—I knew you would do well in life." There was a pause before she added, "The other one too."

"Sadie," I said.

"She was wild but who knows if she had lived..." The old woman wiped her eyes. "God rest her soul."

You're back in the fold, Sadie. Mrs K admits that you weren't all bad, not that she ever thought you were beyond redemption. It was what happened when you began to see things that she didn't trust. And she was right.

"Now you must hurry back to your young man."

"Ben?" For a moment I misunderstood and she shot me a shrewd glance. "Oh, you mean William." I shook my head. "We're not together anymore."

"I saw the ring was missing." Mrs K nodded in satisfaction. "It was too heavy for your finger. You do not need him, Thea. A strong woman needs no

one but herself and God.”
   “I’ll always need you.” I gave Mrs K a hug.
   “You have the cross I gave you?”
   “I have.” *And I’m not taking it off. Ever again.*
   “Then all is well.”

CHAPTER TWENTY-THREE

I drove slowly back along the lanes where dog roses and honeysuckle twined their way through the hedgerows and clumps of pink and purple foxgloves grew in hollows between the blackberry bushes.

The visit to Mrs K had proved as useful as I'd hoped. Our old housekeeper had confirmed that Sadie and I were linked by blood to our adoptive aunt, so that Jane Gordon's previously inexplicable decision to take responsibility for a pair of newly born twins was not as random or illogical as it might have appeared. What I had to do next was to trace the rest of Aunt Jane's family as they were the most likely link between us and Amelia.

Was Amelia Latimer, by any chance, our great-great-grandmother? If so, since Hortense was her cousin, she too was a relative too, however distant. The thought that we might be connected to a woman who'd poisoned her brother's wife and when that plan had been foiled had lied to have Amelia committed to an asylum was not a pleasant one. If Louis had not died beneath the wheels of a runaway wagon what would have happened to Amelia? Would he, at the last moment, have stepped in to save his wife? Or had he run out of the house to bring her back and hand her over to the men from Bradwell Grange?

"How could he do that?" I said as I came to a halt at a red light. "Agree to lock away the girl he'd only just married."

And had never slept with. So they never had children.

"Shit!" The lights changed and I moved forward.

Our connection with Louis and Hortense was becoming more and more distant, and nothing I'd learned so far explained why time had slipped back into those weeks after the wedding when Hortense was plotting to rid herself of her sister-in-law.

Back in Belvedere Crescent the cat was waiting for me on the front steps. It rose languidly to its feet and pressed reassuringly against my calves as I walked into the hall.

What did Mrs K have to say? Sadie was standing by the stairs, her outline nebulous in the shadowy light.

Plenty. I dumped my bag and keys on the table. *It's a shame we didn't ask Aunt Jane when she was alive.*

We did. But when we didn't get anywhere we gave up. You said yourself she could be very scary when we were little.

Anyway, I'm on it. Give me a bit more time and I'll find what we're looking for.

You do that, sis. It's—

The cat meowled loudly and Sadie was gone.

In kitchen I fed it a full pouch of food, took out my laptop and logged in to findmyheritage.com.

Jane Gordon: I discovered the name spawned a web of connections. Father, Frederick Gordon; mother, Amelia Gordon nee Edwards.

"Amelia—" I breathed "—you survived and you married again. You had three children." The elder two, Edward and Susan, were born in the twenties when she was still young; the third, the baby, the afterthought, the accident, was Jane.

"Yes!" I stared at the screen. The cat, smelling of fish, jumped on my knee and butted its head under my chin. If our mother was Jane's niece, then either Edward or Susan must be one of our grandparents.

Edward had died in nineteen-forty and he was unmarried. Susan, on the other hand, had married George Taylor and they had one daughter, Marigold.

That's her. That's our mum. You were right Sadie, she did dump us, though it wasn't something she'd planned to do. What I'd seen must have been the day she died.

~~~

The red-haired girl carrying the Moses basket. Her face hard with desperation. The Poet's sadness when he had to tell Marigold that Aunt Jane refused to see her. That whatever he said only made our great-aunt more and more angry and there was nothing he could do to change her mind.

~~~

The cat shifted on my knee, its paws plucking and kneading my jeans. I stroked its head and it curled itself up on my lap.

Aunt Jane took us in because Marigold died and there was no one else.

That was good of her. Sadie's voice was heavy with sarcasm.

Otherwise we would have been put into care. I struggled to stay rational.

Where we might have been adopted by someone who really wanted us.

Don't be like that. I think, from what Mrs K says, Aunt Jane did care about us in the end.

Or saw us as useful subjects for her research. Wow! Imagine it. A pair of identical twins dropped into your lap, the classic material for a controlled experiment.

Do you really think that?

There was no reply and my elation at having discovered our birth mother, subsided into resignation. Sadie had a point. Twins were a gift for any academic planning a long-term study. Mrs K, who'd never approved of her employer, must have had some inkling about what was going on, so perhaps her insistence that our aunt loved us was purely for my benefit and had nothing to do with the truth.

But we were loved. Mrs K loved us to bits. And we had each other...

I waited. The cat jumped off my knee. The kitchen ached with silence. I closed the program, leaned back in my chair and processed what I knew. Amelia was, as Ben had suggested, related to us so the idea that I might have inherited some of her memories was a possibility though it didn't explain the vividness of my experiences, nor the fact that there were physical outcomes, like being found wandering in the street wearing just a t-shirt.

The only explanation for that was that I had indeed slipped through time, and my desire to survive was the catalyst for Amelia's escape. But where exactly did Hortense fit in? Almost all the other pieces were in place, leaving one significant gap in the puzzle.

She's important because... I mused.

Because she hates you, Sadie replied.

Not me. It's Amelia she hated.

What about any of the others?

I don't know.

I clicked on the icon and findmyheritage.com opened again. As I read I clutched the cross around my neck so tightly that it bit into my palm. The thread that ran through our family history was early death. Amelia's son had died aged twenty; Susan had not lived to see her grandchildren; Marigold had died soon after having the twins. Only Jane survived beyond her sixties and she'd been a bitter angry woman who'd spent her life studying the occult.

Did you make a pact with the Devil? I dismissed the idea. Aunt Jane didn't practise Black Magic. Her studies had been purely academic.

My next thought was more chilling. *I'm the last of the Gordons. I'm the only one left. Did Hortense have anything to do with that?*

"That's not possible. These things don't happen."

But they do.

I switched off the laptop, stood up and walked around the room, trying to calm myself down. At this point Mrs K would prescribe a cup of tea and a biscuit, or rather a plateful of biscuits, or an over-generous piece of cake. Sadie would give me a large glass of wine, while William would sit me down and produce a logical argument to prove that the feeling of dread that writhed in the pit of my stomach was an irrational reaction to a set of unrelated facts. Ben would listen and try to tease out what I really felt. Much as I wanted to talk to him, I couldn't justify contacting him at his work. The other alternative was to ring Dr Radik and ask for an urgent appointment but that meant denying the in-explicable. Dr Radik, like William, would search for a cure for my condition. What I wanted was answers.

There was only one person I could turn to for that – Minerva Beckford with her expertise in the paranormal. I took the phone out of my back pocket and scrolled down the messages. Nothing from Ben or Min. There was, however, text after text from William. The last one read,

My darling Thea, since you have not replied to any of my texts or voice mails I must accept that you won't seek the help I found for you and that our relationship is over. Remember that whatever you feel right now I

There's no kiss. The thought floated across my mind and out of habit my thumb closed on the finger where my ring used to be. I hadn't worn it since I'd come to my decision about the engagement. I ought to return it. If I could remember where I'd left it. I searched all the obvious places and finally found it in the drawer in the dressing table. I'd not put it there so it must have been William. Had he held it, thought about taking it back, then decided to put it away safely where I couldn't lose it?

The ring had always been too big and heavy for my hand. William had chosen it without me and as I'd lost weight it was liable to slip off my finger. It would be a relief to be rid of it and since it was so valuable I'd send it by courier to his office.

Looking for a box to put it in I went to the chest of drawers where Jane Gordon might have kept any jewellery that she didn't regularly wear. In among the jumble of handkerchiefs, gloves, tangles of belts and a silk tie, I found a slim leather case, marked Liberty, and a few necklaces, a ceramic pendant and some bright-red plastic beads. Inside the case was a bracelet made up of swirls of silver surrounding deep-blue stones, obviously of value.

I was about to give up when I saw, at the very back of the drawer, a small square box. Reaching for it I dislodged a tortoiseshell powder compact, which had been pressed against the side of the drawer. As it moved it uncovered a photograph. The edges of the print were crumpled but the black-and-white image was clear and glossy. A young Aunt Jane sat in bed holding a baby to her breast. The child was newly born, her dusting of curls framing a slightly puzzled face.

"No," I said out loud. "That can't be right." A swirl

of cold air brushed over the back of my neck –
followed by a mocking laugh.

*She's not. She can't be. Aunt Jane never had a
child.*

Didn't she? Hortense's voice was as insubstantial
as the movement of air in an empty room. I tightened
my grip on the photograph, my fingers pressing into
the paper until the picture was in danger of folding
over into itself.

*If she didn't what was she doing in bed, in this
room, about to breast feed a new-born baby?*

As if the hand holding it was not mine, I took the
photograph over to the table where I flattened it out
and, not quite able to believe what I was seeing. I
studied it with as much detachment as I could
muster.

Our great-aunt's face was too distinctive to
imagine that this was anyone but Jane Gordon. The
baby, apart from the curls, could be any child. I
leaned forward, resting my palms on the polished
surface and searched for distinguishing features.
Not finding any I turned the photograph over. And
there it was, written in faded pencil: "Marigold,
1965."

Well, Sadie said, *that explains it. Who'd have
thought we were the offspring of Aunt Jane's bastard
child?*

What about Susan? She was Marigold's mother.

*She adopted her sister's baby. Maybe she'd
always wanted a girl. Jane didn't want her so there
was a spare one going.*

Stop it. I put my hands up to my ears, but once
Sadie had begun it was impossible to shut her up. *It
explains why we allowed to stay with her. She must
have had a change of heart in her old age. Or a flash
of conscience. Though that's not likely knowing our*

beloved great-aunt. In any event, the rest of the family were gone and we were her grandchildren, her twin baby granddaughters Whoopee do! What must she have thought when she came down that day to find us wriggling away in our Moses basket like a pair of unwanted kittens?

We weren't unwanted. I repeated what Mrs K had told me. *She might have given her daughter to her sister, Susan, but she kept us.*

Only because Susan went and inconveniently died.

She didn't have to adopt us. She did it because she wanted to. "You have to believe it. *We* have to believe it," I added out loud.

Because if we don't we'll always think of ourselves as useless and unlovable? More pop psychology. I thought you'd given up all that psychobabble when you ditched William.

"It's not..." I began.

Who cares? What difference does it make? I'm dead and you're—

"I'm what?" There was something heavy pressing down on my chest and squeezing the breath out of my lungs.

You're dying too. Your twin is gone. Why would you want to stay? Hortense's voice was smooth and satisfied as if smiling at some private joke.

Spinning through blackness there was a single block of light, the size and shape of a doorway. It was shrinking, moving further away with each painful gasp.

Thea! Sadie was standing by the door, not welcoming me into the next life but gesturing to me to get out of the room.

"Stop. Wait." Speaking grounded me, brought me back. Refusing to be intimidated I put the ring box into the back pocket of my jeans, picked up the photograph and looked around, slowing my glance so that it panned over the chest of drawers, the bed, the long velvet curtains, the walnut wardrobes with their full-length mirrors. I lingered the longest on my reflection, taking in the slightly built woman in jeans and sloppy t-shirt, her dark curls tied back in a ponytail. There were shadows under her eyes and her skin was stretched tight over her cheekbones revealing the amount of weight she'd lost recently. She looked tired and a little worn but she was no Edwardian woman constrained by the expectations of her time. Pulling back my shoulders I lifted my chin and exaggerating my stance gave myself a thumbs up.

Sadie had disappeared but the room had lost its feeling of menace.

"I'm taking charge," I told the cat who'd appeared in the corridor. "Okay, you're on my side too and with you and *a little help from my friends...*"

The song lodged itself in my brain accompanying me as I closed the bedroom door and went down the stairs.

My phone vibrated. Min's message was brief. *Tonight at eight?*

Okay. I texted back. The shadowy warmth of the kitchen beckoned, the comforting tick of the clock, the kettle on the Rayburn, the cat on my knee. With a plate of toast and apricot jam and protected by Mrs K's cross around my neck I'd wait until Minerva Beckford came to banish Hortense's vengeful spirit.

Guests coming and the house in such a mess! In an echo from childhood I heard Mrs K clicking her tongue, saw her running her finger down the banister rail, sending us to work with dusters and brushes while Aunt Jane remained firmly barricaded behind her study door; meanwhile the smell of The Poet's tobacco wafted down from the attic.

I found Mrs K's cleaning basket and set to work. In the drawing room I drew back the curtains, pulled up the blinds and opened the windows. I dusted the furniture, hoovered the floor and emptied the rubbish bins. In the hall I mopped the tiles, working my way towards the stairs, then went up to the next floor to clean the bathroom. On my way I opened all the bedroom doors and windows so a current of late-afternoon air flowed through the house.

Taps sparkled, surfaces gleamed. My hair stuck to my head and my t-shirt clung to my skin. Stripping off, I showered, then wrapped only in a towel bundled my dirty clothes and bed linen into the washing machine. As it chugged and rumbled I saw the cat keeping guard on the windowsill outside. I rinsed its dish, waiting for the first insistent meowl to remind me that it had not been fed for hours, but the cat stayed where it was and didn't ask to come in.

Dirt and cobwebs banished, the house open to the air, I put on clean clothes. My dress was long and loose, skirting my ankles and masking my lack of curves, but with my hair falling around my shoulders it was a romantic, old-fashioned look that suited me and was very different to Sadie's sharper, more angular choices.

Two sides of the same coin. Was it The Poet who had said that? Whoever it was it was nonsense. Sadie and I might share our DNA but we were distinct individuals. Looking at my reflection in the mirror I tried to get a sense of my sister's presence, hoping for some reassurance, or a sarcastic comment, that would help me face what was to come. But Sadie, like the cat, had withdrawn.

Another step that I have to take on my own, I thought as I went to answer the doorbell. The three of them stood on the threshold. Minerva Beckford was flanked on either side by Ben and his brother Ed.

She wore a long gold-and-orange dress. Her hair tied up in a turban gave her the air of a seer or priestess, an image emphasised by the earrings with Egyptian symbols and the ankh around her neck.

"Blessings." She took my hands in hers. "Ben has told me what you've been going through."

"Min's here to help. She knows what she's doing, so there's no need to worry." Ed's gaze swept the hallway.

"The cavalry's arrived," Ben added with a grin.

He's not taking this seriously. A spasm of irritation shot through me followed almost immediately by a sense of relief. For Ben and Ed this was a problem that could be solved. Min would conduct her ritual, Hortense would be banished, and the house and I would be free of her malign influence.

"I'll put it in here, shall I?" Ben carried Min's basket into the drawing room. "Do you want the curtains drawn?"

"Yes, then place the candles and incense burners around the room but don't light any until I say. First we must make sure that we'll be absolutely safe whatever happens." Min took an abalone shell and a bundle of dried herbs, tied with string, out of the basket. She lit the bundle and gently waved the smouldering sage so that the smoke wafted across to the doorway.

"Air, fire, water and earth. Cleanse, dismiss, dispel," she murmured as she circled the room. The beat of her incantation echoed in my brain and I found my lips moving in time with hers as we called on the elements to purify the space.

When Min had decided that we'd done everything we needed to, Ben and Ed lit candles and incense sticks. Pinpoints of light grew in intensity as more and more were added. She told us where to stand and sprinkled a circle of salt around us.

"Have you all got your symbols of protection?" Min asked and my hand went to the cross and chain around my neck. "Okay. Then it's time. Stay calm and strong. Take strength from each other and our belief in the power of good to vanquish unquiet spirits. Ready?"

We nodded. Min spread out her arms and so did we. Taking a deep breath she began the chant. "Unquiet spirit come to us, be with us, show yourself. Hortense Latimer, we summon you." Over and over again Min's words looped and spiralled through the incense-laden air. Their rhythm entered my blood. My eyelids grew heavy and I began to sway. The candlelight faded giving way to an oppressive darkness that grew more and more ominous as the outline of a figure appeared in the centre of our circle. It was vague at first, scarcely more than a shadow, gradually becoming more and more solid until it formed the shape of a woman in a long dark dress. Her features were blurred but I recognised her by the glint of red in her hair.

"She's here," Ed muttered.

"I knew she'd come. She couldn't resist our summons." Min's voice was low and confident. She lifted her head and fixed her gaze on the open doorway. "Hortense Latimer, I command you to leave this house. Go safely from this place and time to which you do not belong."

Yes. I willed her, my muscles tense, my fists

clenched.

"Leave." Min's voice was louder. "Go from here. Go back to where you came from and do not trouble us again."

A deep silence fell over the room. Time stopped as if paused on a screen. Then a gust of energy sent the candles flickering wildly. Hortense's image wavered. She raised an arm. Pointed. The candles flared into bright flame, burning hot and steady. Min gave a cry. She bent over, moaning with pain, and stumbled backwards scattering the circle of salt as she gasped and struggled for breath. Then with a final groan she fell to the ground.

"It's okay. I'm on it." Ed was at her side easing her upright.

Min opened her mouth. "My chest—"

"It hurts?"

Her head slumped forward.

Ben whipped out his phone. "Ambulance. Number fifteen Belvedere Crescent. Suspected coronary."

CHAPTER TWENTY-FOUR

Don't let her die because of me.

While Ed and Ben worked to keep Min's heart beating, I ran to the front door and scanned the street for the first sign of the ambulance. It came in a swirl of blue lights and I hurried down the steps to greet the paramedics.

"All right my lover, where's our patient?" The doors of the ambulance stood open, its interior bright in the gathering gloom. Above the darkening roof tops the sky was streaked with lines of milky blue, bilious green, and pink

Yellow-jacketed, the paramedics moved ponderously with excruciating slowness leaving me outside the drawing room, afraid to enter but unable to keep away. After some time, I have no idea how long, Min was wheeled out on a stretcher.

"I'm going with her," Ed said.

"Call me." Ben put his hand on his brother's shoulder. Feeling helpless I stood beside him as Min was lifted into the vehicle. If she died it would be my fault. I should never have agreed to this exorcism. Hortense was too strong.

One of the paramedics climbed into the ambulance's diving seat. The doors were shut and they were about to leave when I realised that Min didn't have her bag with her.

"Wait," I shouted. "I'll go and fetch it. Her handbag will have all her stuff..." *All the things that make up her life. And keep her here.* "She can't go without it. I won't be a minute."

I ran back into the house. I searched under the table, beside the chair, along the length of carpet where Min had fallen and then inside her basket. I threw out bunches of sage, a box of matches, a plastic bottle of water and, finally, flat along the bottom, I found a gold-leather clutch. My sign that Min would live.

"I've got it," I cried as I ran through the door but the ambulance was a flash of blue disappearing around the end of the crescent.

"Ben—" I clutched his arm "—Min's got to have this. We've got to get it to her."

"It's okay Thea. It'll wait 'til tomorrow."

"No. There'll be people on her contacts list who'll have to be told. And I can't explain it but…" *I have to get out of here. I can't stay. Not when I know Hortense is still in there.*

"If we're at the hospital we'll know what's happening?" Ben suggested.

"Yes." I seized this explanation. Min might be dying and it seemed wrong to be thinking of myself but I knew the house was more dangerous than ever.

"Right. If that'll make you feel better I'll go and get the car – it's not too far. Lock up and I'll be back."

"I haven't got the key."

Ben was halfway down the crescent and didn't hear me. I thought about leaving the door open or slamming it shut and worrying about how to get in later. But I've always been sensible and practical and the key was in the brass bowl only a few steps away. A quick dash in and out and I'd be ready to leave when Ben came back with the car.

I entered. The door shut behind me with a thud. The house was drowsy with incense and candle smoke. The key was not in the brass bowl. I must have left it in my bag. I hesitated, poised to leave. Then decided. It would only take a minute or two to get to my bedroom and back. Racing up the second flight of stairs, a sudden draft caught my dress and it wrapped itself around my legs slowing me down. I disentangled it and hurried along the landing.

The bedroom window was open. A flash of summer lightening leapt across the sky and the curtains billowed into the room. I pulled down the sash, turned to look for my bag – and the wardrobe door swung open revealing a glimpse of white lace and silk. Amelia's wedding dress mirrored the long white shift I wore. It was another link between us and I wished I hadn't chosen this dress to wear. It made me look too much like her and any connection was sure to spark Hortense's fury. Especially now that we'd failed to rid the house of her spirit.

I'm getting out of here. I'm going to the hospital with Ben to see how Min is doing. I'll deal with you later.

Really? There was a hint of laughter in Hortense's voice.

I grabbed the bag and ran to the door. A thick cloud of acrid smoke welled up from the ground floor. I couldn't see beyond the bottom of the stairs. Eyes smarting, lungs heaving, I stepped back. Animal instinct told me to retreat and shut myself in the bedroom but my brain was clear and I knew that the safest thing to do was to get to the attic, barricade the door, put a wet towel over my nose and mouth and wait for the fire brigade.

Run, another voice whispered in my ear. *Run down the stairs and out the front door. Don't worry about the smoke. One quick sprint and you will be out in the fresh air. Think how good that will be, deep breaths of clean cool air.*

Flames coiled around the banister and lapped at the stairs. Scarlet and orange tongues licking at the carpet spreading towards me. There was no way down. That confirmed it: my best chance was the attic where I could climb onto the roof and clamber over the tiles to safety. By then Ben would be back with the car and someone would have noticed the smoke and flames coming through the windows.

I swallowed down a cough and ran along the corridor my eyes focussed on the door to the attic stairs, but as I neared it a black shape reared up in front of me.

I had everything I wanted within my grasp until she took him away from me.

"You planned to kill Amelia." Behind me was the oncoming rush of the fire, in front of me Hortense was blocking my escape. "I heard and saw you."

You! You and your sister were everywhere.

"Get out of my way."

No. You deserve to die. The rest of your family have gone. You've lost your sister so why should you live?

"This is what you want? You want me to give up? Well, fuck you." I lowered my head and ran straight at her.

There was a moment of intense cold, the sensation of being dragged down into the depths of an icy subterranean lake. Then I was through the door. My foot banged against the bottom step, my hands reached out and I clawed my way up the first few stairs. Turning, I kicked the door shut. The sound of the fire was muffled. Hortense was gone.

My chest heaving, I half-stumbled, half-crawled up the rest of the stairs. At the top on the tiny landing was the door to The Poet's rooms. Firmly closed, it would form a fire break and buy me more time.

His sitting room was dark and oddly silent. But

not empty. The Poet, benign but distant, was ensconced in his chair, Aunt Jane standing beside him. Sadie was there too, observing it all with her usual cynical amusement.

If the house went up in flames would they go too? All of them? Perhaps Hortense was right. I should let it happen. Open the door, breathe in the smoke...

We've been here before, Sadie said dryly. *Remember the time on the roof?*

When I didn't jump.

No. You didn't.

Are you going to tell me not to stay here? To get out of the house and live? For you?

The hell I am. I was pissed off. I didn't want to die. I wanted my great career. But you can't live my life for me so there's no point in sacrificing yourself.

Don't worry. I'm not going to do that. What I'm doing is for myself.

Did The Poet look up? Did Aunt Jane nod her head? They, like Sadie, were fading. There was nothing left but the square attic window lit up by the city lights and the garish green of summer lightening.

I piled cushions against the door. I went to the sink. There were no towels so I tore pieces off my skirt and soaked them ready to put over my nose and mouth. Then I went to the window.

Don't go. Hortense's voice was in my ear and I could smell the dry almond scent of heliotrope. *Stay here with them. Forever.*

I gripped the cross around my neck and climbed out onto the roof.

"Get out of my life. Leave this house and never come back."

You killed Louis. I cursed you then, all of you. You're the only one left. Hortense was beside me.

"I didn't kill Louis and neither did Amelia. Face it

Hortense. Take responsibility for what you did. If it hadn't been for you then Louis wouldn't have died."

You're lying. Her hand was on the small of my back.

Thea! Sadie grabbed my arm pulling me sideways.

Hortense, impelled by her momentum, tipped forward. Her skirts spread out and like a speck of burning paper she spiralled downwards.

I got on to the parapet. Far below me were blue lights. People were shouting and gesturing. On the next-door roof a black cat sat by the chimney pot, waiting. Flames leapt towards me curling their scarlet waves around my skirt.

CHAPTER TWENTY-FIVE

"God, Thea you scared us." The voice was familiar, slicing through the layers of light and darkness that cradled me.

"Thea?" It came again summoning me into the bright glare pressing against my eyes. The daylight was so intense that I could hardly bear it and I would have sunk back into the blackness if he hadn't put his hand on mine. Dazzled, I didn't recognise the man sitting beside my bed. His hair was fair but his skin was tanned as if he'd spent time out in the sun. The man I knew was pale, his hair almost ashen, or did he have curls that gave him a rather child-like look? I closed my eyes and when I opened them again the face swam into focus.

"Ben?" My throat was sore, my tongue too big for my mouth. As I spoke the rawness extended down into my chest.

"I'm here. You're in hospital."

"I thought I was going to die."

"Not right now. Your skirt caught fire but the burns aren't deep. It's hard to believe but you haven't broken a single bone. When I saw you up on that ledge..." Ben paused. "I heard a noise and there you were stepping off the ledge. I don't know whether you jumped ... or if you flew but one moment you were there, the fire blazing out behind you, and then you were on the ground."

"I don't remember. I don't remember any of it."

Except knowing that I had to jump. Then Sadie's hand reaching out and taking mine.

"You fainted. If you hadn't fallen so limply you'd have died."

In the end she showed me that I want to live. Whatever it costs me.

"It happened so fast. That house must have been tinder dry," Ben said.

It was all that nicotine. It seeped into the very fabric of the place. That and a good dose of hatred.

"She wanted to destroy our family. She blamed us for what had happened to her brother but I stood up to her in the end..." My voice was growing weaker. Ben lifted a beaker to my lips and the water soothed some of the soreness. "Is the house okay?"

"It's still standing. The fire did a good job of gutting it, but the roof didn't cave in and it seems that the structure is sound."

"So you won't be wanting to buy it?" I croaked.

"In the circumstances probably not." He grinned. "But you'll need a good builder to put it right."

~~~

On a golden afternoon in early autumn the windows of the terrace sparkled in the sunlight, and the trees and shrubs in the garden were a deep rich green. The front of number fifteen was crisscrossed with scaffolding. There were soot stains on the stonework. Plastic covered the windows. A builder's van stood outside. Music drifted out through the house's open door.

I walked into the smell of wet wood and smoke. Where there had been so much evil and hatred now there was a feeling of emptiness.

"Hi." Ben came from the back of the house to greet me. "If you've come for a look we're cracking on, but it's going to be a long job."

I nodded. Much of the interior had been destroyed by the fire so I'd agreed to a complete renovation. Number fifteen was going to be turned into flats. Ben had convinced me. The place I'd grown up in was
~~~

gone, that part of my life was over.

"There's still time to change your mind," he said seeing the look on my face.

"It's not that. I think they're gone."

"You could be right. I wouldn't know. Ed's better at the psychic stuff than me."

Liar, I thought. *You saw Sadie that time.*

"If they're not here is that okay?" Ben asked.

"Yes," I lied. We both knew that, while I might miss The Poet and possibly even Aunt Jane, it was Sadie that I would mourn for the rest of my life. "Min says the dead never really leave. We just find different ways of living with them."

I had a fleeting image of flames roaring out of the attic window, smoke rising from under the tiles, and beside me a figure tipping over the ledge. Bitter, angry, set on revenge, Hortense had almost succeeded in destroying all those she'd cursed. Except for me. I had defied her and I'd won. I waited for the voice that would tell me I hadn't done this alone, that Sadie had been there looking out for me from the very beginning, that without her I would have died up there on the roof.

There was nothing.

I turned to Ben.

"Will you look after the cat?"

"Sure. It's around most days. Whoever buys the ground floor apartment will probably find it comes with the cat." He looked at me.

"If that's a hint I told you I don't know what I'm going to be doing. There's nothing to keep me here anymore."

"Nothing?" Ben raised an eyebrow.

"Apart from the cat." I met his glance and held it.

After the fire all I had left was my car. The furniture, pictures, books, papers and photographs, all the things that had tethered me to the past were gone. It was as if I'd newly arrived in the world. I had no job, no fiancé, no commitments. I was free to start again, reinvent myself, move away, travel, become a new person, or grow into the one I should be. The possibilities were endless.

Sure are sis. Just make sure you make the most of them.

House of Shadows

By

Misha M Herwin

Jo Docherty stood and looked at the wedding ring on the black granite worktop. It would be so easy to leave it there and go.

Desperate to have a child of her own, haunted by a girl in a blue dress, her only hope of saving her marriage is to go back to the place where it all began.

Brooding over the estate at Weston Ridge, the house at Kingsfield hides a violent history. Built by a slave owner for his beloved wife, it is a place of lost children, where time fractures and two lonely girls from different centuries cut their fingers and swear to be best friends for ever. When Jo returns as an adult, long buried memories of her childhood begin to surface. As she slips in and out of time, she realises that she has to face the consequences of her actions, and a friendship forged in blood two hundred years ago will force her to make to a heart-breaking choice...

Picking Up the Pieces

By

Misha M Herwin

Liz, Bernie and Elsa have been friends since their days at St Cecelia's school. Their lives took very different paths but they all have found happiness in their own fashion.

Liz is an independent career woman; Bernie a good Catholic mum with four sons, and Elsa is supported by her wealthy ex-husband. Then, in the space of a few short weeks, everything they have taken for granted is swept away. Money, jobs and partners are all gone.

How will they manage when their worlds are crumbling about their ears? Together Liz, Bernie and Elsa have to find novel ways of avoiding disaster. *Picking up the Pieces* is about friendship, cake, and the mutual support that only lifelong friends can provide.

Shadows on the Grass

By

Misha M Herwin

Every family has its secrets. In the nineteen-sixties Bristol, seventeen-year-old Kate is torn between the new sexual freedom and her rigid Catholic upbringing. Her parents have high expectations of her. She, however, is determined to lead her own life.

Mimi, her grandmother, is dying. In her final hours, Mimi's cousin, the Princess, keeps watch at her bedside. Born in the same month, in the same year, the two women are bound by their past and a terrible betrayal.

Meanwhile, caught between the generations, Mimi's daughter Hannah struggles to come to come to terms with her relationship with her mother, and struggles to keep the peace between her daughter and her husband. She too must find her own way in a land foreign to her, in a new post-war world, where the old certainties have gone and everything she knows has been swept away.

Available from Penkhull Press

Winter Downs

By

Jan Edwards

Winner of the Arnold Bennett Book Prize!

Bunch Courtney stumbles upon the body of Jonathan Frampton in a woodland clearing. Is this a case of suicide, or is it murder? Bunch is determined to discover the truth but can she persuade the dour Chief Inspector Wright to take her seriously?

In January of 1940 a small rural community on the Sussex Downs, already preparing for invasion from across the Channel, finds itself deep in the grip of a snowy landscape, with an ice-cold killer on the loose.